BRYCE

Scandalous Boys #1

Natalie Decker

For those of you who love a little scandal. Ethan and Leeah you're the best parts of me.

BRYCE

Chapter One

Bryce

I repeatedly hit the X button on my PS4 controller. "Die, bitch!"

Graham is no help whatsoever. He keeps taking out the wrong people, and I know he's doing it on purpose. "Seriously, man! What are you doing?" I yell at him.

He pushes pause. "Dude, are you ready to go get Maddy and get this shit done today?"

Inwardly, I groan. He knows how I feel about Madison Issac, my next-door neighbor from hell. As kids, I knew she was too good for me—a dark-haired princess a frog like me could never touch. Not that I wanted to. I learned real quick what girls like her did, thought, and acted. They're nightmares. And Madison is probably the worst kind. She's a priss with a decent face and killer brains but a world-class bitch. I swear she was born with a stick wedged so far up her ass it probably sprouted branches. "Man, she's a freaking buzzkill." I go to unpause the game, but Graham glares at me.

He's my homeboy. We've been best friends since fifth grade, but sometimes he's clueless as all hell. I know he only hangs out with Madison because he uses her to ace his classes. And, okay, I kinda use her too, because I copy off Graham. But that's beside the point. Getting good grades shouldn't require hanging out with her all the freaking time.

The only reason she and I even sort of tolerate each other is because of Graham.

"No, she's not. She's just Madison."

I raise a brow. "Are you trying to tell me you secretly have a spank bank for the girl now?"

Graham frowns and punches me in the shoulder. "Dude, no! She's just a friend."

I shut down the game and nod. "Yeah. You trying for friends with benefits?"

He glowers. "That's not cool. You know I look at her as a sister, fucker!"

"Don't get pissed at me. I mean, don't get me wrong. If she wasn't such a raging bitch all the time, I'd probably try to hit that."

Graham looks as if he's about to punch me in the face. "I hate you. Why can't you two just get over whatever shit is between you? Seriously, it's senior year. I don't want to referee every fight you guys have this year."

"Calm down. I'm not even going to give Smalls any shit this year. But for real, if she starts those jokes about jailbait and then points to me again, I might strangle her."

I haven't dated anyone underage and gotten in

trouble for it. I was tossed in juvie a few months back for tagging a building. Okay, not really me. I was with some people who tagged a building. When the cops showed up, some of us got caught. I smoke, so my lungs aren't exactly in tip-top shape for running distance. I know it's disgusting, and I should quit, serves me right, yadda yadda. I took the rap and got thrown in with the delinquents. Two weeks and some probation. I can't mess up for a whole year, or I'll go to the slammer for defacing property. Well, during the last week of school, I'm standing there talking up my next conquest, and Madison walks by me and says to her friend Emily, "Isn't that cute? She's taking the jailbird's bait. If you two hook up, I'm calling you Jailbait." Then she laughed like she was the funniest person ever.

I glare out my window at her house. Graham sighs. "Oh, come on. That was kind of funny. You know she's just getting back at you for the wet T-shirt bullshit you pulled on her at Greg's party."

Okay, in all fairness, that was a dick move on my part. But I'm an asshole. Everyone who knows me knows this, especially Madison. I'm not going to apologize for being me. She was wearing a white T-shirt, and I happened to stumble upon some water balloons. So, I may have run up to Greg's balcony with a bowl of filled balloons and waited for Madison to come into view. Then I launched them in a way that got her T-shirt soaked, revealing the parts she always keeps hidden. Literally, the girl goes swimming in dark shirts.

I'm a guy. We like boobs and ass. Sorry, ladies, if this offends. Some of us aren't as open about it. Those of us who are are pigs. We know this. We just don't care.

Anyway, Madison's sharp green eyes found me through the laughing crowd, and she made the slit-your-throat sign at me. Pissed off, raging mad, and blushing red, Madison is actually really hot. That's probably why I love tormenting her so much. Plus, it amuses me.

Graham punches me in my shoulder again. "Dude. Come on. We're heading to Maddy's, and then we're getting this stupid list done so my mom can stop riding my ass about being lazy."

"Um … You are lazy."

"Fuck off!"

I shrug and make my way to the door. "You are, man. Admit it—you're only friends with Madison for the homework perks." Because beyond that, I don't see any other reason he'd be friends with her. The girl doesn't drink. She doesn't smoke. She hardly goes to parties. But Graham is a stoner, parties, and drinks a lot.

He shakes his head. "It's called smart tactics. Besides, she doesn't mind. If she did, she'd have said something."

We walk up to her porch, and I dread every freaking minute of it. Graham knocks, and we wait.

Chapter Two

Madison

The shit hit the fan. Literally. Well, not literally. But my dearest aunt's latest crime is smeared on the Internet, televisions, and newspapers all over Arizona.

Apparently, my mom's sister, Aunt Catlin, swindled close to a billion dollars out of this company she works for. She helped hide all these investments and whatever so the head sharks like her got rich while the company went up in flames, and all these employees lost homes, pensions, everything. Now my aunt and uncle are looking at jail time.

Because of the big scandal, my room, my sanctuary, will be invaded by an unwanted guest. My cousin Sarah. She's moving in today. I'm not trying to be a total bitch about it, but we have four bedrooms. Granted, one of those was converted into my dad's personal office, so that really leaves us three. My parents occupy one, me the other, and then there's my older brother, Kyle.

Which means I'm left sharing my room with Sarah, the devilish spawn. Can you tell I'm not a fan of her?

I know part of me should feel bad, and okay, a very, very small part does. But here's the thing you have to know about Sarah: she's such a bitch. I'm not saying that because I'm upset about sharing my room. I'm not even saying that because no one else would take her and now my senior year is possibly ruined. No, she's really a brat! Who knows? Maybe she's actually learned some compassion since Easter, but I highly doubt it.

A yellow cab pulls up to our home, and Kyle walks out to greet the driver. My parents are hugging the little blond, blue-eyed monster. I stare from my window for a second or two, and then I turn my attention to my room. My queen bed is disassembled and up in the attic. Before me now, a twin bunk bed. The brat is going to want the top, and of course I'll have to oblige because she's going through a rough time.

What about me? What about my rough time? This girl tortures me. She takes and takes and has never once given back. If you ask me, all that's happening to her? It's called justice. Okay, maybe that's a little harsh. Maybe she's changed some since she lost her big house with the pool, her rich friends, and her glamorous lifestyle. Maybe she's a little kinder.

Sucking in a breath and feeling a little guilty for being a snot, I go downstairs and greet Sarah. She enters the house as I reach the bottom step of the stairs. Dark shades mask her eyes, and they match her black sun hat and her black dress. If I didn't know any better, I'd say she was dressed for a funeral.

"Hi, Sarah."

She moves her shades down her nose a little and sneers at me. "I see you haven't changed much, Madison. Didn't like the highlights?"

She knows I didn't like them. The evil troll! At Easter, she said she wanted to do my hair. I thought she was being nice. She said we could make it pretty, and I agreed. Stupid me. She said red tints would give my dark brown hair a summery glow. She didn't put red tints in. She made my hair pink. She claimed she picked up the wrong box. I had to go to school with bubblegum-pink highlights in my hair for almost a week before someone could fix it. A hundred and fifty dollars down the tube.

I smile. "Guess it wasn't really my thing."

She rolls her eyes. "Yeah, being cool never has been."

I knew it! I knew the evil monster did it on purpose. She mocks my clothes, says I dress like a hobo, and all that stuff. My clothes are nice; sure, I didn't spend $200 for any summer dresses in my closet, but who cares? I'm certainly not going to spend $800 on a stupid purse. Um, hell to the no!

But my cousin has—excuse me, *had*—over $2,000 to spend per week. I barely have $200 in my bank account. Working five to twelve hours a week for eight bucks an hour is nothing to brag about.

"Where's my room?" She shoves her sunglasses up her nose and makes her way to the stairs.

"You're sharing with me. Come on." I head up to my room, not waiting for her.

She gasps. "Sharing? I'm ... Never mind. Apparently, that will have to do. We'll just redecorate your room."

I stop and turn on the last step to look back at her.

"What do you mean 'redecorate'?"

"Maddy," my mom bites out as she follows us up the stairs. "Change can be a good thing." She walks past me and mumbles, "Remember what the therapist said."

That quack told us we had to make sure we didn't try to force Little Miss Unwanted Guest to conform to our ways. He said we should try to appease her as much as possible and ease her into the change. But right now, I wish she was on a boat to China or some other faraway place.

Gritting my teeth, I say, "You know what? My room could probably use a makeover."

Sarah smiles and enters my room. She looks around, instantly frowning. "I'm getting top bunk." My mom carries in a few boxes, and Sarah smiles at her. "Thanks, Auntie Heather. Where are the boxes I had shipped here?"

"Oh, I'll have the guys carry them in." My mom hugs Sarah. "I know this is a hard time for you, but we're glad you're here."

Pffft! She might be glad, but I'm not, so she can drop the whole "we" business.

As soon as my mom leaves, Sarah removes her sunglasses and hat. She looks around the room and shakes her head. "Well, it's clear you're in need of some decorating tips, that's for sure." She runs her hands over the matching comforters my mom bought for the bunk beds and laughs. "Seriously, this floral motif is so out."

I nod like I care. I really don't. It's a blanket. It keeps me warm. That's all that matters. I'm not the homeless one. She is. I'm not the one with parents going to jail. She is. But, hey, maybe this is her way of coping with all that, so I will bite my tongue and not say a word.

"Maddy! Graham and Bryce are here!" my mom calls to me.

I instantly smile, feeling better. My heart is humming to see Graham. As if in another world, I leave my cousin and race down to the two boys. I'm not really keen on Bryce, but that's because my whole life, he's been in and out of juvie more times than I can count. He's a bad boy with a temper. I don't know why Graham is friends with him.

Graham smiles before I reach the bottom step. "Hey, Maddy! We were … oh, um … Hi." His attention goes from me to the stairs. I look back and see Sarah. I turn back to Graham and realize he's looking at her as if she's the whole moon and stars.

No! This can't be happening. He's the love of my life. Sure, he doesn't know that, but I'm in love with him. And he's looking at her like she just took the one thing I've wanted since fifth grade—his heart.

I blink back some tears and put on the most fake smile ever. "That's Sarah, my cousin. I told you she was coming to stay with us this year."

He nods, not taking his eyes off her. "Yeah. Hi. I'm Graham. This is my buddy Bryce." He glances at me and then back at her. "We were heading into town for our school supplies and then getting some ice cream. Possibly going to the lake. Did you want to come?"

Wait, is he asking her? And not me? Is he ditching me now?

I take a few steps back as Sarah moves closer to Graham and strokes his biceps. I think I'm about to get sick. My chest tightens, and my stomach churns deadly at this display in front of me.

I tear my stare from them and glance over at Bryce, something I instantly regret. Bryce eyes Sarah and then looks over at me. "You okay over there, Smalls?"

I hate that nickname! He only calls me that because I'm five foot two, and he and Graham are well over six foot. I glare at him. "Fine."

"You look like you're about to hurl. There's a no-barfing policy in my ride."

Kyle whips around the corner, ready to haul a few boxes up the stairs, and gives the boys a nod. "What's up?"

"Hey, Kyle. Heading out for school shit. Need some help?" Graham offers.

"That'd be great. Mads can show you guys the way."

Um. No, I can't. These boys have never been in my room. I mean NEVER. And they're not about to start now. That's my … well, it's my personal area. My journal, if you will. Sarah just giggles, though, and starts pulling Graham up the stairs.

"Hey!"

She shoots me a look but doesn't stop.

"Stop! No one is going into my room!"

"Well, technically, it's my room too." And with that, she leads Graham, the only person I've ever really loved, into my off-limits space.

Chapter Three

Bryce

Graham is a freaking dickwad! While he's upstairs, probably nailing the sexy blond, I'm down in Madison's basement sweating my ass off. How did I get stuck helping Miss Priss lug boxes to her room?

This is so beyond the code of helping out a bro in need, it's not even funny. I watch Madison struggle to lift a box and almost laugh as her arms wobble and her body tumbles forward. I snatch the box from her while shooting her a glare. "If you can't lift it, just point to it, and I'll get it."

She rolls her moss-colored eyes and snaps, "I don't want your help."

I'm half-tempted to drop this box and tell her good, because I don't want to fucking help. But I catch the sad glimmer in her eyes, and damn it, it ceases all my asshole retorts. "Look. It's clear neither of us want to be here. Let's just get this done as quick as possible, and we can go back to doing what we love to do best."

She stares blankly up at me.

"Ignoring each other, Smalls."

"Okay."

We get back to work quietly. As we head out of the basement with the boxes, I decide to try and be nice, like Graham suggested. I've got a feeling we're going to be stuck with each other a lot if he's making headway with her cousin. "So, what's up with the 'no one in your room' policy? Got some secrets in there?"

"Everyone has secrets," she shoots back.

I chuckle. "Ain't that the truth. But you, Miss Goody Two-shoes, don't have dark secrets. Bet your room is a picture-perfect, princess pink." I nudge her.

She enters a room off to the right, and I follow. My jaw almost hits the floor. Her walls are not pink, they're white. The way she kept her room off-limits, I expected shirtless guy models posted all over her walls. But there is none of that in here, just paintings. Lots of different paintings.

There's a bunk bed, and on the bottom, Graham has that blond chick practically riding his cock. I'm annoyed, not that he's getting action, but because he stuck me with bitch work I shouldn't have been doing in the first place. "Dude, are you going to help or flirt? 'Cause I don't have 'moving boxes' on my list of stuff to do today."

Graham looks over at Madison, and then me. He has a sheepish smile on his face. "Sorry, man. I guess I got caught up in conversation."

"Yeah. That's what I'd label it too," I say. I glance at Madison, and I swear the girl looks like she's about to cry.

Madison moves toward the door but pauses when her cousin says, "So, Madison, I'm going to head out with Graham here and probably pick up some new stuff. Could you unpack the boxes for me while I'm gone?"

I don't miss the tightening of Madison's jaw. "I'm not one of your maids, Sarah! Unpack your own crap!" Oh, oh, oh! There she is, the girl I've been so well acquainted with all my life.

Mrs. Issac steps into the room. "Madison Lynn Issac! My room, right now!"

"But I didn't …" she starts, but her mom points. Madison bows her head, cheeks flaming red, and leaves the room.

Okay, now this is the highlight of my day. Watching Madison go postal on someone other than me and then getting yelled at by her mom? I might owe Graham for volunteering my help because this was so worth it.

Chapter Four

Madison

My mom scowls at me. "Maddy, we discussed this! Why would you say that to your cousin?"

Is she joking? Because my cousin is stealing everything from me! Like always. She talks to me like I'm her servant, and clearly I'm not. She brought the boy I love into my room. Probably made out with him because that's how she is. She doesn't waste any time. She just jumps on anything she wants.

But I can't say any of this to my mom. She'll tell me I'm being selfish. And maybe I am, but shouldn't I be? "I'm sorry, Mom. I'll go apologize."

"That's better." She ushers me out of the room and back to my bedroom, where twenty-five boxes take up most of the floor space.

Sarah hooks her arm through Graham's as they stand in the middle of my room. I swallow my feelings and start, "Sarah …"

She looks at me with watery eyes. I know it's an act. She does this when she needs something to go her way. And right now, she's winning. It takes everything in me to push out the rest of my words. I can feel everyone staring at me like I'm the devil. Like I'm the one who did something wrong. "Sarah, I'm sorry for snapping at you. It was wrong. Of course I'll help you unpack. Forgive me?" I ask, pasting on a smile.

Sarah strokes Graham's arm and sniffles. "Sure, I forgive you, Madison." She pulls Graham out of the room with her. My mom follows. Bryce, for some reason, remains.

He shakes his dark hair and smirks at me. "Have fun being her bitch, Madison."

I glower at him. "You'll know all about being someone's bitch in a few years, Bryce! That looks more and more certain."

He stops smiling. I immediately regret what I said. He helped me without complaint, carrying these stupid boxes up here. And how do I repay him? By telling him he's heading to jail eventually. Smooth, real smooth, Mads.

Bryce flips me off and leaves my room before I can apologize.

Her clothes take up over half of my closet. Instead of shoving some of them back into the boxes, I remove more of my own clothes. Why? Because we have to appease the princess.

Of course, you'd figure she'd be happy. She isn't. She gives me a sour expression as she thumbs the closet. "Madison, you can't cramp my bags like this. And this dress needs to breathe. What were you thinking? Are you trying to ruin my things?"

"Sarah, we have to share a closet. I let you have most of it. What do you want me to do?"

She yanks my clothes out and tosses them onto the bed. "How about I get the closet, and you can have the dresser?"

I'm on the verge of blowing up again and need to escape. I run from my room, but it's not far enough, so I leave the house. Once my feet hit the paved road, I sprint. Where am I going? I don't know. I could run my usual route that I do every morning. Of course, I've got on the wrong shoes and don't actually want blisters on my feet, so maybe not. I just need to get out of this place.

At the park about a mile from my house, I slump down on a bench and let go. Tears fall—hard, snotty sobs. Oh yeah, I let it all out. Heaving deep breaths, I soak the palms of my hands with my sorrow. No one is here, so I'm not worried about anyone seeing me. Definitely not worried about anyone asking me what's wrong.

At least that's what I think until I hear someone clear their throat nearby. I jerk my head up and look around. Bryce is puffing on a cigarette.

"Damn, Smalls, who died?"

"No one! Go away!"

He looks around and laughs. "Not happening. This is public property. I'm allowed to be here as much as you are." He takes another drag on his cig, and I glare at him. I don't want him seeing me like this.

"You know those things kill people." I point to the cancer stick.

"Really? I thought they increased your life span."

I know he's joking, but I don't find it funny. "I like living. You might not enjoy it so much, but I don't want to breathe that crap in. So put it out or take a hike."

He throws up his hands and drops his cig to the ground, then grinds it out with his shoe. "Better?"

"Much."

Bryce takes a seat beside me and looks up. Evening is settling, turning the blue Tennessee sky into an orange and pinkish wonder. "So … why are you out here? The park is usually my domain."

"I just needed to get some air. My house became too much." I shrug. It's an honest answer. Not the full answer, but I'm not spilling my guts to Bryce.

He nods.

We sit in silence for a few more minutes, and then I stand up. I need to get away from this bench, and him too. He looks me over and then shakes his head while his dark eyes look down at the ground. He chuckles.

"What?"

"Nothing."

"No. What's so funny?" I demand.

He meets my gaze. "You. Well, all good girls are the same. Always running from the criminal as soon as they can. You owe me a cigarette."

"I don't owe you anything!"

He laughs louder. "Jeez, Smalls. Couldn't even deny running away from me. Wow. Just wow."

"I'm not running away." I fold my arms over my

chest and snarl, "I need to get back home."

"Yeah. Whatever you need to tell yourself." He waves, and I leave him.

Stupid Bryce. Why do I care what he thinks anyway? I don't. Why couldn't he just let me cry?

Footsteps fall close behind me, and I make the mistake of looking over my shoulder. Bryce is right there. "It's getting dark, Smalls."

"And?"

He sighs. "I'm being a gentleman and making sure you get home okay. All right?"

"I can get home by myself."

"I know. Humor me."

Chapter Five

Bryce

When I came to the park, I thought I could enjoy my smoke, and it would be a good ending to a good day. I didn't expect to see Mads bawling her eyes out on a bench.

Shit, the way she was crying, I thought someone died. Apparently, that wasn't the case. At the same time, I'm not buying her story of feeling overcrowded. No one would cry like that over feeling a little cramped. Something else is bothering her. And a good person, well, a person who isn't me, would make her tell them. But I'm me. So I let whatever is worrying her go.

I have my own problems to deal with.

We're silent most of the walk to her house. Not that I mind silence, but with my last cigarette until I can get another pack tomorrow snuffed into the ground, I need to end the quiet between us. "So, your cousin Sarah bought some paint for your room. Did you see?"

She makes a noise that sounds like a growl. "Well, my mom said she could."

"Yeah, but it's your room. Do you really want her to paint your walls hot pink?"

She squeezes her moss-colored eyes shut. "Not particularly, but it doesn't matter. It's her room just as much as it's mine now."

"Why is that?" I know she probably won't answer.

She sighs. "Her parents got into some trouble with the law. It's all over CNN. You know, the news?" She makes her jab at me. I let her. Mads has been surprising me a lot today. "Anyways, now she's living with us until she finishes high school. And goes off and becomes a supermodel or whatever."

I nod. "You don't like her much, do you?"

"I don't know."

"Graham likes her a lot. Guess you better start getting used to it."

And that's when I see it. Clear as day. She nods once, but the tears glisten.

"Holy shit! You like Graham."

"As a friend," she lies as she swipes a hand under her eyes.

"Nah. You like him way more than that." I laugh. I shouldn't, but damn, I should have seen this coming. All the homework she did and never once denying him a chance to copy, the tests she helped him through if they were in same class, and all the surprise gifts.

She shakes her head as she bolts down the street.

Shit. Should I run after her?

Nah. It's not like she wants me to. She hates me. Always has. Always will.

So I let her run to her house, which is only four

houses away. But I do watch her. I guess it's the least I can do.

But Madison doesn't run to her house. She runs to mine. More specifically, my tree house. A decent person would say they were sorry for bringing up a sore subject. I'm not one of those people. Especially when I'm not really sorry. It's not my fault the girl waited so long to tell Graham how much she liked him. It certainly isn't my fault her cousin snagged him away. And it also isn't my fault Graham will probably never look at her as anything more than a good friend and sister type.

But I'm not about to tell her I know how Graham sees her. Girls say they want to know stuff like this all the time, and I've fallen for it too often. Truth is, no girl wants to know that the guy they like sees them as nothing more than a friend. Especially if the girl is really holding out for that dude. Yeah, they definitely don't want to know.

I make my way to my room and watch her from one of my windows.

An hour passes and Mads is still there inside my tree house. So I gather up a couple of blankets and a pillow and head out to the back of my house. Good thing my mom isn't home, and my dad, shit, he's barely around much. Not that it matters, but I hate when they're all up in my business asking me what I'm doing. Then they'll give me a lecture on how I better not be smoking or doing drugs. It's basically the same song and dance I get from them every freaking time.

I snatch a couple of bottles of water from the fridge and go out the back door. I can't believe I'm carting any of this shit out here. What's wrong with me?

Glutton for punishment, I suppose.

Climbing the ladder to the top, I throw the latch and toss the blankets and pillow inside before I hoist myself in. The wood creaks under my feet as I shut the door and move a chair over it. Mads sniffles in the corner. "Sorry, I shouldn't be here. I know that."

"Smalls, I don't care." I toss her a blanket and pillow. "I got a water here too."

She wipes her eyes again and nods. "Thanks." She looks around the tree house. "I remember it being bigger for some reason."

"Well, you're barely four feet; of course everything looks bigger."

She shoots me a glare and snorts. "Yeah."

I hand her the water as she fans out a blanket on the floor and lays her head back on my pillow. "I didn't know how long you planned on staying. Didn't want you to freeze. We're supposed to get a cold front tonight."

She looks over at me with a surprised expression, and I smile. "Yeah, I watch the news."

"Didn't think you would."

"I know. Because I'm heading for a prison in less than a year."

She props herself up on one elbow. "I didn't mean it, Bryce. That was out of line. I'm sorry."

"Eh, it's cool. I don't really give a shit what anyone thinks about me." I wave it off because that's the truth. I've always known she sees me as a low-grade piece of shit. Truth is, most of those times I've gotten busted was to save someone else's hide. Yeah, I'm that idiot.

But it doesn't matter. Only a few people actually see me as anything else. Everyone else believes I'm a shady character. An asshole. They believe my future will be a four by four with bars. And that's okay. I know where I'm going to be next year—up in Michigan.

Madison frowns. "I really am sorry. And I didn't mean it."

I nod. I know her words are just that, words. I'm not putting stock into them. "Well, here's another blanket to cover up with." I start to move the chair from the door.

"Stay. For five more minutes. Please."

I turn to her and ask, "Why?"

"Never mind."

I shrug and then leave.

Chapter Six

Madison

I'm sleeping in Bryce Matthews's tree house. His pillow doesn't smell of smoke but of cedar and soap. He brought me blankets so I wouldn't be cold. All this surprises me.

I can't believe I asked him to stay. Why did I do that? He's a jerk most of the time. He's the same kid who tossed gum in my hair in first grade, and I had to get it all chopped off. I got mistaken for a boy more times than I could count that year, and it was awful.

Emily, my only girl friend and also best friend, lives ten minutes from my house. That's driving-wise, so of course I can't go stay with her. Besides, Emily is in Florida on vacay. If she wasn't, I still wouldn't attempt the trip. My mom might tell me to take Sarah with, and I'm done losing people to her. I check the screen on my phone and sigh.

I missed a couple texts. One from Graham, asking

if he could come hang out tomorrow. Pfft. I'm not answering that. Next one was from Emily, asking how my day was going.

> Me: My day sucked.
> Emily: Yeah. Is she bossing you around?

I call her. The phone rings once. "Holler at your girl."

"She's a nightmare. She took my whole closet. She's going to paint my walls pink. Oh, and she took Graham."

"What do you mean 'she took Graham'?"

"He's totally in love with her. Whatevs. I can't do anything about any of it because we're supposed to walk on eggshells around her and kiss her butt. I hate her, Em."

"Girl! Eff that crap. Go kick her fat ass! Please tell me she has a gigantic booty."

I giggle. "No go. She's flawless in the whole appearance area."

"Well, she can't just take up space in your room and push you out."

I can picture Em parading the beach with her face all scrunched as she voices her thoughts into her cell. This is the reason she's my best friend. She's always got my back. I sigh. "She kind of did. You wouldn't believe me if I told you where I am right now."

"Why? Where are you?"

I inhale the scent coming off the pillow and laugh. "Bryce Matthews's tree house."

"Shut up! You are not, liar. You and Bryce are like oil and water."

I laugh harder. "I know, right? Oh, Em, I've

completely lost it, haven't I?"

"Nah, it'll be all good. I come home this weekend. We'll go do school shopping and figure out a way to get Sarah to stop treating you like her personal doormat. God, I just want to punch her in the face for being a brat."

I smile. "Thanks. And how is Florida?"

"It's awesome. Totally wish you could have came with."

"I know. I had to work."

"I know. What would two weeks be without those pesky people getting tickets to watch movies?" I laugh. She kids now, but she totally loves that I work in a movie theater. "Well, I'm heading to this beach party right now. Talk to you later, girl."

"Okay."

We hang up, and I feel a little better. Not a lot, but a little.

I wake up to my phone buzzing softly against my palm. I groan slightly as I stretch and look down at the number on display. I don't know who is calling me, so I ignore it. As soon as I do, the door to the tree house swings open.

Bryce glares at me. "I called you."

"That was you? How'd you get my number?"

He gives me a look like *Are you kidding me right now?* "Freshman year. We had English together. We had to give our numbers out to the people in our group. You were in my group." He says it all slow and deliberate like I'm a moron.

I blink, trying to remember this, and I eventually do, but why would he keep my number? "Oh" is all I can manage.

"You can head back to your house now. Graham picked Sarah up, and they went somewhere. Probably the lake."

Great. The most romantic place in the world, and Graham's there with her. Again. I nod and toss Bryce's pillow at him. He catches it, and his head jerks back a little when he does. "Ease up, Smalls."

"Stop calling me that." I stand up and fold his blankets to distract myself and also to help shield my outburst. I've never told him how much I hate that name. I've never acknowledged how much it bothers me. Usually I could ignore him. Graham was always around, so it was easier to do. But Graham isn't here now. So being around Bryce is awkward.

I finish the first blanket and start on the second. My backside bumps into him, startling me. When did he get so close? His deep laugh follows. "Relax. I was coming to help you." He drops the pillow and picks up one end of the blanket. "Why can't I call you Smalls?"

"Because. I don't like it." It also reminds me of all the parts of me that are small—like my chest. I swear, if I didn't have a decent butt and long hair, I could probably be mistaken for a boy.

He shrugs. "Okay. You could have told me that a long time ago, you know."

"I guess. I'm sorry. I'm not a morning person."

He nods. "I know. That's why I got you some

coffee." I start to tell him how he didn't have to do that, but he waves me off. "Had to make a run into town anyways." He shows me a pack of smokes, and I glower at him.

"You should really stop that."

"I should, but I'm not. I can quit whenever I want. I just … don't want to."

I roll my eyes. "That's a stupid reason."

He narrows his eyes and sets his pack down. "Don't touch those. I'm going to get your coffee."

He leaves the tree house and comes back up in less than two seconds. "This is the reason I was calling you. So you could open the door for me while I carried these up."

I mouth the word *Oh*. I don't know why he's being so nice to me. Bryce and I don't usually have nice conversations, and he doesn't do nice gestures, at least as far as I've seen. This is weird and almost dreamlike.

"What?" he asks.

"Nothing. Well, okay, what's up with the nice act?"

Bryce smiles his perfect white teeth at me. I never noticed before how straight they are. "I'm not a complete asshole all the time." He hands me a cup. "It's a caramel latte."

"Thank you." I take a sip. He picks up his pack of cigarettes and smacks it against his palm. I give him a look.

"Don't start, Smalls. I need one."

"Fine. Blow it out the window." I don't know why I'm giving him orders; this is his tree house. Just like I don't know why I'm staring at him. Besides if I'm being really honest, minus the disgusting habit and his bad reputation, Bryce is actually pretty hot.

He looks over at me, sticking one of his cancer sticks in his mouth, and then lights the end. I watch him take a few drags, and then he blows the smoke out the window. He takes a sip of his own coffee and then another drag from his cigarette.

"How did you sleep?" he asks.

"Fine. Thanks for letting me crash here."

He nods and blows another bout of smoke out his tree house window. Then suddenly, he mouths *Shit!*

"What'd you do?"

He stomps out his cigarette and tosses the pack to me. "Hold on to these for me."

I'm about to refuse, but he looks desperate, and he did let me sleep here. He also brought me a coffee. I tuck his pack of tar-filled crap into the back pocket of my shorts. Bryce grabs a can of air freshener and sprays the air as well as his clothes. I stifle a giggle when his mother's voice calls out, "Bryce Alexander Matthews, you better not be doing what I think you are up there, young man."

He drops his half-smoked, squashed cig into a tin can and shouts, "No, Mom! Just hanging out with Madison."

"Graham's girlfriend?"

"Why does she think I'm Graham's girlfriend?" I ask.

He shrugs and flips open the door. "Mom, I told you she's just our friend."

His mom pokes her head into the tree house, looks around, and settles her stare on me. "Hello, Madison." I give her a shy wave. "Bryce, why does it smell like apples? You've been smoking, haven't you?"

"No, Mom."

"He farted. It was so gross. I told him to cover it up before I barfed," I lie. I don't know why I'm lying for him, but he looks grateful for it.

His mom scoffs. "Bryce, that's terrible. He has manners somewhere." Her eyes land on the pile of blankets and the pillow on top. "So what exactly is going on up here? I better not have to warn you two about the consequences of having sex at your age."

My eyes widen. Oh. My. God. She actually thinks Bryce and I were either about to or have already done it. Ew. I can feel heat spread across my cheeks.

"Mom! No! I slept out here last night. Jeez." He snatches up the blankets and his coffee and heads toward the ladder. His mom descends, allowing her son to come down. I glance at my back pocket and make sure Bryce's stupid cigarettes aren't noticeable. They aren't, thank goodness. I grab my phone and head down the ladder.

Bryce's hands wrap around my waist when I reach the middle rung, and he helps guide me down. I bite the inside of my cheek as I notice his grip. It's firm but gentle at the same time. As soon as I reach the ground, he lets go, and I give him a nod.

He guides me across the yard away from his mom. "We're going to go to the lake," he tells her. "Graham's meeting us there."

"Oh, okay, honey," his mom says.

I look up at Bryce. "I'm not going to the lake," I whisper.

"Neither am I. It was the quickest excuse I could think of. Besides, I need my cancer sticks, as you call them, and I can't have you handing them over to me right now."

His mom enters the house, and Bryce and I head to his car. He opens up the passenger door and waits.

"Um …"

"Get in."

Right. I do as he asks, carefully removing his pack from my pocket, and then I set them in the middle console. Bryce closes my door and slides into the driver's seat a moment later. "Where are we going?"

"I don't know. I'm hungry."

"Bryce, I'm not eating a meal with you."

He laughs. "Yeah, you are. Sorry. My mom's watching us. I think she thinks we're dating."

I laugh. "That's ridiculous."

He pulls out of his driveway and asks, "Why?"

"Are you serious?" He gives me a look that suggests he is. "Fine. For starters, we don't have anything in common."

Bryce narrows his stare at the road. "I'm sure we have more in common than you think."

I'm pretty sure we don't, but I don't say it. I just hope he doesn't take me to some gang hangout or whatever.

Chapter Seven

Madison

Bryce takes me to IHOP. Which, all things considered, is sweet but also a little weird. I order a stack of pancakes and tell him I'll pay him back when we get to my house, because I don't have my wallet with me. He brushes it off, though, as if the very idea insults him.

This wasn't the only weird thing. He keeps opening doors and even pulls a chair out for me. It's almost as if we're on a date. And that right there seems so wrong.

So as he pulls up to my house, I don't wait for him to put his car in park. I bolt from it like it's diseased. He probably thinks I'm crazy. Probably will tell Graham how much of a nutjob I am.

I slam the door to my bedroom and lean, panting, against the wood. Hot liquid streams down my cheeks as I slide down to the plush carpeted floor. I'm a walking mess.

My door jerks open, pushing me toward my desk.

Kyle runs a hand through his sandy hair. "Was that Bryce Matthews's car I saw you get out of?"

"W-what?" I stammer.

"Don't." He glares at me. "Look, I know Graham hangs out with the kid and you guys all chill together. But jeez, Mads, you can't be with that dude by yourself! He's a criminal. What would Mom and Dad think?" He shakes his head.

"I'm not hanging out with him. I just … We were going to go to the lake to meet Graham and Sarah, but I got sick so he brought me home."

He looks at me, I mean studies me for longer than usual, and it makes me uncomfortable. "Good," he says after a long bout of silence. "I couldn't go off to college if I thought you were interested in hooking up with Bryce."

I glower at him. "What's that supposed to mean? I can't make wise choices or something?" Why do I sound so defensive? No, why do I sound like I'm defending Bryce?

He raises a brow. "It's supposed to mean that you can't fix him. So don't try."

"I'm not trying to fix anyone. Just get out."

"Where were you last night?"

I shove him. It's not an answer, but it's all he's getting.

"Because I know Em is still in Florida, and Graham came by around eight to take Sarah to a movie. So where were you?"

I shove him again, pushing him right out of my room. Kyle can stop acting all brotherly. He certainly wasn't brotherly last week when he could have offered up his room for the witch to stay in. He certainly wasn't brotherly enough to tell Mom what kind of things Sarah has done to me. And he most certainly wasn't brotherly when Sarah stole Graham from me.

I shut the door in his face and flip the lock. Maybe I'll get a good hour to myself. Maybe I can paint or draw. I pick up my sketchbook and flip through the pages. It's really my journal. Some people write down their feelings. I draw mine. Sometimes I put little phrases beside them, but most of the time I just draw.

However, as I skim through the pages, something catches my eye. I stop on the picture of Graham in a relaxed pose on the lawn at school. I remembered the image so clearly that as soon as I got home I sketched it out. I added a little saying: *A holder of my heart. Never knowing. Always careful. Always growing.*

Beside it, someone has scribbled: *How sweet. Well now, he knows, FREAK!*

My eyes widen at the words. My anger is beyond the point of control. She looked through my things. She wrote in my journal. Oh, this brat is going to pay.

I snatch a pair of scissors from my desk and make my way to her closet. "Take my things. Take the only person I love. Trash my journal! Ugh!" I slice through one of her beaded tops. Glittery beads instantly shower the carpet, and oh my goodness, does it feel great! I mean absolutely liberating.

I slice through a few more of her tops. Cut up some of her jeans. Pick up some of her shoes and decide they need to go too. When I'm finished, my closet looks a little thinner. Not too noticeable, but good enough for me.

But when I look at the mess on my floor, panic sets in. How the hell am I going to get rid of this stuff? I glance over at my door and decide that's a bad idea. I look at the window. Gathering up the ruined clothes, and without a second thought, I open the window and toss the material down to the ground. I shove her shoes, purses, everything I need to get rid of out the small, second-story opening.

Once it's out, scattered across the lawn and a couple of bushes, I hurry downstairs and out to the side of the house where most of the evidence is. I'll vacuum the beads up later. As I'm collecting all the stray pieces, I hear someone laughing. Like a hard-core, deep-within-the-belly laugh. I turn my head and see Bryce looking over his fence. "You know you could have taken that stuff to Plato's Closet and got some money out of all that shit."

Ugh. He's so right. But I don't want money. I want to feel justified. She ruined my sketchbook and my life, so I can ruin her flipping clothes.

"Money couldn't fix it," I say.

He shakes his head at me. "Money fixes a lot of stuff. Have problems? See a shrink, pay them some bucks, and feel better. Need to get away? Get a bus ticket to wherever, pay some bucks, and enjoy the ride. See? Money fixes things."

"What do you want, Bryce?" I pick up a piece of her stupid top near the fence and glare at him.

He scratches his head. "Look, it's none of my business, but I'm pretty sure those aren't your clothes all butchered up." He checks his watch and sighs. "And I'd say you have about ten minutes to hide what you've done. So I was going to suggest you toss it in our trash can." He hands over a garbage bag and waits for me to say something.

Problem is, I don't know what to say. "Thank you"? "What's in it for you?" "Why are you being so nice to me?" I take the garbage bag and start putting the ruined clothes in it.

I look over at him, hoping he's not watching. Turns out he is. I mean, he's still staring at me, probably waiting for a response or for me to toss him the full bag. "Why are you helping me?"

"Because, believe it or not, you've actually helped me out a lot. In school. You know all that homework you let Graham copy?" He winks. "Consider this a way to get even."

And there it is. He's only doing this because I've apparently helped him get better grades. Well, I can accept that. I fill the bag and toss it over the fence to him. "Thanks."

He nods. "No problem."

Chapter Eight

Bryce

I haven't spoken to Mads in two weeks. I mean, I've seen her in quick, snapshot moments like her getting in her car. Her coming home from somewhere. Her sitting by her window with her sketchpad in hand. The other day, she helped her brother load his car for college. I thought about asking if she needed some help, but then I remembered how she looked at me the last time I helped her.

I've never paid much attention to her before. One of the windows in my room gives me a direct view of hers. I never noticed until the other day when I saw her sitting by her own window.

Today is the first day of school, and honestly, I'm not in the mood to go, but there are some perks. I get to see all the girls who perfected their tans over the summer, showing off their legs in short skirts or short shorts. Oh yeah, school is almost worth that viewing. Making my way to my car, I spot a pair of legs going on for miles attached to a nice butt barely covered by skintight shorts bent over the passenger's seat of a car next door. I almost whistle but stop myself when the person straightens.

Madison pulls at the shorts a bit and walks her backpack to the trunk of her car.

Holy fuck. That's what's been hiding under all those layers and baggy jeans? A whole lot of fuck-me sexy. "Hey, Mads." Calling her Smalls today just wouldn't be fitting. Although she's still short, she's just a whole lot of wow today.

"Good morning, Bryce." She drops her bag into her trunk and shuts it.

"You know, we should think about carpooling. Doing whatever we can to save the ecosystem."

She shakes her head. "Right. Because you're looking to save the world." She rolls her eyes. Damn, why do I want her to sit here and talk to me so bad? It's like the universe flipped, and now everything is all out of order. My usual routine would be to chuck an insult or two at her.

"You look good today."

"As opposed to every other day when I look like butt, right?" She shoots me a glare and starts to head back to her house.

"No. That's not what I meant. You look good every day. It's just today you look really good."

She flips me off and walks into the house.

This is why I shouldn't talk to the girl. Or at least never try being nice to her. She just acts like she's so much better than everyone else. Well, she can screw herself. I'm never giving her another compliment ever again.

Halfway down the road, I snatch a cigarette and light it. Inhaling the menthol flavor and then blowing it out instantly makes me feel better. Piss on Madison Issac. She's nothing but a nightmare.

I finish my cigarette as I pull into Graham's driveway. He runs out of the house as soon as I honk the horn and practically jumps into the passenger seat.

"Dude, I've got something to tell you," he says.

Pulling out of his driveway, I ask, "Yeah, what's that?"

"Well, you know Sarah and I are dating."

I narrow my eyes. "Yeah, I kind of figured that out. That's not really newsworthy shit this early in the morning."

"Don't be a dick. Anyways, she found Maddy's sketchbook, you know, the one she never lets anyone touch, and there's like a shitload of sketches of me in there."

This doesn't surprise me. Girls like Madison always go for the good boys like Graham. Problem with this is Graham is hardly a good little boy. "Yeah, and?"

"And? Dude, why is she obsessed with me? Sarah says it was like serial-killer shit. What the hell am I going to do? I've been avoiding her for two weeks now. We probably have a bunch of classes together, and she's like the best damn study partner I've had in the last four years. I'm screwed."

"Just tell her you aren't interested. I don't know. I don't think she'd make a move on you since you're dating her cousin."

He looks at me. "Yeah?"

"Yeah, man. I don't think Mads is exactly the go-getter type." I mean, the poor girl has been crushing on him for a while and hasn't said shit. Why would she just say something now? Of course, it's not like I really give a damn if she does or not.

Pulling into a parking spot, I notice Madison getting out of her car. Sarah and Emily are getting out too. Sarah sneers and says something to Mads, and Madison's eyes widen but go back to normal just as quickly. I get out and hear Emily yell, "Don't talk to Maddy like that, you ungrateful little bitch!"

I move closer because I have to pass them to get to the front entrance.

"Drop it, Em," Madison warns. "I don't even care."

"You should care! She went through your stuff. Painted your room. Shrank your shorts! Girl, those things could be classified as hoochie. You need to put your damn foot down, Maddy!"

Maybe this is why she was in a pissy mood with me earlier. Damn it. If it is, I feel bad.

"Good morning, Madison." Jake Foster whistles. "Summer did you some good."

I turn around. Between his cocky grin and his eyes glued to Madison's ass, I want to beat the shit out of him. "Dude! Leave her alone."

Graham walks past us with Sarah. Jake is staring at me like I've lost it. And Madison is blushing while Emily's jaw is completely unhinged. I motion around Mads to help shield her backside from onlookers like Jake and follow her up the steps.

"Thanks," she says when we get into school.

"I've got a hoodie in the car if you want to use it to cover up."

She shakes her head. "I'll be okay. Thanks, though."

I have a feeling she's lying, but I don't call her out

on it. I let her continue down the hall with Emily, and I head to my homeroom.

Mr. Jenkins is probably one of the coolest teachers here. But I honestly have no idea what he teaches. His salt-and-pepper hair is cut short, military-style. He swivels around in his teacher's chair, rocking every so often, while flipping through a paper copy of *USA Today*.

The daily, repetitive motions have officially begun. I rifle through the stack of yellow, printed schedules on his desk, grab mine, and then have a seat. Other kids in my class file into the room, including Sarah and Graham. Graham sits down in front of me. Sarah takes a seat beside him, and I swear I want to gag all over my recently whipped friend. He coos praises to Sarah, and she cackles like a hyena.

I should bitch-slap the back of his head and ask him where the fuck his balls went. But then I think better of it, because he could ask me the same damn thing about what I just did for Mads. Why the hell am I letting a girl like Madison Issac get to me? Lately, she's been all I think about. Her butterscotch scent has imbedded itself into my pillow, so now all I smell is her.

"Dude, let me see your schedule," Graham says, snapping me back to reality.

I toss him my schedule. Sarah leans over and groans. "I don't have any classes with you. You're in all the supersmart ones."

Graham laughs. "Yeah. Wonder if Madison's got any classes with us." He tosses back my schedule. "We've got second through sixth together. I hear we'll get to pick our lab partners in chem, so we better get someone who takes notes. Like Jenny Gardner."

"Or Smalls," I offer. "Oh wait, she's in chem 2, isn't she?"

"Yeah." Graham makes a face but looks over at Sarah. "Let me see what classes you have."

She giggles and hands over her schedule. I covertly take a peek and shake my head. I took biology my sophomore year, and she's taking it as a senior. Holy shit—algebra? The girl is in all the remedial classes. I stop looking. Graham better wrap his shit up because I wouldn't put it past Barbie here to get knocked up and suck the life out of him.

"Mr. Jenkins?" There's a knock at the door. I turn and see Madison making her way into the room. Most of the guys in the class are gawking at her. One, Jeff Nibs, actually makes catcalls. Madison's cheeks turn cherry red, but she doesn't take her eyes off Mr. Jenkins.

"What's up, Madison?"

"I have my schedule, and it says I have you for psychology, and although I think that class would be fascinating, I didn't sign up for it. I really need my weight-training class back."

"Ew. Weight training? She isn't serious, is she?" Sarah scoffs.

Mads runs track and cross-country. All athletes are encouraged to take weight training. I don't tell Sarah this because it will probably confuse her. Her comment does set me off, though. "What's wrong with weight training?" I ask.

Sarah gives me a look like I just spit hellfire in her face or something. "Um, hello. Only girls who want to look like men take those classes. And Mads's chest is pretty flat as it is."

Graham laughs. I don't have a retort to her comment. At least not one she'd understand, so I just let it go. Besides that, I'm looking at Madison's chest right now, and it doesn't look flat at all. In fact, she's got a decent amount up there.

"Did you speak with your guidance counselor?" Mr. Jenkins asks.

She nods. "He told me to have you sign this form."

He looks over the paper and then eyes her up. "Madison, I can't sign this. You need my class or another form of social science to graduate. Unless you plan on taking my class this summer, I won't sign this. I'm sorry."

"But …"

"I'm sorry, Madison."

She nods again. "It's okay. Thanks, Mr. Jenkins." She hurries out of the room just as the bell rings.

Chapter Nine

Madison

My life is in full-on suck mode. Yes, I forgot all about the social science requirement. They still didn't have to take my weight-training class away. I need that to ensure my leg strength for track. Now, I'll have to try to squeeze lifting into my already busy schedule. As if this day couldn't get any worse, I've also got a front-row seat to the Sarah and Graham make-out show before every class I have with him.

That should be me. Not her. But what can I do? He's clearly head over heels for her. And who wouldn't be? She's beautiful with her long legs and perfect hair. Sure, she lacks brain cells, but guys apparently love dense girls.

Class is killing me, though. Not because the work is hard or because the person I want most is totally in love with my cousin. Nope, it's the silence. He doesn't say hi. He doesn't look at me or smile at me.

He doesn't even ask for my help on problems I know he's struggling to get the answer to. Do you know who does ask for help? Bryce.

Bryce Matthews is asking me for help. Graham actually looks up at him in calculus 2 and gives him a faint shake of his head. I see it. But he coughs and turns away when he catches me looking at him. I ball my fists and try to hold back my emotions. I try to hold in the scream that's begging to be released.

"What's your problem with me? Did I do something?"

I feel Bryce's stare on both of us, but I don't care. I don't care if the whole class is looking at us. Graham fumbles with his pencil and mutters, "Y-you have p-pictures of me."

"What?"

He looks over at me, finally. "I'm with Sarah. And I don't think we should be friends anymore. Because I'm a little creeped out by your obsession."

Any blood in my body drains. My heart twists, and my stomach knots. Eyes are on us. Ears hear every word. I'm so humiliated. I stumble to a stand and refuse to look at him. At anyone really.

I won't cry in front of him either. That will only confirm the thoughts he just projected aloud. I walk over to Mrs. Vixen's desk and drop my worksheet into the basket. "May I please use the restroom?"

She hands over the paddle that has the words "hall pass" etched into the wood underneath her name and "room number 106." I don't know how I managed to walk out of the room without crumbling, let alone spilling one tear. I do it, though.

In the bathroom, I stare at my reflection in the

mirror. I'm no beauty queen. I've got freckles all over my nose and across my cheeks. My hair isn't as sleek as it should be. Not without serious help from a flat iron and some product. But I don't have misshapen eyebrows or a hooked nose. I don't have eyes too big for my face. So why am I always alone?

Why do boys only want the insanely perfect, flawlessly skinned girls? Why not me? What's wrong with me? And who knows what Sarah told Graham? He thinks I'm obsessed with him. He doesn't even want to be my friend anymore.

Tears spill. Anger ebbs through my body. I should let it go. Let karma take care of Sarah. But karma is taking her sweet-ass time, and I'm done waiting.

Swiping the stray tears away, I splash some cold water on my face and observe my reflection again. Sarah wants to play dirty. I can do it too.

Heading back to class, a plan is concocted in my head, and I swear my steps feel a little lighter. Everyone will see her for the devil she really is, including Graham. Once that happens, he'll be mine.

Sliding back into my seat, I don't let my eyes go to Graham like they usually do. I don't even look up at Bryce, although I can feel him staring at me. My attention is focused on my calculus 2 book.

A note flies over the page.

Hey, I'm serious. Will you help me with this last problem? Please.

I look up at Bryce and sigh. I snatch his paper and start working on the problem that's giving him so much grief. It's the least I can do since he did safeguard my butt this morning. He also offered me his sweatshirt to cover up these scandalous shorts and all they are showing off.

I hand him back his paper, and he reads through the problem all worked out. "Seriously?"

"Y-yes." I sound unsure, because I'm not sure if he was really asking or being sarcastic. I never can tell with him.

"I could kiss you right now, Smalls."

The comment makes me reel. He doesn't mean it. Bryce doesn't kiss girls like me. He's all into easy, gothic, bad girls. I'm none of those things. And it's not like I want him to kiss me anyway. For some reason, I do end up looking at his lips. His upper lip is not really thin, but it isn't all plumped up. The bottom lip is a little plump, though, and it is begging to be sucked and nibbled on.

I blink a few times and look back at my notebook. I can't believe I actually pictured myself sucking and nibbling on his lower lip. Oh. My. God. What am I saying? I don't want to kiss Bryce. He smokes. He's always in trouble. Kissing him is all kinds of wrong, and thinking about doing such thing is even worse.

"You okay over there, Smalls?"

I make a noise. "Pfft. Yeah. Are you okay?"

He gives me the almighty "You're so freaking weird" stare and then shakes his head. Serves me right. I'd be shaking my head at me too. My thoughts were crazy—thinking about kissing criminals. Just to summarize, my love life: really sucks. My friends: well, now that Graham no longer wants to be my friend, I'm down to one. Wow, I need to get out more or get a life.

"Class, I'd like each of you to exchange numbers with the group you're in. In this study group, you will have to set up study sessions, and homework will be graded as a group project, not just an individual grade.

This means double points."

Wait a second. I'm writing my number down but stop because both of them have my number already. Also, the last part of what my teacher just said freezes me in place. Homework is worth double points and graded as a group? In what universe is this even fair? I look over at my group and literally want to cry. Well, there go my sick days. If I rely on these two while I'm ill, my grade will go straight in the toilet.

Graham seems to be thinking the same thing, because he looks over at me, then at Bryce. I want to tell him this isn't my fault.

Bryce hands me his number with a smirk. "Now, Smalls, I know you'll have this urge to sext me tonight. But you shouldn't because my mom takes my phone after ten." He winks.

My mouth falls open in disgust, and I glare at him. "Don't flatter yourself, Bryce."

"Kidding. But for real, my mom takes my phone every night at ten."

I shoot a look over at Graham, but he looks uninterested in our conversation. I don't even want to clue him in because he doesn't want to have anything to do with me. At least for now, he doesn't.

I turn my attention back to Bryce. "We should probably do the work together so we all have the same answers and we're all on the same page. I can't keep carrying you two knuckleheads every year."

Bryce nods. "I'm down. I've got to work until five, but I can be wherever after that." He smacks Graham. "Hey, did you hear us?"

"What?" Graham asks.

Chapter Ten

Bryce

Madison is in my room, sitting on the floor listening to whatever the hell is playing on her iPod. She taps her foot, working on some other homework while we wait for Graham. If he's not here in ten minutes, I'm going to suggest we start without his ass.

"Bryce, is Madison joining us for dinner?" my mom asks through the small opening in the door.

I snap my fingers in front of Madison's face. She pulls out an earbud. "Hmm?"

"You hungry?"

She looks down at her stomach and blushes. "Was it growling?"

"What?"

She chews her lower lip. "Was my stomach growling?"

I laugh. Jesus, she's so cute when she's all embarrassed about stuff. "No, it wasn't. I was asking if you want some food, though. My mom's setting the table."

"Oh! Um. Okay. I mean, if that's okay."

"Mom, she'll eat with us," I say, knowing my mom heard her, but I want to confirm it without answering Madison.

Madison returns to her other homework, tapping her pencil against her notebook while a loose strand falls from her hair clip. I am mesmerized by her. She looks up, catching my stare, and asks, "What?"

"Nothing." I grin like an idiot.

She tucks the strand behind her ear and sighs. "I don't—"

"Okay, kids! Come on down for dinner," my mom shouts, interrupting Mads.

I help Mads up off the floor, and we head downstairs. I know we're waiting on Graham, but I kind of hope he doesn't show up. This kind of hoping will get me into deep crap. I've already fell for this girl once. Way back in kindergarten. And do you know what she said to me? "Ew! Never!" After that, I knew exactly where I stood with a girl like Mads. So why in the hell am I wanting to spend time alone with her? To touch her hair? Her face? Why do I really want to do all these things as well as kiss her? Especially when I know she only has eyes for guys like Graham?

"Bryce?" Madison asks, bringing me out of my train of thought.

"What's up, Smalls?"

She crinkles her nose. "Where's your dining room?"

"Huh?" Why is she asking about my dining room?

She scowls. Oh, that's right; we're eating dinner together. I lead the way, and she follows. Once we enter the dining room, I notice only three plates are set. Dad's not coming again. Mom looks over at Madison and smiles. "I hope you like pot roast."

"Love it," Madison answers with a smile. She takes my usual seat, and I sit down beside her.

My mom wears a wide smile from ear to ear as she serves food to Mads and me. I shake my head. That look alone means trouble—questions and a slew of ideas I want no part of. My mom sits back. "So, Madison, how's school?"

"It's fine."

"I see you've been spending a lot of time with my son, without Graham, lately. Are you two … ?"

Madison blushes. Full-blown, deep apple red. I groan inwardly. Mads looks over at me, then swallows, and says, "Graham is running a little late today. But we're just friends. All of us are just friends." She drops her gaze to her plate and begins shoveling food into her mouth.

If only she knew that this will not protect her from my mom asking her questions. "Hey, Mom," I said, "when's Dad getting back?"

"Not sure. Probably late this week." She frowns and starts on her own dinner.

There. I saved Mads for at least a few minutes.

An hour later, there's still no Graham, so Mads and I do our homework. I catch her glancing at the clock every ten minutes. I catch her glancing out the window and over to her own room. She grumbles and then taps her pencil harder against her notebook.

We come to the last problem, and I ask, "So which one of us is going to share and explain this to Graham?"

Her green eyes look up at me, and she snaps, "Funny. It's obvious he thinks I'm obsessed with him, and he's not going to come here because of me. So you can share with him."

"Mads, I don't think—"

"He said it! You heard him say it." She drops her gaze. "I draw. I'm always drawing. Sometimes there were perfect moments that I wanted to capture. Like our time at the lake. He was looking out at the sunset, and you were by this set of rocks smoking." Mads's gaze draws up to mine, and then she sighs. "Never mind. You don't care."

And usually, this is true—I don't care. Today, though, I do. Mads is awkward. She's great at sports, but socially, she's awkward. She has like, what, two friends. She doesn't go to dances. I don't think she's ever dated a guy. But, hey, what do I know? She might have.

"Smalls, I think it's cool that you draw."

Mads isn't listening to what I'm saying. She's rambling about something and stuffing all her books and notebooks into her book bag. I step in front of her before she reaches my door to leave. "Hey. Why are you bailing?"

"I'm tired. I have to go." She sidesteps me and heads out. I let her. Anyone else would have held her up. Comforted her or said something to make her stay. But that isn't me. None of this is me. I can't be like this with Mads. I can't get sucked up into falling for her again.

It doesn't stop me from watching her from my window. She makes it to her house and disappears behind the brick walls. The light to her room flicks on, and then, like some pervert, I watch her take a seat at her desk. I turn away before she can glance out the window and notice me looking at her. I pick up my phone and call Graham.

"Yeah?"

"Dude, I should punch you in your nutsac. You ditched Mads and me today."

"I'll just copy what you guys got. Wait, she did work out the problems with you, right?"

I hear a splash and a giggle and then, "Who are you talking to, baby?"

"Cute," I say. "Playing at the damn lake while I stay behind and do our homework. You're such a dickwad."

"Oh, piss off. I can't do it, man. All I keep thinking about is Madison planning out our wedding and shit!"

I groan. "First off, have you even seen this drawn-out plan?"

"No. But Sarah has. She lives with her. Why would she say something like that if it wasn't true?"

"How the hell would I know that? Look, I'm telling you that you need to go talk to Madison about this. Seriously, man. Grow a pair and just figure it out, because a group grade is not some shit to be joking about."

I hear him grumble. "Fine, I'll talk to her."

"I'll hook you up with the homework after you talk to her. Just swing by."

"Whatever, man."

"Later."

"Later."

I hang up and look over at Madison's window. She looks deep in thought. There is no way she's doing homework. Nah. She's probably drawing.

Next thing I know, I'm throwing on my shoes and heading over to her house.

Chapter Eleven

Madison

My cell rings. I look at the caller ID and see it's Graham. I push ignore. I've never ignored Graham—ever. Even if I was deathly ill, coughing up a lung, I still answered his calls. But today, I'm not in the mood.

I don't want to hear his voice, which I swear is as sweet as honey. I don't want to listen to whatever he might have to say, because I'm mad. Yes, I'm beyond mad! I'm downright livid with him for not only ditching me but for what he did to me in class. It's like ... well, he can just go screw himself right now.

Soft tapping against my door pulls me from my thoughts. "Yeah?"

My mom enters. "Bryce is here to see you. Can I just send him up?"

I nod. My room isn't exactly secret anymore. I swivel back to my sketchpad.

"She's in here." Heavy footsteps fall near me, and my mom says, "Leave the door open, sweetie."

I roll my eyes and cringe at whatever crap my mom thinks will be happening in my room. I look over at Bryce. "Hey."

He tips his head up. "I see you're drawing."

"Yep."

He walks over to my bed and asks, "May I?"

"Yeah, sure."

He takes a seat on my bed and leans back on his elbows. "Will you show me some of the stuff you drew?"

For some reason this makes me smile. It shouldn't, because it's Bryce asking. "Sure."

I hand him my sketchbook. He starts to crack open the book. "I'm sorry if you hate any of them," I warn him ahead of time. Because there are sketches of Bryce in there. As well as Graham and Emily, my family, and other things, like places.

He nods and starts to look through the pages. He pauses on one of him. In it, his shoulders are slumped as he leans against the hood of his car and smokes a cigarette. He looks up, and his eyes lock with mine. I'm about to grab the book back from him. I don't need him thinking I'm obsessed with him too.

He must know what I'm about to do, though, because he stands and starts walking around the room, still flipping through the pages. "Wow," he says. "Smalls, I really had no idea you were so good."

My jaw hits the floor. "Really?"

Bryce looks at me. "Yeah. Can I … can I take this one?" He points at the one I drew of him when we were all at the lake. Normally, I'd say no, but today, I just nod. He smiles and carefully rips the page out of the book. "Thanks."

"You're welcome."

He hands back my book and rocks on his heels. "So, the reason I came over here was to see if you were all right."

Placing my sketchbook back into my desk, I sigh. "I'm okay. I guess." For some reason I laugh. "Well, besides the fact that Graham hates me, he's dating my awful cousin, and all my clothes look like something a stripper should be wearing. All in all, I say, yeah, I'm okay."

Bryce frowns. "All of your shorts are like the ones you wore today?"

I nod. "Some are worse. Wanna see?" I've completely lost my mind. I'm asking if Bryce wants to see my shorty shorts. Next thing that'll come out of my mouth will probably be worse—like, "Wanna see me in them?" Ugh!

Bryce follows me over to my dresser, and I pull out the drawer with all my now really shrunken shorts. He picks up a pair and groans. "There's no way in hell you'll walk out of the house in these. I bet your ass hangs out, and if you bent over, someone could get a crotch shot."

I go to take the pair Bryce is holding just as Sarah and Graham enter the room. Graham's eyebrows are raised, and he glances over at Bryce and then me. My hooker shorts are still in both of our hands. Bryce lets go and nods to Graham. A red-hot flame of mortification spreads across my cheeks and down my neck while my stomach knots.

"What's going on here?" Graham asks.

If my blush didn't already burn, it was smoldering now. "We were hanging out," Bryce says.

"Aw, maybe there is hope for you yet," Sarah chimes in as she pulls Graham into our room. She takes a seat on my bed and starts kissing him. It's one thing when this is at school. But seriously, on my bed?

I storm out of my room.

I wake up to my phone blaring, "Fear is a danger." I hold my head and look around. Definitely not in my room. Definitely not in the tree house either. Crap! I'm in Bryce's bed. I pat myself down and take comfort that all my clothes are still on—well, minus my shoes.

Looking to my left, I notice that the sheets are untouched, and it's empty. I shift to plant my feet on the floor, but they land on something lumpy, and it groans. I pull my feet back and peer over the side of the bed.

Bryce is asleep on the floor. Why did he let me have his bed? I can't remember last night very well. This is what happens when I'm really upset. I tend to blackout and forget things. I haven't done it in years. And only a few people know I've done this. Bryce was never one of them.

God, I hope I didn't destroy anything. Or worse—embarrass myself by confessing how long I've liked Graham. The thought causes a wildfire blush to heat my face.

I roll to the other side, about to make my exit, when I hear, "Smalls, give me a second."

Blinking, I look back and notice Bryce standing. He isn't wearing a shirt, and oh my, he is cut in ways I never imagined. Not even on my wildest days. He never takes his shirt off at the lake, so of course I never knew about each of those ripples.

I tear my eyes away from his sculpted frame and look down at the floor. His breath brushes my ear, and I shiver. "Let me check to see if my mom is up."

He steps out of the room, and I release the air I'd been holding in. "Oh my God." My body needs to quit reacting to him like this. It's Bryce. I do not have feelings for Bryce.

So why is my heart pounding as if it's on overdrive? And why did I feel utterly mortified checking him out while he had no shirt on? I mean, it's normal for girls to check out guys, even guys they have no interest in, right?

Bryce returns just as I'm about to make a mad dash out the door. I kind of don't care if his mother is here and awake or not. I charge at him, and he puts his body in front of the exit, causing me to stop. I glance up and ask, "Will you move?"

He steps aside and lets me pass. As I'm making my way toward the stairs, he says, "You're welcome, by the way."

I don't know if that was a sarcastic insult or he really meant it. Either way, I will not care. This has gotten way out of control. I need to get a grip on my feelings. The only way to do that is to confront my evil cousin.

Chapter Twelve

Bryce

Madison practically stormed out of my house like it was on fire. At first, that kind of stung. I know I come off like the bad boy, the guy every parent sees as their worst nightmare for their daughter. But Madison should know after last night I'm nothing like that guy.

So yes, when she ran away, it put a dent in my armor. Well, I'm not letting my defenses down again. Not for her. I've learned my lesson. She can kiss my ass if she expects me to feel sorry or worry about her or give her a place to lay low so she can gather her pathetic thoughts about Graham. Yup. I'm officially done.

I light another cigarette. It's the third one since I left to pick up Graham. He waves his hand in front of his face and snaps, "Dude, ease up. I know you don't care what people think, but I've got a girlfriend. And she doesn't like me smelling like an ashtray."

"Then get a fucking ride with Mads if it bothers you so much. Or walk your ass to school for all I care." Last thing I need right now is Graham getting on me about my habits.

He shakes his head. "What's the deal with you and Madison, anyways? I thought you guys hated each other."

"I don't hate Mads. She's just a real bitch sometimes. Lately, though, she's been a little nicer. Why do you even give a shit, anyways? You ditched us because you're worried she's obsessed with you."

"I don't … care. Not really. It's just … I don't like you guys hanging out together."

I glare at him. "We've done it before. Only difference is you were always there before. So …"

He shrugs as I pull into the school parking lot. "Exactly. I was always there. Now I'm not, and I guess I don't like you two hanging out. That's all."

I throw my car in park and flick my cigarette out the window. "This is the stupidest conversation we've ever had. And by the way, I don't give a fuck if you don't like the idea of me and Madison hanging out. You ditched her the moment you met Sarah. So what gives?" I'm seething. He better watch his next response, and he seems to know it.

He mumbles, "I just don't like it."

If he wasn't my best friend, I'd deck him. Instead of cocking my fist back and wailing on him, I get out of my car and stomp off into school. Others must know I'm in a bad mood because even the freshmen, the people who probably don't know where most of their classes are, dive out of my way. I storm right up to Madison's locker. She's the reason I'm so mad. This is all her doing, and I'm going to make her suffer for it.

Her friend Emily sees me first. Her big brown eyes bulge. Madison is clueless, digging in her locker, carrying on a conversation. I think Emily is in too much shock to pay attention, but I'm listening. Especially when she says, "And I woke up in his bed. Why do I keep ending up at Bryce's place? He probably thinks I'm a lunatic." She straightens and grips the side of her locker. "It's so hu*mil*iating. Why do you look like you saw a ghost or something?" She shuts her locker, and her stare lands on me. Her cheeks turn bright apple-red. I admit I'm starting to like this look on her. Kind of suiting.

She swallows. "Hi."

I give her a nod. "I let you stay because you were too upset to return home. I gave you my bed because I'm not a complete fucking asshole. But you're welcome."

Mads's jaw drops open, and Emily taps her shoulder. "I'm going to head to class, Maddy. I will catch up with you later."

Madison frowns at her friend. Once she's gone, Mads says, "I am sorry. I didn't ... How long were you standing there?"

"Long enough." Her stare drops from mine. "So what, exactly, is humiliating?"

"Everything. My behavior. Not ... um ... never mind. I'm sorry. I just keep popping up in your life unexpectedly, and I'm sure you have better ... uh ... things to do."

There's something more to this than she's saying. I just don't push it. "Maybe you should talk to Graham. Get him to see you aren't obsessed with him so you don't feel the need to tag along after me or constantly keep me company. Because, honestly, you're a little too whiny."

She blinks. And just nods her head once. Then she starts down the hall. I'm an asshole. Not only because of the statement. But because I follow her to her first class, which we do not have together.

Madison sets those green eyes on me and snarls, "I got the point. There is no need to follow me."

She's right. But for some reason, I can't stop this sick cycle. The one that wants to be near her. The one that actually tries to get under her skin. Knowing, in the end, I'm going to get my nuts kicked in by this irritating yet addicting girl.

Madison comes by my house around seven. "Sorry. Had to run," she says as she barges into my room wearing yoga pants and a tight T-shirt. She looks amazing, even with her hair all pulled back into a ponytail and one of those ugly headbands wrapped around her head. Her forehead glistens with sweat, so I know she didn't even bother changing.

I need to stop observing her like this. She made it clear she wants nothing to do with me, and I'm not getting shot down by her again. My door flies open again right as Madison takes her spot on the floor. Her eyes widen a bit, and then she looks down at the carpet.

Graham clears his throat and walks into my room. He's done it a thousand times before—given the old "what's up" nod and taken a seat at my computer desk. Only problem is, this time, he doesn't cast his eyes on me or at a spot on the wall. No, his fucking stare is on Madison, and that sets my blood boiling.

"So, how far did you all get?" Graham asks.

"We didn't," I grumble.

He looks over at me and then back down at Madison. "Is that true, or are you two screwing with me? You know, to punish me for bailing on you the other night?"

"I just got here," Madison says. "You know, because I had cross-country practice."

Graham opens his book with a smile. "Great! Well, how are we going to do this? Mads, you answer all the questions, and then we copy—"

"Or we all work on the problems together, because I told you before I can't keep carrying you knuckleheads."

Graham glares at me. "Are you going to say anything?"

I shrug. "I think her idea is better. She's not going to be with us when we get to college. And yeah, she knows this shit better than we do. But it's not fair for her to keep carrying us."

Graham glances at Madison and then back at me. "All right." He slams his book down on my desk. "What the hell has been going on with you two lately? Because I know damn well you don't give two shits about learning this crap any more than me"—he looks from me over to Madison—"and you hate being here. So out with it now."

Madison's cheeks turn bright red. I roll my eyes and shake my head. "Nothing is happening. I just don't want to go off to college pretending I know something that I actually have no clue how to do. And she's not going to be there to tell me what's what." I stand up and head to the door. "Even if there was something going on, you would have no say in it. It would be between her and me. But because we're friends, Graham, I'm going to lay this all out for you. She'll never want someone like me. So you don't have to worry about Madison and I hooking up. What you should be worrying about is doing this fucking work and learning it, because I've got news for you: she's not going to be a hop, skip, and a jump away for you either. When college rolls around, she won't be there giving you the fucking answers."

I glance over at Madison, whose eyes are wide, her face completely red. And Graham has his mouth hanging open. One more second in this room and I'll burst, so I leave.

Chapter Thirteen

Madison

I'm a sweaty, disgusting mess. It made no difference before—I wasn't going to get all cleaned up and decent for Bryce. That was before Graham showed up, though. Then everything instantly turned awkward.

Graham glares at the door Bryce just walked out of. I tap my pencil against my notebook and stare at the list of problems we're supposed to be working on. "Well, that was messed up," Graham says.

I glance over at him. "Seemed pretty normal to me."

"Are you serious? When has Bryce ever blown up on me and defended you of all people?"

I shut my book and start shoving everything back into my book bag. I don't have to take this kind of crap from Graham. He ditched me and treated me like I've got a contagious disease. He's the one who changed.

"Where are you going?" he snaps.

I stand, slinging a strap over my right shoulder. "Home."

He reaches for me before I make it to the door. "You can't bail on us. This is a group grade worth double points."

I narrow my stare. "You certainly didn't care about that the other night. And honestly, I don't give a crap if we fail. I'm going to request a transfer."

"Why? Did something happen between you and Bryce?"

I jerk away from his grip. "No. Between you and me? Yeah. Him? No. You're the one who has a problem. My art journal is no one's freaking business, but your girlfriend seems to think it's everyone's damn business. So here's a fact: I draw everything and anyone I find inspiration in. Even Bryce is in there. Don't believe me? Go ask him. That doesn't mean I want him or I'm in love with him." I turn the knob. "And another thing: I thought we were friends. But clearly I was wrong about that, because you only want me when it's convenient for you. So go screw yourself, Graham." I yank the door open, and right there in the hallway is Bryce.

His nostrils are flared, and he glares at me. "Where are you off to, Smalls?"

"Home. I don't feel very well. I'll do the work and give it to you later. You two can just copy."

He steps into the room but takes me along with him. "Smalls, you aren't leaving yet. If you don't feel good, fine, I'll let you go. But not if you're just going to do the homework by yourself. That's not right." He guides me to the bed, and I follow him. Each and every step. I don't know why. I take a seat on the edge of the bed, and he smiles. "Good."

He hands me a water bottle he had stuffed in the back of his loose jeans. He pulls out another and starts to take a drink. I start to take off my backpack when Graham snarls, "Did you bring me something to drink?"

"No," Bryce says in a cold tone. "You know where the fridge is. Go get something."

I notice the exchange between both boys and swallow. What's going on with them? Why are they acting like this? I almost say, "I thought you two were best friends," but Bryce takes a seat next to me, and I let my comment go.

Graham huffs. "Fine. You two want to be all chummy now, great. Don't tell me a thing about it. You know it wasn't that long ago we used to all be friends. It also wasn't that long ago you two couldn't stand each other."

I rise from the bed. "You know what, this isn't working out. Tomorrow morning I'm going to request a new group. You two … you two are on your own." I face Bryce. His fists are clenched. "Thanks for the water." I gather my things and leave.

I'm not even halfway down the hall when the yelling reaches me. Bryce is shouting at Graham. Graham is hollering back. I shake my head and walk down the stairs to the front door. Mrs. Matthews spots me before I can exit. "Madison?"

"Hi, Mrs. Matthews."

"Hi. Are you done with homework so quick?"

"Um … not exactly," I start, but then Bryce yells, "You know what? I don't fucking care what you think!"

Mrs. Matthews's eyes widen. "I better go see what's going on upstairs."

"Okay. Bye, Mrs. Matthews." While she heads upstairs, I slip out the door.

After I finish all my homework, I take a seat by my window. I look at the house next door and notice Bryce is pacing around his room. A hand runs through his hair, and it almost looks torturous.

An ache settles inside me. This is somehow all my fault. I pull out my art journal and sigh. This is what started all this trouble between them. My stupid hobby. I should stick to running. I riffle through the pages and begin tearing them out.

Once I toss the pages into the trash, I turn in for the night. I pull the covers up over my shoulders and turn to face the wall. It's pink. Even in the dark, the damn thing looks bright and annoying. I'd face another wall, but Sarah got her way and did all my walls in this awful color. She wouldn't let me have even one in just white. Like in everything else, my wants or opinions didn't matter. Not after the snot-nosed princess cried.

Groaning, I close my eyes and pray that this will all be over soon, and I can go back to my life. The one that made sense. The one that didn't have a cousin ruining my things. Taking over my closet with her crap. Stealing my crush, my friends, and making them hate me. Yes, I can't wait to get back to that, but I have a feeling it won't be soon.

Buzz ... Buzz ... Buzz ... I open my eyes slowly and peer over at my clock. Sometimes I sleep through my phone's alarm, so I use my clock as a backup. The springs in the mattress above me squeak, and then I hear, "Shut that damn thing off!"

I almost let it keep going just to piss with her, but my mother's stupid reminder to be nice to Sarah pops in my head. With a groan, I shut off my alarm and head to my dresser. Using the sliver of moonlight spilling into my room as a guide, I make my way over there safely. I pull out my sweats and a long-sleeve shirt. I throw them on over my PJs, which is just a ratty T-shirt and cotton shorts. Yeah, I know, super sexy stuff right there.

I gather my hair into a ponytail, snatch my running shoes, and go straight down the steps. Making barely a sound, I slip on my shoes and out of the house. I stretch out my legs using the front steps, and then I glance around the silent, sleepy neighborhood. It's three forty-five in the morning. The only people awake are people with babies and people coming home from second shifts.

I run hard, down the road past all the things that are familiar to me. The large blue mailbox at the end of the street. The row of three white houses with black shutters. I always wonder why they all have the same red door. And if the occupants have ever mistakenly gone to the wrong house while intoxicated.

I keep a pace that's probably considered a medium speed for about a mile down the road and then whip back around. I can't run too long out here, as much as I might want to. I still have to shower and go to school. Plus, there's a cross-country meet today, and this Friday is our rival meet.

My team is running against Greenville High today. I'm not worried about that meet at all. Not to brag, but I could probably walk faster than most of the Greenville girls' team can run. What I am worried about is my meet on Friday against Westminster High. It's the toughest team to beat on our schedule. In fact, each year they've stomped us in track, baseball, cross-country, and football. Plus, my archnemesis, Kathy Wheeler, is on the Westminster team.

My cousin and Kathy could become BFFs, that's how much this girl gets under my skin. She's all smiles when coaches, judges, and refs are around, but once they turn their backs, BOOM! Out come the claws, and she's jamming them into your back. She's dirty too. Not like she smells and needs three baths but like she'll do anything to win—including cheating. Last year, she managed to trip me. The year before, she elbowed me as I attempted to pass her on a bend. She never gets caught either. Not by people who matter.

My coach caught her stunt last year and threw a major fit, but no one else saw it. So that cheater walked away with a smirk on her thin, glossed lips. And all I wanted to do was pop her in her big fat nose. My team had to hold me back when she made the comment, "What's that? It's the sound of you losing to me once again."

Images of Kathy crying because I beat her fill my head. I barely register a car driving toward me. I make a dive for the sidewalk as the car stops and the passenger-side window rolls down. "Jesus, Smalls, what in the hell are you doing running in the middle of the road for? And without bright clothing on."

I stand and brush off my sweats. "No one is ever out at this time. What are you doing?"

"Breakfast. Want some?"

I look around. My house isn't that far. I glance down at myself. Jeez, I'm a sweaty mess. I start to shake my head, but Bryce leans across the seat and opens the door. "Come on. I promise I'll have you back in time for a shower."

"I'm not worried about you getting me back on time. I'm worried I won't have any hot water for a shower. Plus, I'm a mess."

He looks at me as if I smacked him in the face or something. All confused and silent. He looks over at his dash and drums his fingers on the steering wheel. "All right. Well, I'm in my grunge form too, so what you're wearing is fine. But how about this, I promise to have you back in time for a *hot* shower. What do you say?"

"Fine. But this is not going to change my mind about what I said yesterday. I'm still requesting a new group today."

As soon as I slide in and shut the door, he nods. "Fair enough. But I'd like you to know I'm still going to argue my case, if that's okay."

I nod. "Doesn't mean I'll change my mind."

He laughs. "You might not want to make that statement just yet."

We're driving down the road, but he's either being really cautious or driving overly slow on purpose. I roll my eyes. "Think you better get a move on if I'm supposed to be getting a hot shower today, Grandpa."

He glares at me. "First, I'm going the speed limit. And second, next time, you can drive."

Next time? Why does the thought of that scare me and delight me at the same time? I mean, this is Bryce. He's a whole lot of wrong, yet … I don't know. Sometimes I get the feeling there is way more to him than he lets on.

Chapter Fourteen

Bryce

She's a bad idea. I keep telling myself that this is getting way out of control. I mean, fuck, I told my best friend he could kiss my ass yesterday because of this girl. The same guy that I know she wants. And someone like me really doesn't deserve a girl like Madison. She's smart, sweet, and funny, and I'm trouble. At least that's all anyone in this fucking place sees me as.

I know all this, and yet, here I am being stupid and inviting her to breakfast. Well, not just any damn breakfast. It happens to be my cousin Hailey's birthday. She drove down from Michigan, where she goes to college—Michigan State University, to be exact. My aunt and uncle live a town over from us, but the reason she attends a school three states away is because Hailey is kind of like Madison—supersmart and into sports. She got a basketball scholarship.

Hailey is the only one in my whole family who actually understands me and doesn't judge me. She's also the one who bailed me out and picked me up in bad sections of town when I needed it. She's always in my corner. But she's also nosy as hell, so Mads is the perfect person to help deflect weird questions this early in the morning.

"So, do you always get breakfast at five in the morning?" Madison asks.

I smile. "Not really. Do you mind if I … um …" I need a cigarette. Thank goodness I don't have to finish the sentence.

"Do you?" She scowls. "Just do it."

"I'm quitting."

She rolls her mossy eyes. "Uh-huh."

I pull out a cigarette and roll it between two fingers. "I am."

She turns her attention away from me. My stomach plummets. I don't know why or what's wrong with me, but all of a sudden, the craving is gone. I drop the cigarette right back into the pack and growl, "Happy?"

She's the only logical explanation for all this. Not that it's a bad thing, but man, she's so frustrating. And why do I all of a sudden give a shit what she thinks?

"I wasn't going to give you a lecture or anything. But I am proud of you."

This will sound weird, but I like the fact that she's proud of me. Yes, it's for not doing something stupid that I know is bad for me. But still. The fact that she's proud of me for something makes me smile.

"Look, about yesterday," I say, "if I promise it won't happen again, will you at least stay in our group?"

I glance over at her and catch her twiddling her

thumbs. "I don't know."

"It wasn't your fault. Graham is an asshat sometimes. Plus, I think he's just mad. Not because he has to do his own work for once. But because I think he's realizing what kind of asset you were in his life."

She starts to argue, but I interrupt her. "Plus, I think a part of him loves the fact that you idolize him. I know he acts like he's all freaked out, but he secretly he loves it. That's why he's jealous of us hanging out. He's mad you'll stop looking at him like he's some flipping god."

"If this is supposed to convince me to stay, you're doing a crappy job."

"I'm not finished." I run a free hand through my hair and then place it back down on the steering wheel. "I was pissed off yesterday because he acts like you and I can't be friends. And honestly, a few weeks ago, I would have agreed. But now, no. I think we just never really gave ourselves that choice. Here's the thing, though, now that we have, I don't think we should stop. I don't care if Graham gets jealous. He'll get the hell over it."

She sighs. "It doesn't matter much. Like you said, we'll all be going our separate ways in the end. And okay, I admit, I did like Graham. I thought he was perfect. But … I guess I was wrong. Doesn't mean I want to get in the middle of your friendship with him. You two are best friends, and you were about to clobber each other. And over what? I think it's better if I ask for a different group."

I'm not going to admit why I was about to beat Graham up. She can't know how I feel about her. Not right now. I'm not ready for her rejection. Not that anyone is ever really prepared for that. "You're right."

We remain silent for the rest of the ride to Bob Evans. I open the door to the restaurant, and no sooner than we're in the entranceway do I hear, "Bryce! Bryce! Over here!"

Madison looks back at me with a raised brow.

"That's Hailey."

Madison slows her pace as we approach the table. I notice her posture is a little stiffer. Her fists are clenched at her sides, and I almost laugh. If I didn't know any better, I'd say Mads is jealous. Well, well, well, who would have thought that was possible?

"Hey, Hails. This is Madison," I say as I wrap my arms around my cousin. "Happy birthday!" Hailey pulls back and moves toward Madison.

Madison stares at her with wide eyes as my cousin hugs her. Mads looks over at me and glares, right as Hailey returns to her seat. "Bryce, you're the world's biggest asshole. Why would you drag me along to this?"

I start laughing. "Madison, sit down. It's not what you think."

She looks over at Hailey. "I'm so sorry he dragged me to your date. It was nice meeting you and all. I'm going to go get a cab."

"Date?" Hailey kicks me under the table, and I groan from instant pain. "You had this poor girl believing I was your girlfriend? What's the matter with you?"

I shake my head. "I didn't do that. She just assumed it." I lock my stare with Madison's. "She's my cousin. Jeez. What kind of dickwads have you been seeing that take their friends on dates with them?"

Madison blushes. "I don't go on dates," she

mumbles so low I barely hear her. She glares at me. "Why didn't you say something when you picked me up?"

I shrug. "I didn't think it mattered."

Hailey laughs. "Take a seat, Madison. Oh, I needed a good laugh this morning. She's a little riot, Bry. So how did you two meet?"

Madison settles into the seat next to me and picks up her menu. "We attend the same school. We're also neighbors."

"Get out!" Hailey smacks the table and says to me, "When did the priss and her family move out? And why didn't you tell me? We could have had some fun."

Oh, boy. From the corner of my eye, I see Madison drop her menu and shift in her seat. "So that's what you think about me? I'm a priss?"

Hailey stares at me. "Oh, shit."

Yeah, that. And a whole lot more. I face Madison. Her glare speaks volumes. She wishes I were dead. Right now. "That was before we started hanging out."

"We hung out before this, though. You were rude. How was I supposed to act? All you did was make fun of me. Snap at me. Roll your eyes. You were nothing but an asshole. Who wants to be friends with an asshole?" She looks at the ground. "You ruined my hair in first grade. You took all the pencils from my desk every day in third grade. Mrs. Christopher wrote on my report card 'not responsible.'" She looks up and narrows her eyes. "Stop smirking. It's not funny. And how about the time freshman year you told Danny Livingston that I had a crush on him? That kid followed me around for weeks."

I can't help it, I burst out laughing. Oh, those were

some damn good times.

"Who's Danny Livingston?" Hailey asks.

"He's this kid in our grade who has rotten breath and smells like B.O." I smile at Madison. "Oh, come on. If it were anyone else, you'd laugh."

"But I'm not. And it's not funny." She crosses her arms. And I know she's mad, but she looks adorable.

Hailey snorts. "Oh, Bry, you made her out to be so horrible, but I can see now she's your match. Don't pay any attention to him, hon. Once you get past his prickly layers, he's actually really sweet. Almost like a puppy."

Madison purses her lips and raises a brow. A waitress with strands of gray in her hair stops by our table. "You kids know what you want?"

"Order what you want, Mads. I gotcha," I say.

Hailey smiles at me, and I shake my head. "I want a stack of apple pancakes," Hailey says. "I'd also like a cup of coffee."

"All right. Home fries or hash browns?"

"Home fries." She looks over at Madison and adds, "I don't trust shredded potatoes."

I smack my palm to my face and drag it down. I hope to hell my cousin doesn't start talking about weird food things. Like how she doesn't eat canned corn or why she won't eat fries that aren't fresh cut. She seriously watches way too much investigative documentaries.

"And for you?" the waitress asks Madison.

"I just want the Sunrise Bowl with biscuits. I'll have a water to drink."

When the waitress gets to me, I order two coffees and a water. One coffee is for Madison because I know she wants it. Why she didn't order one, I'm not sure. And maybe it's weird of me to order her a cup, but I want her to know I pay attention. Even when there are times, like right this minute, I wish I didn't.

"So, Hails, how is college?"

She looks up at me. There's a slight frown on her face, but she changes it to a smile. "It's good."

I clench my fists and tighten my jaw. She just lied. Something's off, and I'm going to get to the bottom of it.

Chapter Fifteen

Madison

Bryce stiffens beside me. His cousin looks away and tries to divert attention away from herself. I know this because I do it often enough.

"So, I have a question. You got up at five in the morning to have breakfast with each other?"

"He practically kidnapped me. I was running when he pulled over and demanded I come with him." I try to laugh it off, but Hailey looks at me and then over at Bryce.

"So … are you two dating?" she asks Bryce.

The waitress returns with our drinks, saving Bryce from answering. He slides a cup of coffee to me, and I start to shake my head, but he grumbles, "I know you want it."

Okay, so he's right. I do want the coffee. But the fact that he knows that is making whatever this is between us really awkward. I mean, we're not really friends. Not in the real sense of the word. We might be getting there, but we're still a ways away from that.

Plus, there are moments like earlier, before I knew Hailey was his cousin, when I imagined ripping every strand of her hair from her scalp. Total animal-like, I know. If that's not weird enough, these past few days he's been constantly on my mind. God, knows I don't want him to be. Not in the ways he is.

Last night, I kept wondering what he was doing. If he was upset with me. Whether he would he miss me or even care if I switched groups. Which is all really stupid. But that's not the only problem. Sometimes I wonder what it'd be like to kiss him. Or what his hands would feel like going through my hair. Or how his cheek stubble would feel against my fingertips. Yeah, its weird thoughts like those I know I shouldn't have but do.

I'd ask Emily what all this means and what could possibly be wrong with me. But I'm scared of the answer. If I don't admit to it, it can't be true, right?

"We're just in the same study group in math and neighbors. Don't go making it into something that it isn't," Bryce says with a shake of his head.

My heart instantly plunges to the bottom of my stomach. That's not right. I thought I'd feel relieved. I thought I'd jump for joy. Oh crap! Crap! Crap! No, no, no! I'm not falling for Bryce Matthews.

I've got to get out of here. I just … I need to leave now.

I stand up and mumble my apologies and then dart toward the restrooms. I whip out my phone as soon as I've locked myself in a stall and call my mom. She won't give me a bunch of crap for hanging out with Bryce. At least I hope she won't.

Emily digs into her locker for something, and I'm listening to her jabber on about this party happening this weekend when a loud *bang* sounds right behind me. Emily looks up, and I turn to the noise. Two steps away from me stands Bryce. He looks livid.

"Explain to me why you won't answer your fucking phone. And while you're at it, how about you explain ditching breakfast." His hand fans his ear that's tilted toward me. "Come on. I'm dying to know."

I swallow and look back at Emily. She shrugs and gives me the "What the hell have you been hiding from me?" glare.

"I remembered I didn't make a reference page for my report in psychology." It's a total lie. I actually have a packet to do in class, which is due Friday. But I already did it.

Bryce stares at me. He leans a shoulder against the locker. "Yeah? Let me see it."

"What?"

"Did I stutter?"

"No. But … why do you want to see it?"

Emily whispers, "Because you're full of it, and he knows it."

I narrow my eyes at her and turn my attention back to Bryce. "I already turned it in."

"Bullshit! Do me and yourself a favor, Smalls. Quit lying."

I fold my arms. "Why do you care so much?"

"I was worried something happened to you. You fucking left without saying good-bye. Decent people at least say, 'Hey, I'm leaving.' You just left. I searched everywhere for you. I called your fucking phone. You could have answered, but I know that's too much to ask of you. Right, princess?"

He's right. I should have answered. I just ... I didn't know what to say. That sounds so selfish, but I didn't want to tell him why I left. This is already awkward enough. And he had me meeting his cousin on her birthday. That just seems too personal and, well, it's just getting to be too much.

I lower my lashes and sigh. "I'm sorry. It was wrong."

"You know what? Thanks. I knew there was a reason I didn't want us becoming friends. Thank you." He bows and starts to ease away from me. "Oh." He places a finger against his lips. "You should put in that request for a new group during calc today."

I watch him as he turns his back to me and disappears down the hall. Emily smacks my shoulder. "What was that?"

"Nothing." She glares at me. "All right. I was doing a run this morning, and Bryce picked me up. We were going to have breakfast with his cousin. I left before the food arrived."

"And you didn't tell anyone you were leaving?"

I groan as we walk in the opposite direction Bryce went. "Not you too. Look, it's getting weird. Graham said he thought me and Bryce hanging out was a bad idea. Then Bryce argued with him, and when has that ever happened? Never. Well, before yesterday it had never happened before. And …" I stop when I see Graham and Sarah yelling at each other in the crowded hall. She smacks his arm, and he winces. "That doesn't look good."

"Let me get this straight," Sarah yells. "You think we should hang out less because Madison isn't helping you anymore?" Is this really happening? Emily tugs on my arm, but I can't leave.

Sarah snaps, "Don't you see she's pulling this stunt to have you all to herself? She's crazy. Look at these. Tell me she's not obsessed with you!" She pulls out a stack of drawings I know I threw in my trash can and shoves them at Graham's chest.

He unrolls a few pages, and then his eyes turn toward me. Sarah follows his gaze. She gives me a look that says, "He's all mine now." Graham's face, though, says it all. He's completely freaked out.

I'm about to tell him I can explain. But he just shakes a fistful of the drawings. "Seriously? How many have you done? Why? I've never liked you like that, and I never will, Madison. You need to get some help."

I feel my left arm being tugged again, and my body stumbles toward the jerking. My eyes blink, and I feel the tears sliding down my cheeks as well as my heart snapping. But when my stare lands on Sarah again, rage fills me. I want to punch the smirk right off her face. Give her a black eye, maybe a broken nose. Doesn't matter, just as long as she's not so pretty tomorrow.

"Come on, Maddy," Emily commands.

"I feel sick."

"Yeah, well, you have a meet today, so suck it up and get your butt in class. Besides, he's not worth it.

Never was."

But wasn't he? He's just doing and saying these kinds of things because Sarah is manipulating the situation. She has to show everyone that she's the pretty one. The popular one. The girl everyone either wants or wants to be.

Emily pulls me to my first period class and levels her gaze at me. "Maddy, you need to forget what just happened. Let it go. Trust me when I say there are way hotter, sexier, smarter, and sweeter guys out there. Graham will seem like a total D-bag when you meet one."

I nod. There is nothing I can really say. This is my senior year, and I've never been on a date. I haven't really been kissed. Frank Russell does not count. That was a peck on my lips and in eighth grade while playing spin the bottle. Again, that doesn't count.

"Yeah."

She smiles. "I'll see you at lunch."

"See ya."

I walk into my class while she shuffles off to hers. Emily has civics this period. I'm just grateful Graham isn't in my chemistry 2 class. I think I might die if he were. The wound he put in my chest is way too fresh. I might have to find somewhere to disappear to for second period. Maybe I can try seeing my coach or something.

"Madison Issac?" Mrs. Walters says.

I look up.

"You're to go to the office."

"Oh, um … okay."

I grab my bag, snatch the slip from my teacher, and head down to the office.

Chapter Sixteen

Bryce

She thought she could just ditch me at breakfast and I wouldn't tell her off at school? Madison had another think coming. As soon as I found her, I let her know exactly what I thought about her. I believed it would make me feel better. Truth is, after I laid into her and saw her eyes glisten with tears, I felt worse.

Around third period, I notice she isn't in class yet, which is odd. She's always in here before me. Graham walks in and settles into his usual seat before saying, "Oh, thank God she's not here."

"Who?"

"Madison. Her obsession with me has gotten way out of hand. I had to tell her off."

I give him a puzzled look. "What are you talking about?"

Graham leans closer to my desk. "Dude," he says in a low tone, "I guess she tried to pitch her drawings or whatever. Maybe she was going to lie about it later or something, but I saw them. They had hearts and phrases like 'mine forever' and 'XOXO' shit all over them. I hope to hell she requests a new group, because I'm not doing assignments with her ever again!"

I shake my head. "I don't know what you were looking at, man, but I can tell you firsthand, I've seen her drawings. There wasn't any kind of 'XOXO shit' like you claim."

"Whatever, man. I know what the fuck I saw this morning. And I'm telling you, you need to bail on her now if you don't want to end up on her list."

Pretty sure that won't be happening. She made it clear how she sees me, so I'm not worried about her becoming obsessed with me.

I ignore Graham for most of class. That's up until Madison enters the room. Mrs. Vixen sets down her marker and smiles at Madison. Madison hands her a slip and then steps back out of the classroom. What the hell just happened?

I raise my hand.

"Yes, Bryce?"

"May I use the restroom?"

"Sure. Come up here and grab the hall pass."

I rush to her desk, snatch the wooden paddle, and then head into the hall. Looking left, then right, I decide to head toward the restrooms near the stairs. I spot her walking slowly down the hallway and run to her.

"Hey," I say as soon as I reach her.

She looks over at me and sighs. "I don't have time for this. What do you want?"

"I want to know what's going on. Graham said he saw your drawings and that you wrote a bunch of weird crap on them."

She stops walking and glares at me. "I didn't write that stuff! But it doesn't matter. I've already gotten an earful from you and Graham today."

"I'm sorry." She drops her head and starts walking again. I continue to follow and explain. "I was just worried about you. It was just breakfast, though, not a date or marriage. There was no reason for you to freak out and take off like you did." I brush my arm against hers. The small contact sends a zing down my spine, and my stomach flips.

She slows her pace and pauses right by the other set of stairs. "You're right. Both times. I shouldn't have left like that. Also, I should have told you I was leaving. It was rude, and I'm really sorry I made you worry. I really didn't think you'd care."

I want to touch her chin and lift it so she can see me, not my shoes. But I think if I touch her it might be too much and she'll run off again. "But I do care. Shit, Smalls, I like hanging out with you. I think you're pretty cool. And I think we could be good friends, so of course I care."

Her green eyes find mine. "I ripped all that stuff out last night. After you and Graham started fighting over me." She looks away. "I feel like none of this would have happened if I didn't leave my journal out for people to see. Or maybe if I'd let you both see what I drew instead of hiding it away from everyone like a dark secret. This wouldn't be an issue at all."

"Smalls, who gives a shit what Graham or anyone else thinks? I think you've got amazing talent. As long as you like doing it and it's what you want to do, then screw everyone else. Just do it."

Madison smiles and then wraps her arms around me. "Thank you." She pulls back quicker than I want her to. She smiles and starts to head down the steps.

"Wait. Where are you going?"

"I've got a meeting with my coach and a scout. I just had to give a note to Mrs. Vixen to tell her why I wasn't in her room. I've got to get back, though, or I'll miss fourth and lunch."

I nod. "Okay." She goes down two more steps. "Wait. Did you request a different group?" She shakes her head. "Good. Don't. We'll figure something out. Are you going to Greg's party this weekend?"

She shrugs. "Bryce, I really have to go. I'll talk to you later. Okay?"

"All right."

I let her go, and I head back to class.

Chapter Seventeen

Madison

After my long day of school and the meet, all I want to do is take a hot bath and go to bed. But as soon as I step into my house, my mom calls me into the kitchen. I sluggishly enter. The smell of tomatoes, onions, and sausage hits me.

The homemade pasta sauce I love wakes my tired body. I stroll over to the pot of deliciousness. I spot a loaf of bread cut up and grab a slice to dip into the sauce. My mom slaps my hand before I even get a chance to plunge the slice in. "No. Your brother always did that, and that's where you picked up that habit. I will not be chasing you off with a spoon now just because he's not here. Go set the table."

I roll my eyes, and as soon as she turns away from me, I dunk my bread in the sauce and head over to the table.

"I saw that."

"'Aw what?" I ask while chewing off a chunk of the evidence.

"Madison, just go set the table, please." She grabs a container from the fridge and looks back at me.

"I'm going. I'm going."

"Five plates, Maddy."

"Ma, there's only four of us. Kyle won't be home for couple of weeks."

She closes a cabinet near the stove. "I know. But tonight there will be five. Graham is eating with us."

I almost drop the stack of plates in my hands. This was the only good thing about studying over at Bryce's house right after practices and meets—I avoided this. Graham and Sarah pawing each other, throwing their love-fest in my face like a bunch of animals. It's bad enough I have to see that at school; now I have to look at it during dinner?

I love my mom's homemade spaghetti and sauce, but there's no way in hell I can stomach a bite. I set down four plates. "Crap! I forgot I've got to go to the theater and pick up my work schedule before it closes. Sorry." I rush over and peck my mom on the cheek.

"Wait. Oh, okay. Be careful. I'll make you a plate."

I nod. "Thanks. I love you." I head out of the kitchen and out the door with my backpack. Barely two steps away from the porch, I'm face to face with Graham and Sarah in a whole lip-lock session. They look like two octopuses attacking each other against his car.

I feel the bread I ate earlier forcing its way up. Tearing my gaze from them and focusing on the lawn, I quickly make my way to Bryce's house. I don't know why I'm going there. I shouldn't.

Instead of turning around and heading to the park

or basically anywhere else, I lift my knuckles to the front door of his house. Three raps on the door and Mrs. Matthews stands before me. "Madison? Was, um … Bryce expecting you?" She clutches the upper half of her button-down shirt. Her skin appears flushed, and her hair is falling out of the tight bun she usually has it in.

"Uh … no. I, uh …" *Jesus, think of something. Leave. You're clearly seeing something you shouldn't.* "You know what? I forgot we were supposed to meet at the library today." I smack my forehead to help make the lie believable.

"Oh. Okay. Well, when you see him, can you remind him it's Hailey's birthday and he should give her a call?"

"Sure." I backpedal off the porch as she shuts the door. Reaching the last step, my back collides into something hard. I turn and see Bryce, fists at his sides and staring ahead. "Oh, hey, I was just looking for you." I grab his hand and pull him along with me. "Library today. Right?"

Bryce looks down at me and then up at the door. "What are you doing?"

"I, uh …" I glance over at my house and then over at him. "I actually was coming over here to see if you wanted to have dinner with me. Your mom is always feeding me, and I figured it was time to return the favor."

He follows me to my house. As soon as we're at my front door, he says, "Stop for a second."

"Why?"

"I know, okay, why you're really doing this. And thanks."

I frown. "I'm so sorry. I actually … You look like

you're about to strangle someone to death. Trust me, I know it's not my place or business but … did you know?"

"Yeah. For about five months now. My dad has been gone a lot actually. He says he's working at the office. What he really means is he's working his new assistant over a desk." I gasp, but he shakes his head. "Don't. He's an asshole. My mom knows. She just refuses to leave. So she started having her own little affair."

"And you?"

"Say nothing. I let them both think what they want, that everyone is happy. Faking happiness is very easy."

I squeeze his hand. "I'm sorry."

He shrugs. "Nothing you can do, Smalls. Thanks, though."

I open the door and guide Bryce into the kitchen. My mom is setting a huge serving dish on the table and looks over at me. "Madison, I thought—"

"Hey, Ma, I'm so silly and forgot that my schedule is online. Bryce here reminded me when I ran into him outside. I was wondering if Bryce can join us for dinner?"

She smiles. I peer over at my dad, who looks Bryce up and down. Then his gaze stops right at my hands. "Bryce, please join us," my mom says.

"Madison, I'd like a word with you," my dad grinds out.

Sarah snickers, and I let my glare drop to her and Graham. Their backs are to me, so if I attacked them they'd never expect it. I study them a little longer than I should and notice Graham's hand resting on her upper thigh.

My father clears his throat, and I follow him out of the room and to his office near the living room. He shuts the door behind us and steps over to his bookcase on the far left of the room.

"What's up?" I ask.

"Is there something going on between you and Bryce Matthews I should be aware of?"

I snort. "No. He's just a friend, Dad."

He looks at me. His forehead wrinkles, and he rubs the bald patch on the back of his head. "I don't think it's a good idea to be friends with someone like Bryce. He's got a knack for trouble."

I grumble. "Dad, seriously, you need to relax. We don't hang out all the time. Just for study group. Graham is in it with us. Nothing to worry about."

He nods. "Okay." He closes the space, kisses my forehead, and we leave his office.

I return to the kitchen and take a seat next to Bryce. My mom already filled his plate with pasta. "Smells and looks great, Mrs. Issac. Thanks for having me over."

"Oh, you're more than welcome, hon." She looks over at me and scowls. "Madison! Stop hoarding the garlic bread."

I drop one of the pieces onto Bryce's plate. "I was sharing." Okay, really I hadn't planned on sharing at all. Mom's garlic bread is to die for. Literally. It's butter, garlic, and Italian herbs brushed over the entire bread slices. With melted parmesan and mozzarella cheese on one side. The only good thing about Sarah moving in—she doesn't eat bread. Something about carbs will make her ass huge or something. Hey, more for me.

Sarah sneers at me. "Do you have to eat like a cavewoman?"

My mom glares at me. "Manners, Madison. Stop stuffing your face and eat like a lady. We have guests."

"They aren't watching me eat," I mumble.

"Well, you're across from me, and you sound like a cow," Sarah says.

I drop my fork. "Your ass is as big as a cow's, so I guess you laying off the bread doesn't really work."

"Madison! Go to your room right this minute!" my father says.

Sarah smirks at me.

"Keep smiling over there," I snap. "I'll make sure you have two black eyes tomorrow!"

She gasps. My mom stands and moves toward me.

I snatch the bread from my plate and grab Bryce. "Bring your plate," I say to him. He does and follows me.

My dad growls, "Madison."

"You said I had to leave. We need to study. It's a win for everyone."

My mom shoots my dad a look, and then he waves us off.

Chapter Eighteen

Bryce

"I actually had no idea you could be so entertaining," I say to Mads as I take a seat at her desk.

"I'm so grounded as soon as you go home," she says as she buries her face in her hands.

I roll her desk chair over to her. "Hey. It's going to be okay." She lowers her hands, and I grab them. I pull them the rest of the way from her face and smile at her. "I've got your back, Mads."

"Why, though? I mean … isn't this all weird for you too?"

I shrug and lean back in her chair. "You keep forgetting something about me. I don't care what people think. Not about us becoming friends. Not about if this turns into something else." I edge toward her and tuck a strand of hair behind her ear. She gasps as soon as it's secure, and I pull my hand away. "And I don't care if it all blows up and we go back to avoiding each other again." Well, that's a lie. I'll care a little more than I say if she goes back to avoiding me.

She rises from her bed, causing me to move back a few inches. She brushes her hands over her T-shirt and wipes her eyes with a sniffle. "Let's, um … get to work."

She walks around me and over to her desk. She plops down on the floor and starts tugging books out of her backpack.

"Mads, you should take the chair." I roll back to the desk.

Madison shakes her head. "That's okay. I like sitting on the floor. It helps me think better." She laughs. "This is going to sound really strange, but I feel freer on the floor than confined to a desk when I'm doing homework."

I nod. "Not strange. I know what you mean. It's like a floor is infinite space. A desk only has so much room."

"Yes! Exactly!" Her mossy eyes brighten before fading again. "So, um … since I didn't switch groups, and, uh, that stuff just happened downstairs …" She chews on her bottom lip. Which makes me want to grab her and kiss that mouth of hers. "We can work out the problems, and then you and Graham can do them, I guess."

I want to tell her piss on my best friend. He's the one being an idiot. We shouldn't have to make stupid arrangements like this in order for him to get the same answers as us. But on the other hand, I'm glad he's being a jackass. I get to spend time with Madison without having him stare at us like we're aliens or something. I get to talk to her and watch her laugh or suck in her bottom lip with her teeth. It's like these moments are all mine, and excuse me for not wanting to share.

"Bryce?"

"Hmm?"

"Did you hear what I said about tomorrow?"

No, I was too busy staring at your lips and imagining all the ways I'd get you to moan against my own mouth. "Uh, no, sorry. What about tomorrow?"

She sighs. "Do you need to smoke?"

"What?"

She pushes herself to a stand and opens the door. "I'm not judging, but your leg bounces and you rub your hands against your jeans right before you put a cigarette in your mouth."

I raise a brow. "Oh, do I? Are you studying my habits now, Miss Maddy?"

She rolls her eyes and snorts. "Don't take this somewhere it's not meant to go. I've just been around you long enough to know when you're about to light up or in the need to light up."

I honestly wasn't thinking about a smoke. But I can't tell her what I was craving. She'll run off like she did this morning. "It's cool. I can wait."

"Okay." She pulls out some paper and hands it over to me. She gives me a pencil, and we get started.

We're almost done with the problem sets when her door opens. Sarah strolls into the room with Graham trailing behind her. He looks like a whipped pup. Pathetic. I shake my head at him, and Madison clears her throat, pulling my attention right back to her. "Want to take a break?"

"Sure."

We get up from the floor and leave. She stops at the bottom of the stairs and glances back at me. "Tree-house break?"

"Sure."

Madison sits at one end of the window of my tree house, and I sit at the other. She looks over at me a few times, and I laugh. "What's wrong?"

"I don't know. I just … If you'd asked me two months ago the last place I'd be, this would have been it. Well, hanging out with you alone would have been it."

"Oh, trust me, Smalls, I would have had the same answer. But now, what would you say?"

She chews her lip. "I don't know. Being in Mr. Clement's class. His breath is god-awful."

I laugh and slap my leg with my hand. "Oh, I know. I have to sit in the front row near his desk, and his shit breath reaches everyone in the first two rows."

She makes a gagging noise. "That's so gross. I'm lucky; I sit closer to the back. But as soon as he finds out you play sports, he is always coming over and talking to you."

"Yeah. Henry Byers sits next to me, and he gets a double dose of the dragon breath."

"Poor Henry."

I shrug. "Henry is kind of a dick, so it's actually quite funny to me."

"Is he? He's always nice to me and Emily."

"That's because Henry has the hots for you and Emily. He'd be stupid not to."

She elbows my ribs. "You're just saying that so I don't shove you out the door and possibly to your death."

"Is that any way to treat me after I let you take over my tree house, and my bed?"

Her cheeks turn scarlet. She fiddles with her hair.

"Relax. It was just a joke," I say.

"I know."

I lean toward her and ask, "Do you?" Her gaze bores into mine, and I smile. "I meant what I said—that Henry would be stupid not to have the hots for you. Anyone would."

She rolls her eyes. "I can think of a lot of people who don't have the hots for me."

"And they're all fucking stupid." I get closer. Our lips are mere inches from touching. I want to kiss her, but I don't want to go down as the guy who kissed her with garlic breath. I need to back off.

"Right, well, it doesn't matter."

I pull back a little. "Why?"

"Because no one has ever asked me out. I know what the guys call me behind my back. Drunk parties bring out the honesty in everyone, don't they?"

I look away. "I guess." Fuck. Did I say anything about her? It was probably when I thought she was a little prissy princess.

From the corner of my eye, I catch her movement. I glance back at her and see her stand. "We should get back."

"Okay."

Chapter Nineteen

Madison

My heart is racing like it does after running ten miles and sprinting the last lag of the mile. My palms are all sweaty. Other parts of me are probably sweating too, but I don't exactly know how to check without Bryce seeing.

So I play it as cool as possible. Even though I can hear *thump-thump-thump* hammering in my ears, and I'm sure he can hear it too. Maybe if I create a lot of space between us I can pass it off as something else if he asks. There is only one spot in my room, though, that can create that distance, and I'd rather lick the backside of a slimy toad than sit on my bed. Because directly above it is Sarah and Graham giggling, kissing, and watching some video clips on her phone.

Bryce looks about as annoyed as I feel as soon as Sarah says, "Stop it." And playfully shoves Graham.

He tickles her again. "You stop it."

"No, you," she says through giggles.

It goes on like this six more times before I finally can't take anymore. "Both of you knock it off. We're trying to do our homework in here. If you can't stop being a bunch of bubbly idiots for more than five minutes, then get the hell out!"

Sarah sits up and glares at me. "Or what, Madison? This is my room too. And if I want *my* boyfriend in here with me I can have him in here." She emphasizes the word my like I needed a reminder that Graham's her boyfriend. Which really just pisses me off more. I'm done being nice and kissing this little bitch's ass!

"You know what, Sarah? I've had it." I glare at her from my spot on the floor. "I let you have my closet. Let you paint my walls. But I will be forever damned if I let you do one more fucking thing to *my* room. Because that's what it is. It's my room."

She starts a rebuttal, but I interrupt her, "Does anyone even know why you are here?" I look around the room, and when no one says anything, I laugh. "Wow. Well, I hope the wardrobe, shoes, and purses that you remind me every single day are so much better than the rags I own are worth it. I'd be ashamed to wear anything my parents bought me with stolen money. But you go ahead, wear your dream-crushing merchandise like a badge of honor."

Her jaw clenches, and Graham stares at her, then at me. "What's she talking about?"

"Nothing. Right, Madison? She's just jealous because you love me and not her. She's always been jealous of me. Isn't that right, Maddy?"

I've got her. She knows it, too. "Oh, sooooo jealous. Jealous my parents aren't facing a trial for stealing millions of dollars from their employees. Sooooo jealous that I'm not homeless, and no one else was willing to take me in."

"Shut up, Madison! Or I swear I will ruin you."

Bryce whistles beside me. "This has been fun, girls, but Mads and I really need to finish up this last problem. Graham, take your girlfriend downstairs, or I won't let you copy off me later."

Graham swallows and somehow convinces Sarah to follow him out of the room. Once the door is shut, Bryce shakes his head at me. "What?" I ask.

"Stellar move, Madison." He presses his finger against his lips. "You know the secret to revenge is to do it in a way that destroys your enemy without them knowing it was you."

"Sounds like you've made your fair share of enemies."

He shakes his head. "Forget it. The answer to the last problem is zero." Bryce stands, and I stare at him. He leaves my room without another glance back at me.

The whole stupid evening plays over and over inside my head. I should have stopped him from leaving. I shouldn't have said what I said. He doesn't deserve my cruel remarks. He's been nothing but nice, and what have I been? A little bitch. Like someone else I know.

Lying in bed, I toss my head back and look straight up above me. I see dark cherry wooden slats almost resembling the underside of a deck—or a tree-house floor. I squeeze my eyes shut. I can't think about the tree house. That'll make me think about Bryce all over again.

My alarm blares beside me. I turn over and stare at the big red digits. I swear it feels like I've only been lying in bed for ten minutes, not eight hours. Smacking the off button, I shift to my back and rub my aching eyes.

I've got to get up, get energized, and focus on my meet today. If I drag ass, my times will suck. And if I want a scholarship anywhere far away from this place, I need to have good times. Well, if I want to go to college, period, I'm going to need a scholarship.

Okay, I've probably laid here long enough. I chuck the covers off and sluggishly head to my dresser. I grab a pair of white undies from the top drawer, shirt, bra, and jeans. Yeah, it's going to be a muggy, hot-ass day, and I'll be miserable, but there's no way in hell I'm wearing the last three pairs of shorts left. I haven't gotten to my laundry yet.

Stepping into the bathroom, I turn on the shower and wait for the water to heat up. While I wait, my attention lands on my panties. I pick up the soft cotton and examine them from front to back. They look normal, but when I open them, there is a giant hole right where the crotch is.

What the heck? I leave the bathroom and return to my room to hunt for another pair of undies. Inside my drawer, every pair, I mean even the granny-style panties I wear on those PMSing days, have a hole cut into the crotch area. I clench my fist and release it, then clench it again. I'm going to beat her so hard, she'll be put in the hospital with a possible coma!

At least that's what I want to do. She stirs in her bed. She glares at me, but then her eyes lower to my hand and she smiles. Like that stupid Cheshire Cat from *Alice in Wonderland.* "Good morning, Madison."

"Madison!" my mother calls out, interrupting the verbal rant inside my head. "Did you leave this shower running?"

I turn from Sarah and head into the hall. My mom is standing beside the bathroom door with a scowl on her face. I can't hold back the tears forming. As much as I don't want to be that brat who tattles, I'm going to. It's low, but I can't do this anymore.

"Madison, what's wrong?"

I hold up my underwear and point back at my room. "She ruined all my underwear!"

"Madison, I'm sure that's not true."

My jaw drops. "Are you kidding me? Yes, it is. Go look. She did this to every pair!"

"Are you sure it was her? Bryce was in there yesterday. And so was Graham."

I shake my head and push past her into the bathroom. She starts to say something along the lines of, "You can't blame Sarah for everything," and I slam the door closed. Yeah, end of discussion. If she wants to play hard, fine by me.

I shower quickly and dress, commando-style. I grab my backpack and keys and walk past Sarah. "Afraid I'll steal your homework and keys?" She giggles.

"Nope."

She narrows her eyes. "Whatever." She stomps off to the bathroom, and I head downstairs and out the door.

I feel like yelling, "Oh, by the way, have fun taking

the bus, bitch!" But I'm enjoying this moment of her being so unaware of me leaving her. And also, if my mom heard this, she'd make me come back, wait, and take the horrible leech to school.

Settling into my seat, I sigh. I'm about to turn my car on when someone taps on the glass. I look over and huff out a sigh of relief. It's only Bryce, not my mom. My car is kind of a POS, and I have to roll down my windows by hand.

Bryce folds his arms against the door and eyes me up. "Smalls, I wanted to … Wait, why are you in your car at six forty? We don't have to be at school for another hour."

"Yeah, so? Are you going to arrest me for going in early?"

"No. But it's a ten-minute drive."

I nod. "I know. Do me a favor—get in or stop talking so I can go."

He smiles. "You're ditching her?"

I don't answer him. His smile widens. "Nice. All right." He moves around my car over to his. He snatches his bag, then returns to mine, and takes a seat in the passenger side.

I don't wait for him to buckle in. I just put the car in reverse and pull away from the house. Should I feel slightly guilty about leaving Sarah to fend for herself? Possibly. But you know what? I don't care. She's gone too far this time.

I could handle the walls turning pink, my paintings going to the attic for storage, my closet being taken over. I could even handle her turning Graham against me and posting my drawings all over the place. But it wasn't enough for her to ruin my clothes? Now she had to violate my underwear too?

My fingers tighten around the steering wheel as we head to school. "I can't believe my own mom took her side over mine!" I snap. "She has everyone wrapped around her damn finger. No one can see the evil bitch she really is!" I slam my palm against the wheel and growl, "Do you know that because of what her stupid parents have done my mom decided to split our college funds so we can help Sarah better herself too?"

I shake my head. The anger inside me boils. I move my right hand to the shifter. "It's such a waste. I don't even have to be a mind reader to tell you the first thing that will happen. First semester in, she'll party so much, probably do blow or who the heck knows what, and fail out. She'll be back at home with my parents, and they'll go broke supporting that miserable, spoiled brat. Because they'll be too afraid to tell her no. They'll feel sorry her parents are locked up. She has no one. That's what they told me and Kyle when we learned she was staying with us."

Bryce's hand covers mine. The warmth of his touch causes my stomach to flip. I peer over at him and then back at the road. I should pull my hand from his. Is it weird that I don't want to?

"I'm sorry," he says. "Your parents are really good people, though. It would have been very out of the ordinary if they didn't do something like this. They don't strike me as the kind of people who would stand by and let someone suffer, you know?"

I mumble, "I know. That's what makes this worse. I want to be mad at them. But I can't blame them because that's who they are."

I don't head to school. I drive straight to Emily's

house, even though it's early, and there's a good chance Emily isn't even up. You'd swear by looking at her on any given day that she takes hours to make herself look like that, but in reality, it's only ten minutes.

"Where are we?" Bryce asks as I ease into her driveway.

"Emily's house. I drive her every morning."

We both get out of the car after I shut it off. He looks up at the large, mansion-like two-story and then over at me. "She's got some nice digs. She doesn't throw parties here like the other snobs, I take it."

I shake my head as we approach the front door. "Her parents are always here. And if they do leave, she has to go with." I ring the doorbell and wait.

Bryce coughs, and I glance over at him. "You're not getting sick, are you? Because I have a really big meet today, and I can't afford to catch anything."

"No. I just had a tickle. You're so high-strung today. Chill."

I narrow my eyes. "You chill. I've got—" The door opens, and Deanne, the maid, greets us. "Hey, Deanne, is Emily up?"

"She is, Miss Issac. Should I tell her you are here?"

"No need. I'll just go right up." I smile and enter the house. Bryce tags along. I start toward the long, winding staircase and glance back at Deanne. "Is he okay to come up? Or would he be better off down here?"

"He can enter Miss Emily's room."

I grab a hold of Bryce's hand and pull him up the stairs with me.

Chapter Twenty

Bryce

Madison's hand in mine feels amazing. It's not too small and not too big but just right. I know I went a little *Goldilocks and the Three Bears* there, but it's true. I hate when girls' hands feel like they're the same size as mine. Not a fan of the overly tiny hands either. Makes me think of little children, and that just creeps me out.

Madison pulls me up a flight of steps and down a long hallway. She pauses by an ajar door. Madison doesn't knock. She just pushes it open, and I follow. "Emily, don't freak."

Reddish hair with blond tips fans out across a pillow. A zebra-striped mask covers her eyes, and she grumbles "Ten more minutes, Maddy."

Madison lets go of my hand and lightly shakes Emily. "Em. Emi-lou! Wake up."

Emily doesn't seem to be stirring. "Come on, Smalls, I don't think the maid knows she's not awake."

Emily props up on her elbows and lifts the mask from her eyes. "Oh my God! What are you doing in my room?" I point to Madison. Emily gives Madison a wild look. "What the hell is going on?"

"You need to get ready. We have to go hit up a Walmart or something before school," Madison says.

Emily groans. "You came to my house at …" She looks over at the clock on her nightstand and tosses the covers off . "Are you insane? It's seven. And you want me to go shopping at Walmart? Ugh. No. I'm drawing a line on our friendship."

"I need to go. Or I need to …" She leans in close and whispers in Emily's ear.

Emily raises a brow. "Why?"

Madison whispers something else, and Emily snaps, "That little bitch. Okay, I have a solution to this, but he needs to go."

I throw my hands up in the air. "Fine by me. I'll be downstairs."

"No," Madison says. "Don't go that far. Just stand outside the door. I'm going to need you for something in a couple of minutes."

"We don't need him for anything," Emily starts.

Madison interrupts as I make my way closer to the door. "Yes, we do." I glance back at her as I step out of the room. She smiles. "I need you."

"Okay." Is it weird to be thrilled by this simple statement? Because I'm stoked. And, with a probably goofy smile on my face, I leave the room and wait out in the hallway.

"You want me to give you pointers on how to be bad?" I ask, sliding into Madison's car.

"Yes. No. Maybe," Madison says with a shrug.

"I told you we don't need him," Emily pipes up from the back seat. "Besides, I think there's a difference between bad and totally dark and pure evil. No offense, man. But you're like on every cop's go-to list when a crime occurs, aren't you?"

I glare at her. "You know what, Smalls? The rich weirdo is right. You don't need me for this mess because I actually want no part of it."

"Please. I'll do all your homework for two months," Smalls offers.

"Madison!" Emily snaps.

A phone rings as Madison starts the car. She glances down at her cell in the cupholder and shakes her head. "That little witch is ruining my life. I need both of you to help me. I literally can't take it anymore."

I glance out the window and sigh. "All right. I'm in. But if we get caught, I'm not going down in this mess. I can't. Do you got me, Smalls?"

"I got it. But it won't be that kind of trouble. Not really."

"What do you plan on doing?" I ask. "Building a bonfire with all her clothes?"

Emily laughs. "Oh, that's so disturbing how well he knows you. I told you that idea was lame."

"What do you suggest I do?" Madison says. "Steal bunch of stuff and put it in her closet? She'd know that was me."

I look back at Emily and then over at Madison. "You're both missing the main point. You have to do this without getting caught. No one would suspect either of you. So you need to get some friends who gossip a lot."

Madison frowns. "I don't talk to those types of people. And how exactly would this work?"

"Sure you do. You've got the two biggest gossips on your cross-country team. And Emily knows a few from band."

"Hey!" Emily says. "There is no way I'm going to get all chummy with Ash and Penelope."

"Anyways, from what I gather about Sarah, she seems to want whatever you have. Right? So hanging out with new friends, chances are Sarah won't really know much about them, but she'll steal them. You want this. Once this happens and you randomly turn on the news that's broadcasting her parents' scandal, and say something like 'oh sorry, we need to change this,' but don't tell them why those girls will find the reason." I say. "And then they will spread it all over. Emily can help by having shopping days or whatever the hell you girls do with the Harper twins and just casually mention little things like 'so I heard Penelope hung out at your house.' Watch the rumors fly from there."

We pull into the school parking lot, and Madison's phone rings again. She groans and ignores the call. "Who is that?" Emily asks.

"Who do you think it is? My mom, probably calling

to yell at me because I left Miss Perfect at home. Boo. Hoo."

I laugh. "Oh, Smalls, if I hadn't known you most of my life, I'd say you were already on the dark side."

She glares at me and then opens her door. "What's wrong with being good?"

"Nothing, if you're into goody-goody gumdrops and rainbows. I actually like reality, and that is not all nice."

"Don't listen to him. He's the devil," Emily quips as we walk up to school.

I trail behind a bit. What am I doing? If I get caught bailing out one more imbecile friend, I'm screwed. No Michigan State like planned, just jail time. Maybe I should back out. I mean, yeah, I'd love to help Madison, but it's not really worth the risk, is it?

"Bryce!" I turn and see Graham marching up the sidewalk. I glance at Mads and Emily. Mads is making her way back to me, but Emily is tugging on her arm. I whip around to Graham, and he's practically nose to nose with me. "What the hell, man? You didn't come pick me up and didn't bother telling me." Sarah is right beside him looking smug.

I roll my eyes. He sounds like a flipping chick. "You had to drive yourself one effing day. Get over it. I'm not your personal taxi!"

"No, but you used to be my friend. I can see where your loyalties lie now." He shoves past me and storms over to Madison. "Can't have me so you take my friends now?"

Sarah snickers. Madison lowers her head and mumbles something.

Graham glares back at me and throws his hands in

the air. "Real cute. You know what, never mind! You two deserve each other!" Then he makes his way into the school.

Madison doesn't look at me. She makes eye contact with Emily, and then the door Graham stomped his little pissy ass through.

It's the last period of the day, which is study hall for me. We're in the library today because Ms. Rose is sick. Mrs. Quinton, the librarian, is watching us today. She pushes a large metal cart filled with books down one of the nonfiction aisles way in the corner. Once she disappears, the door to the library opens, and Sarah enters.

She's holding hands with a junior, Ryan Fitz. World-class asshole. His family owns most of the lake property here. Rumor has it Ryan has been kicked out of all the board schools and private schools in the state, and apparently his dad had enough. Guess public school was supposed to be a punishment. And, okay, school is a punishment for some, and maybe his dad was expecting his son to get his ass kicked the first day. But let's be real, if you saw a Hennessey Venom GT pull up to school, would you kick the ass of the kid who gets out? The answer to this would be *hell* no. Because that person has money and probably a big house and will be throwing parties.

I pull out my cell and snap a few pictures of the pair. Ryan leans in, and Sarah giggles. They kiss a few times, and yeah, I'm getting it all. I should say something. I should send these photos to Graham. But I don't. I shove my phone in my pocket and hunt down Mrs. Quinton.

She's wedged in the back corner, climbing a long ladder, when I reach her. "Mrs. Quinton?"

"Yes?" She looks down at me and smiles. "I can't remember your name, hon."

"Bryce Matthews. I was wondering if I could use the computer lab for a second."

She nods. "Sure, hon. Go ahead."

She continues stacking books while I grab my things. I head straight to the computer lab and sit down in a cubical. The scent of lilac and vanilla hits me. I turn, and sure enough, there's my ex. Ginger Fields. "Hey, Ginger."

"Bryce. What are you doing here?"

"Working on a couple of papers."

"I meant don't you have a class this period?" she asks as she twirls a strand of neon-green hair around her finger. She's always dying her hair different shades of green. Before we dated, I thought it was kind of cool. Now it just makes me hate all things green. Plus, she's crazy. Like, take-a-baseball-bat-to-my-car crazy. Which she did when I broke up with her.

"Yeah."

She stares at me with those deep brown eyes that used to remind me of chunks of chocolate. "There's a rumor going around you're trying to date Madison Issac."

"And you know what they say about rumors." I sigh and turn back to my computer.

Out of the corner of my eye, I see her plop down

and scoot her chair as close as she can to me. Great. "It isn't true, then?"

"No."

"Good. Because when I heard it, I started laughing. But then it hit me, what if you really did like her? I mean, Madison is like in a whole other world compared to everyone else. She's like alien or maybe a robot or committed to a convent."

I turn my chair and glare at Ginger. "Why does everyone at this school think Madison is some sort of freak? Yeah, her social skills need some vast improvement, but she's smart as hell. She doesn't look like a mutant. She's actually pretty cute." I stop talking when I notice Ginger's eyes narrow. I face my computer and shrug. "I'm just saying she's not bad."

"I knew it was an act. You two hating each other like cats and dogs. I bet you wanted her the whole time we were dating, huh? What did she do, turn you down?"

"No. I'd have to ask her out in order to get shot down. And I'm not into her. Madison is just a girl who happens to be my study partner in math. Nothing more."

A throat clears, and a few cubicles down from me a person stands. Her moss-green eyes and dark hair make my heart squeeze. It's Madison. I'm sure she heard every word. I've never in my life wanted to be anywhere else so badly. Even when I was thrown into the back of a police car and hauled into juvie. Nope. This even beats that.

Madison picks up her things in silence and walks slowly out of the room. I know if I run after her things will only get worse. She'll make me eat my words. She'll make me feel a thousand times worse than I already do. So I let her go.

Chapter Twenty-One

Madison

I sit on the grass and stretch with my teammates. Westminster High is a few yards away doing the same. I scan the competition and easily find Kathy Wheeler.

She readjusts her blond ponytail, and we lock stares. I glare at her. She forms an L with her index finger and thumb and presses it to her forehead. I grit my teeth and smile. We'll see who the loser is in a little bit.

"Issac! What are you doing?" Coach Dockers yells.

Still bent forward touching my toes, I say, "Stretching?"

"I can see that," he snaps. "Why are you over here when the team is over there warming up?"

I glance around the open field. "Oh. I ... uh ... had to stretch a little longer. My muscles were tight."

His face softens. "All right. How are they now?"

"Better."

"Good. Go join the rest of the team."

I nod and hurry over to the line of red and black jerseys. Penelope Kline, world's biggest gossip, leans into her friend Ash Simons and whispers something. They both snicker, and I pretend not to notice. Bryce's words form in my head. I need to become friends with these girls. But another set of words replays themselves. "I'm not into her. Madison is just a girl who happens to be my study partner in math. Nothing more." I'm a whole lot of nothing to plenty of people lately. Nothing to Bryce, my parents, Graham, and probably more, I just don't care to list them all.

I take a deep breath and line up to do a short wind sprint, when Penelope says, "Are you and Bryce an item now?"

I cock my head at them. "What?"

"You and Bryce? Don't deny it. We saw him getting out of your car this morning."

"Yeah," Ash chimes in.

I shake my head. "No. And maybe you two should worry more about warming up than my love life." There goes being friends with these girls.

"Ohhh, someone is snippy," Ash chides. "What's wrong? Did the bad boy decide he didn't want a good girl?"

I take off. Her words sting. It's not the fact that Bryce doesn't want me, but the fact that no one does. Being good gets you nothing. Emily isn't exactly innocent—she's done some evil things—and boys like her just fine. She's been on more dates than I have. And my evil cousin gets guys, not just the good ones, all kinds. But me? What do I get? The friend award. The girl who is good enough to do homework with but not awesome enough to ask out.

I sprint back and get in line again. Penelope doesn't make any more comments. Ash looks at me every once in a while, but that's it. Their insults shouldn't have affected me for this long, but my blood is still boiling.

"Alright team, come over here!" Coach yells.

We hurry over to him. It's hot and muggy, the kind of weather I don't enjoy running in. Sweat beads and drips off my forehead and along my neck. Even my boobs are starting to get sticky and itchy.

Coach is giving us the typical pep talk. I practically have the thing memorized, so I zone out. Between the heat and my mood, I'm ready to just start this race and go home. Someone elbows me, and I glare to my right. Freda Hills darts her stare from me to the coach. He has his hands on his hips and snaps, "Are you even here today, Issac? This is the second time I've caught you blanking out. If you don't want to be here, let me know."

"I do want to be here."

"Then act like it. What's your objective today?"

"Don't let Wheeler anywhere near me."

He shakes his head. "No. But I'm glad to see where your mind is."

Penelope and Ash snicker again, and I don't bother giving them anymore of my time. We all place our hands in the middle, count down, and yell, "Go, Panthers!"

We all head over to the starting line and get ready for the gun to sound off. As I march up to my spot, Penelope says to Ash, "After this, it's Greg's house for some much-needed drinks. Right, ladies?" Then she looks at me. "Well, most of us."

I wasn't planning on going to Greg's because I have to work at the Movieplex tomorrow but screw it. As soon as I run this 3.1 miles, I'm going to call Emily, and we're hitting up a party. People think I'm such a goody-goody, wait till they get a load of me tonight.

"God, even your own team hates you," Kathy sneers.

I clench my hands until my fingernails dig into my flesh. I'm ready for the gun to go off. Ready to nail such an unbelievably amazing time that even Kathy will be shocked into a decade of silence. Yes. I am so ready.

A tall man dressed in white and black holds a gun up to the sky and shouts, "Runners, take your mark!"

I lean forward just a smidge, waiting patiently for the sound. A loud *bam* sounds and I take off. The trail is winding. It's mostly dirt, going through an open field first, then through a bit of forest, over a small creek, and circling back around to the field. I like to call this freedom. It's strange, yes, but here's the thing. In track, I kind of feel like a hamster. Running in a circle, sometimes two to four times, tends to make me think of hamster wheels. This, though, this makes me feel like I can go anywhere.

The wind caresses my face while my legs stretch and my arms pump a comfortable rhythm. I dart to my right and notice Kathy is keeping pace. I'm not running my hardest, I know this, so I decide to increase my speed. Kathy grunts. "Always one for shooting out too early."

I refuse to respond. I'm not going to let her get to me. She does this to mess with my head, just like her other insults. I'm going to win today no matter what. I increase my speed a little more until I'm probably putting in eighty-five percent effort. I don't want to give it my all in the first mile; I'll be toast by the second and begging for air by the third.

We hit the trail leading into the woods, and I notice most of our team has thinned out. There is no one in front of me just Kathy on my left. As I round a corner in the trail I glance back and spot Ash and Penelope a good fifteen steps behind me. Two Westminster girls are neck and neck with them. I dart my attention back to Kathy who's a little ahead of me. Normally I'd speed up, but every time I've gotten close to her, she's done something to get me to trip or remain behind her.

Ash yells, "Madison, stop lollygagging! You're letting her win."

She should worry about her own race. I speed up again, hop over a branch that magically lands on the path in front of me, and stride past Kathy. I don't slow my pace and head to the bridge. My legs ache as I race across it in no time at all. My lungs are churning with what feels like the fiery pits of hell. But it doesn't matter because I'm winning and the field is just ahead.

It's like my body is in overdrive. I pump my arms faster; my feet barely hit the ground. I'm almost to the finish line when someone screams, "Snake!"

I see it. Slithering along the path. It's tan and has hourglass-shaped saddles along its back. It stops moving and looks like it's about to strike. If I get bit, today of all days, by a copperhead, it'll confirm my worst fear—that I truly ticked someone off in another life, and now I'm being punished for it in this one. I try hurdling over the scaly beast, but it launches and catches my ankle. I feel the teeth sink in, and I yelp.

Heat and pain circle my ankle. I refuse to stop

running. I will crawl to the finish line with this darn thing leaking poison into my veins before I let Kathy win again. This is my year! My leg is starting to tingle as if it's slowly falling asleep. This isn't good. I'm almost to the finish line. Refs and coaches are running toward me. I wave them off. I will finish this race.

I stretch my left leg, then my right, which is turning from tingling to feeling numb. I glance down, and holy crap, my ankle looks like a cankle! My chest is tightening, and I don't know if it's from the poison or the running, but I'm about to pass out. Eight more steps. I can do this. Eight more steps and I can go night-night in the grass.

"Issac! I'm coming!" my coach screams.

I shake my head. I'm not about to let him stop me from finishing. Six more steps. Coach is three away. Four more steps. Coach is at arm's length, and I huff, "I'm crossing!"

"Issac, you don't have …" I stride out of his reach and get two steps from the finish line. My lungs burn for air. I can't feel my right leg. My ankle looks like a football on steroids. Oh, this is not pretty. Not by a long shot. But I rush through the tape and drop to the ground.

Kathy crosses after me. She glances down at me and shakes her head. "You're one crazy person, you know that?"

"But I won."

"Yeah, but at least my body isn't deformed. You, on the other hand, have one ankle the size of my dad's pickup." She helps me up, and I hobble over to the medic.

Coach Dockers is standing alongside me. "For God's sake, Issac, I didn't want you to take the phrase 'finish no matter what' literally!"

"I did good, though. Right, Coach?"

He smacks his palm to his forehead and walks away grumbling. The cute medic taking care of my ankle laughs. "You know, you're the first person I've ever met who finished a race after being bitten by a copperhead."

"Do people often get bitten during races?"

"No. But I'm pretty sure they wouldn't have told their coach they were going to finish before getting medical attention. In fact, it's the stupidest thing you could do."

I shrug. "They didn't lose to Kathy Wheeler three years in a row then."

He smiles and tells me to rest for a bit. My coach hops into the back of the medic truck. "I called your parents. They're meeting us at the hospital."

"Thanks."

"You drive to school, don't you?"

I nod. "Looks like I'm not going to be going to work tomorrow."

"Or running in Tuesday's meet. Next time someone yells 'snake,' will you at least do what the other girls did? Don't hurdle it. Make a huge loop around it."

I give him a thumbs-up. "I honestly didn't think it would launch toward the sky like that."

"You shouldn't assume anything."

"Yeah, I definitely shouldn't assume this sport isn't dangerous. Animals and reptiles can attack you at any given moment. I had no idea I was signing up for this kind of craziness."

The doors to the vehicle close after the medic climbs into the back with us. "How's the patient?"

"I think I'm good."

He hands me a large bottle of water. "Drink up."

Chapter Twenty-Two

Bryce

I make my way through the crowd of people at Greg's party. Heading toward the kitchen, I spot Graham kicking back some shots with Greg and Ryan. Graham nods at me. "What up, man?"

He's clearly forgotten about our argument this morning. He no longer seems to be in a pissy mood, and I'm glad. I also notice Sarah isn't around him, though. Maybe he got that anonymous e-mail after all. Although that wouldn't really explain why he was taking shots with Ryan instead of throwing him to the floor and beating him to a pulp.

"Where's Sarah?" I ask.

Graham shakes his head. "At the hospital."

"Why? What happened to her?" Ryan asked.

Graham gives him a funny look and then stares at me. "Madison got bit by a copperhead at her cross-country meet. How insane is that? Anyways, she was hauled off to the hospital. Mrs. Issac was in super freak mode and kicked me out of the house, and then they all took off to TriStar."

I leave the kitchen and turn toward the crowded party.

"Bryce, where the hell are you going?" Graham yells after me.

"Outta here," I shout back.

I'm stepping outside when a hand lands on my shoulder and tugs me back. I shift. "Wait up. If you're going, I'm coming. Giving moral support."

I glare at Graham. "For who? For weeks you've been telling Madison she's a freak and a stalker. And in case you haven't noticed, Sarah doesn't look like a fan of Madison's."

"Oh, like you are? Don't think you're fooling me. You're using her in order to get a good grade in calc."

Any other time, I'd tell him he was right, just to shut him up. But right now, he's barely walking a straight line, so I know whatever I tell him won't matter. He won't remember it, and even if he does, I really don't care. "I like her, Graham. Maybe even love her."

His mouth hangs open, and then he laughs. "Bullshit! You're not in love with Madison."

"I am. So what?" I get into my car and start the engine.

He slides into the passenger seat. "So what? I'll tell you what! She'll never date you, man. She hates you. Really hates you. I don't know what's wrong with you two lately. It's like a damn magical arrow stabbed you both in the ass, and you both magically forgot how much you loathe each other."

"People change."

He doesn't say anything else. Fifteen minutes of silence; that's how long it takes us to reach the hospital. When I step inside the emergency entrance, I feel panic take hold of me. What the hell am I doing here? Would she really want to see me after what she overheard me say in the computer lab?

I step up to the glass, and a woman in pink scrubs asks, "May I help you?"

"Hi. I was told my friend Madison Issac was admitted her for a snake-bite wound."

The nurse punches some things into her computer. "Yes, she's in the west wing. Check in at the nurse's station there, and someone will be able to help you."

"What the hell?" Graham suddenly shouts. "I'm going to kill him!"

I glare at him. "Dude!" I turn back to the nurse and smile. "Thanks." I yank Graham toward a hallway on my left. "What is wrong with you?"

Graham holds up his phone, and there are the pictures I took of Sarah and Ryan making out in the library. Aw, shit.

"Maybe that isn't her," I say.

"It's her. I can't believe she cheated on me."

I tug him along. "Come on, man. I've got to see Madison. When we get there, you can tell Sarah off, or you can confront her."

He doesn't say anything; he just follows me to the desk. The nurse working is dressed in dark blue scrubs. She is plump and doesn't look very happy to see anyone. "Yes?" she growls.

"I'm looking for Madison Issac."

"Are you family?"

"No. I'm a friend."

"Name?"

"Bryce Matthews."

The woman peers at her comphuter and shakes her head. "You're not on the list. Go wait over there. I'll send someone to you."

"I can't believe she made out with that dick!" Graham snaps as the nurse stands. She glares at us and waddles off.

I smack Graham. "If you get us kicked outta here before I can see Madison, I'm going to kill you."

Graham starts to say something, but a jingling of keys and clacking of heels followed by, "Oh my God, oh my God!" makes us both turn toward Emily. She's running down the hall and stops when she sees us. "What the hell are you two doing here? Is she okay? Did you see her?"

"We just got here," I say. "I'm not on the list. He just tagged along."

Emily hits Graham on the arm. "You're an asshole! You used to be her friend. What's wrong with you?" Then she wallops me in the shoulder. "And you! Don't even get me started on what an asshole you are. Don't even like her, huh? Could have fooled me the way you went off on her for sneaking out on you during your breakfast date at IHOP. Oh yeah. I'm not stupid."

I'm about to say something, but the nurse is back. "Mr. Matthews, I'm sorry, but you can't see her today. Tomorrow, visiting hours are from seven in the morning to eight thirty at night."

I don't care when the hours are. I'm not leaving. Not until I see her. Graham has other plans. He stumbles up to Emily. "Go get that nurse to go get Sarah."

Emily folds her arms. "Why?"

"Because I wanna know why she's been screwing around on me," he says in a raised tone. People from behind the desk start to stare at us. I see one of the nurses pick up the phone, probably to call security. It is after visiting hours, and he's making a scene.

"Shut up!" I growl.

Graham shoves me. "No. I know you hate her, but I love her and want to know why. Is it money?"

I almost ask him where's the last place they went and when. Because if it's only been hanging out at Madison's house or his house, that's not a date. Even I'm not stupid enough to think any girl will count that as a date. Instead, I observe the nurse's station and then Emily. "Do you think you can get in there?"

"I might be on the list. Let me go see."

"If you are, will you give her something from me?"

Emily nods and walks away. Graham starts to follow, but I get a hold of him and jerk him back. "What are you doing?"

"I am trying to see if I'm on the list," he mumbles.

I shake my head. "I wasn't talking to you. I was talking to Emily. Go have a seat in the corner before you piss me off and I hurt you."

He jerks his arm away and snaps, "Don't be a dick." He stomps over to the small waiting area off to the side of the hall near the nurse's station.

Emily hurries back over to me. "I've got five minutes. Her parents approved me. What am I giving her?"

I walk over to the counter and ask for a sheet of paper and something to write with. They hand me a piece of white copy paper and a pen advertising an erectile-dysfunction pill. Nice. Normally I'm a klepto when it comes to pens, but this is one I don't plan on pocketing.

I scribble a note, fold it, and give it to Emily. She takes it and tries to open it. I scold her, "That's not for you. It's for her."

She sticks her tongue out, then says, "This better not upset her." Then she follows the nurse leading her to Madison's room. I take a seat in the waiting area with Graham.

He's pacing around, running his fingers through his hair. Maybe I shouldn't have sent those photos. At least not right now. I should have waited a couple of days, a week, or until I took Madison on a proper date and convinced her I was the guy for her. At least then, I wouldn't have worried about her falling back in love with Graham. Well, maybe she never stopped loving him, and this is all a lost cause.

The *clack clack clack* of heels echoes in the hall, getting louder and louder. Graham stills and looks back to the open doorway. Sarah steps into the room, gives me a smile, and then heads over to Graham. "Hi! I can't believe you came here to see me." She throws her arms around him, and I watch him cringe. She pulls back slightly and asks, "What's wrong?"

"Did you think I wouldn't find out?"

"Find what out?"

I can't see her expression, but I can see Graham's, and his cheeks are flaming. He narrows his brows and roars, "Do you think I'm an idiot? You've been hooking up with Ryan Fitz for how long?"

She takes a few steps back, and I'm waiting like an eager little kid in a candy store. The juicy shit is about to hit the fan. She's either going to tell him flat-out, lie, or lie and get caught all in the same sentence. Either way, I'm practically on the edge of my seat waiting for the massive blowout. And wishing Madison was right beside me to see it.

"I love you!" Sarah shouts.

"Is that what you call it?" He holds up his phone. "It sort of looks like you kissing another guy."

"Folks, I'm going to have to ask you all to either leave or keep your voices down. We have patients that are in need of rest," the woman working the desk says. Graham lowers his head and mutters, "I'm sorry."

Sarah doesn't look like she cares either way, and they both exit the room. A few seconds after they leave, Mr. Issac enters the waiting room, and I stand. "Hi. How is she?"

"She's fine. Bryce, I don't want to be rude here, but may I ask what you are doing here?"

I frown. "I heard she got bitten by a snake during her meet, and I wanted to make sure she's okay. I know you won't like when I say this, sir, but I really do care about Madison. As a friend, of course."

He nods. "I get that. But both of you will be living different lives very soon. Madison's will be at either Vanderbilt, Cornell, Brown, or Northwestern—she hasn't decided, but she has her pick. Do you get what I am trying to say, son?"

"First, I'm not your son. And second, yeah, I get it. Loud and clear. You don't want someone like me hanging out with your very bright and gifted daughter." I nod and leave the waiting room.

I'm usually the guy who lets this shit roll off his shoulders. But today I can't. Her dad actually made me feel like a lowlife piece of crap. Because he's right—someone like me isn't worthy of Madison. Yeah, I may be smarter than people give me credit for, but I have a record. Vandalism, breaking and entering, stealing, and possession.

Mind you, none of this would be on my record if I wasn't hanging out with my older cousin Joe, who's always pulling me into some shit. And yeah, I should have said no, but at age twelve, when I first got introduced to the system, my cousin was seventeen. What twelve-year-old tells their seventeen-year-old cousin to piss off? None of them. So I went along for the ride. He didn't tell me what he was doing at the electronics store. He handed me a bat and said, "My buddy Mark told me that this glass doesn't break. So let's see."

Again, being twelve and wanting to make my cousin proud, I took the bat and hit a rock right into the window. Glass shattered. Sirens blared. And when I turned around with a smile for my cousin, his ass was gone. Cops surrounded the place within seconds before I could even drop the bat and run. That's how I got my first vandalism charge.

As the mid-September air hits my face, I take a breath and wish for the first time ever that I didn't have a record. I wish I looked like the straight-and-narrow kid Graham appears to be. But that's a lie. He does everything I'd probably get labeled for doing. Drugs—he's always carrying some weed on him. Alcohol—he's always hitting up parties or stealing from his parents' stash.

I head to my car and slam a fist down on the roof. I will never have Madison. Not with everyone reminding her of my past. The things that will haunt me forever. The mistakes I made. The stupid times I stuck my neck out and took the fall for someone else. All that can never be erased, but I wish it could.

Chapter Twenty-Three

Madison

Emily smiles at me with tears streaking her cheeks and throws her arms around me. She squeezes me so tight I think I might explode. "Hi to you too," I manage to get out.

"Oh my God! You could have died!"

"Emily. Maybe if I never got it treated, yeah. But I'm fine. They only have me in here under observation. I'll probably be able to go home tomorrow."

She looks about the room and chews on her lip. "I have something for you. Don't kill me. He just … oh, he's in the waiting room and looks so lost. I've actually never seen him like this ever, and you know we've been in like every school together since kindergarten."

She hands me a crumpled note, and I sit up a little in my bed and begin to unfold it.

Call me when you feel up to it. I miss your voice.

It's from Bryce. I stare at the note and then look at

Emily. "Seriously?"

She snatches it away from me and gushes, "Oh, come on. You have to be a little awed by it. He said he misses your voice."

"Was he sober?" I grab the note back and examine it again.

"He showed up at Greg's but left within like seconds of arriving. I don't think he got trashed that fast."

My heart is pounding really hard. My father enters my room and smiles at me and then at Emily. Then he looks back at me. "How about we get some rest? What's that in your hand?"

"Nothing." I hand the note to Emily, who crumples it up, and then I fake a yawn. "Yeah, I'm beat. Em, I'll try calling you tomorrow."

She nods. "You better." She exits the room.

My dad flips through some of the channels on TV until my mom comes into the room and places a black travel bag in the chair near my bed. "Everything you need is in there. We'll be back in the morning, okay?"

"Okay." I'm about to ask my parents if anyone came by to visit me, but my mom interrupts my thoughts with a question.

"Where's Sarah?"

"She was in the waiting area with Graham and Bryce," my dad explains, "but she left when I, uh …"

My mom frowns at him. "What did you do?"

He leads her outside the room, but it's not far enough away for me not to eavesdrop. "I told the staff he wasn't on the list to see her. I told him to go home because this was a family matter. That boy has no business hanging out with our daughter. I have disliked it since the moment he got himself in trouble. But you kept telling me it's probably not what I think."

"It's not. He's a good kid who made some bad choices. You had no right to butt into her life like that, honey."

I stop listening to their conversation. My heart twists, and my stomach tightens. Bryce probably hates me. I can't believe my father told him to leave. Well, okay, no, I can, but it still upsets me all the same.

But I think what really hurts is Bryce leaving. Nothing bothers Bryce; he's even told me so himself. But something my father said set him off. I'll just have to wait this little storm out for a few more minutes, or until my parents decide to leave, to call Bryce and apologize.

It takes until almost nine thirty for my parents to leave. I pull out my cell and find his name. The line rings one, two, almost three times before I hear, "Hey."

"Hi. I got your note."

"Yeah. Um … I shouldn't have given that to Emily. I'm sorry."

"I'm glad you did."

"Okay. Well, I just wanted to make sure you're okay. I've got to go."

"Hey. Are you trying to get rid of me?"

I hear him sigh. "Listen, coming there was a mistake. Sorry. It won't happen again." He doesn't even give me a chance to say anything back. He just hangs up. That's the end of our conversation.

Two weeks go by. It's almost Halloween, and Bryce has yet to speak to me. Graham, funny enough, has loads to say every day. And Bryce answers him just fine, but as soon as I say something, he clams up. Seriously, do I have a curse on me? Will all the men who become friends with me turn into giant icebergs or something if they continue to hang out with me?

I've had enough of the silent treatment. I march right over to Mrs. Vixen's desk before class starts. "I want new partners. I realize it's late in the semester to request a change, but I need one. Both of my partners have been giving me the silent treatment. Neither of them want to meet up to go over homework. I'm not certain we're getting the same answers, and I can't have my grade influenced by them."

Mrs. Vixen raises a slightly gray brow. "Have you asked your group why they seem to be excluding you from their study sessions?"

"No. But I don't see the point of homework being counted as double the grade and the whole group having to come up with the same answers. How is that even fair?"

"Madison, I realize you may find my methods a little odd. But here is the thing I want you to learn from my odd method: There is always someone who knows something you do not. Later in life, you will probably face difficult things and will need more than just yourself to solve the issue. Groups are formed to find more solutions for simple problems. This is why I grade group homework the way I do. If one of you did the work and let the other copy, is this really helpful? No. Because when the tests come, this person still won't know how to do a darn thing. And it will show. Therefore, your grade as a group will drop. Would a person benefit from everyone doing individual work more than collaborating with a team?" She shakes her head. "No. Because three brains are always better than one."

"But—"

"Madison, if this is really that big of an issue for you, I will try to place you in another group. But it'll take me until Friday to find a replacement."

I try to smile, but inside I'm dying. I have to endure this silent treatment for another week? Slowly, I make my way to my seat. Stepping over backpacks haphazardly thrown in the aisles, I overstretch myself on Maggie Sender's bag and trip. My body lurches forward, my face within inches of smashing into the probably-never-been-shampooed fifteen-year-old carpet, when something grips my waist and pulls me upright. I gasp. Smoothing my hands down my front, I straighten. Turning slightly toward my savior, I'm instantly stunned speechless to see it's Jake Foster.

"Be careful where you step."

I nod stupidly and drop my gaze. A book being slammed closed causes me to jump. I shake myself from my daze and take a seat at my desk. Maggie whispers loudly at Kelly, a girl I know, but I'm not really friends with, "Oh my God. I would totally trip over my own shit in order to have Jake Foster catch me in his strong arms."

Kelly giggles. "I know, right? So lucky."

They both turn to me, but I pretend I don't hear them. Instead, I dare myself to look over at Bryce. He's staring at me as if he'd love nothing more than to shoot lasers at me and turn me into ash. I swallow hard and pull out my books.

I don't understand why he's so mad at me. I called him. He's the one who told me it was a mistake and then hasn't talked to me since. What's sad is I miss him. I didn't think that would be possible because he's an asshole. Well, okay, he's really not, but he's certainly acting like one now.

Class seems to drone on. I'm drawing flowers, swirls, and scribbles in the corner of my notebook when an elbow shoots into my side. I glare at Graham, and he says, "We're supposed to get into our groups."

I roll my eyes and move my desk toward him and Bryce. I notice both of them are flipping through a packet of problems. "What's that?" I ask.

"The problems we're supposed to do tomorrow. The study guide. Weren't you paying attention?" Graham asks.

I groan. "Oh." Bryce reaches over to untuck mine from my book and drops it on top of my notebook. He returns his attention to his own packet, and I sigh. "Don't worry. I requested a new group. You two will have someone else on Friday."

Bryce finally locks eyes with me. "Why?"

"Clearly you two don't want me here. The silence makes me uncomfortable."

"Not everything is about you," Graham says.

Bryce doesn't say a word; he just stares at me.

I stop looking at both of them and riffle through the packet. Most of the questions I already know the answers to. I lightly pencil them in and will fill in the work on them later. I'm on page four when Bryce asks, "Don't you have a meet tonight?"

"Not tonight. I've got to work at the movie theater until eight."

"Well, I've got stuff to do after eight. Some of us have a life," Graham adds.

I glance up from my papers. Graham is slouching in his chair, chewing some gum, his arms crossed. Bryce is flipping through his packet and doesn't bother acknowledging either of us. I want to scream, "Look at me!" but I don't. Instead, I shrug. "I'm sorry some of us don't have college entirely paid for."

"What's that supposed to mean?" Graham asks, looking completely offended.

"Um, I'm pretty sure it was straightforward, dude," Bryce mumbles. "You're lucky your parents only had one kid and saved up enough for you to go to any college you want to without having to take out loans."

Graham stands. "I've gotta use the restroom."

Bryce shakes his head but goes back to working on problems silently. I can't take it, though. He's so close, yet it feels like he's halfway across the globe. "What did I do to make you hate me so much?"

He lowers his pencil and tilts his head in my direction. "I don't hate you."

"Then why are you acting like I'm not here? In school, at your house, you and Graham don't even say hi to me anymore. I know why he acts like that, but I don't get why you are. I thought …" I can't finish the sentence because the word "friends" catches in my throat.

"Mads, you don't need someone like me in your life. I mean, before Graham turned into a walking asshat when your cousin came to town, did you even care if we never spoke to each other?"

I shrug. "I don't know. You never seemed to have anything to add to any conversations I started."

He raises a brow. "Okay."

"Never mind." I start working on my packet. Screw the whole "three brains are better than one" crap. I don't need him, and I don't need Graham either.

Chapter Twenty-Four

Bryce

A voiding her is the hardest freaking thing I've ever done. I like Madison way more than I should. She makes me want to make her laugh, blush, and smile at least once every day. Lately though, she's been frowning, close to tears, and just generally looking miserable. And I know it's my fault. When she asked me if I hated her, I almost grabbed her face and kissed her. I don't want her thinking I hate her, but she can't know my real feelings. Her father made it perfectly clear she's got her future lined up. And me, well, I'll just get in the way, and that's not what I want.

Graham's in my room, sitting on my bed, glancing out the window to Madison's room. I know he's not looking for her, but for Sarah. He's been doing this for the past two weeks, and it's annoying as hell. He mutters curses each time he sees her and then yells profanities about Ryan. So mostly, I've been ignoring him. I can only take so much of, "She left me," before I want to hit him.

I perk up as soon as he asks, "I thought Madison had to work tonight."

"She does."

"Then why is she in her room?"

"What?" I roll my chair over to the window, and sure enough, there's Madison sitting at her desk. I snatch up my phone and click on her name.

"What's up?" she answers.

"I thought you had to work."

"I am."

"Bullshit! I'm looking right at you."

She looks out her window and then draws the blinds down. "Fine, I'm not at work. I got fired."

"Why?"

"I had to lock up Saturday. My boss didn't come in until tonight, which is when I was supposed to return the keys. But I didn't have the keys."

"What happened to them?"

I can hear the sob in her voice. "I don't know. If I knew that, I wouldn't have been fired. I have a feeling who has them, but I've torn my room apart looking for them."

I sigh. "We're coming over." Graham looks at me and starts to shake his head, but I smack him. He groans and shoves his books in his bag.

"No, Bryce. Graham won't want to be here, and I don't blame him. Plus, my room is a mess."

We're already walking down the stairs and out of the house. "All right. I'm going to say this one last time. I don't care if he doesn't want to be there; he'll man up and deal. I'm coming over there because I'm going to help you, Madison. I don't want to hear any more excuses. In fact, I want you to come downstairs and let me in."

"Bryce …" She breathes my name, and I swear I'd do anything to hear it again.

I knock on her front door. "Smalls, I know you hear this. Let us in."

I hear her stumble over some things and then run down the steps. She opens the door and looks at me. Her face is flushed, but she looks beautiful.

"Hi." I hang up my phone and smile at her.

She smiles back. "Hi."

"Oh, jeez. I think I barfed in my mouth. Let's get this shit over with because I don't want to be here when she comes home. She isn't home, is she?" Graham asks.

I almost turn around and punch him. He might be my friend, but he's acting like a stupid baby. I can't stand it.

"Sarah's not here. She left with her new friends Karen, Blair, Ginger, and Maggie." I don't miss the way she says Ginger's name like it's vomit in her mouth.

Graham and I follow her up to her room. I glance at the open door to Kyle's room, and Graham asks, "When's he coming back?"

She shrugs. "Don't know. Probably Thanksgiving. Like he did last year."

"Do you ever think about staying in there until he comes home to visit?" I ask.

"No. I'm not letting her have another thing."

She pushes open her door, and holy shit, she wasn't kidding. She has ripped that room apart. Sheets are tossed in the middle of the floor, along with clothes, shoes, and purses. It looks like a department store took over her room. "Smalls, what the—"

"Jesus, Maddy," Graham finishes for me. "What the hell did you do?"

She rolls her eyes and steps over the mess. "As you can see, I've gone through everything."

She certainly has. There are drawers dumped out; everything in the closet is gone.

"I flipped the mattresses. That top one was a challenge. But no keys. So I've got to get everything back before Sarah and my parents get home. And then I have to get homework done."

I close the space between us and brush my fingers along her cheek. "It's okay. Graham and I will help with the heavy stuff, then we'll start on the homework, and you can copy."

She gives me a weary look. "I don't know."

Graham huffs, "Maddy, you bailed us out enough times that we owe you. Just direct us, and we'll get it done."

She hugs me and then Graham. I clench my jaw when I see his hand skim her lower back. The thought of ripping his arms out of their sockets and smacking him with them makes me smile. "Smalls, what do you want us to do?"

She pulls back from Graham and points to the beds. "I need to put the sheets back on them. Bryce, who makes your bed?"

I glare at Graham because he starts chuckling like a damn schoolgirl. "I do," I mumble. I'm not embarrassed. But there is some shit a guy just doesn't announce to the world. This would be one. The other would be that he always tells his mom he loves her and good night.

Maddy grabs my hand and squeezes it. "Can you make Sarah's bed then? I'll do my own later."

"I can make yours too," I say without thinking.

Graham walks past me and coughs, "Pussy."

He has no right to talk.

I notice his eyes wandering over to Madison's ass, and I smack his arm. "Don't," I say through gritted teeth.

"What?"

"You know what," I growl.

He shrugs and grabs the sheets. I climb the ladder on the front of the bed. Remaining on the third step, I hunch over and tell Graham to hand over the sheets. Layer by layer, I get the top and bottom bunks all made. I then move on to helping Madison put boxes in the closet. She chews on her lower lip, and I have a strong urge to pull her into my arms and nip at it. Standing this close to her and watching her teeth bite and release that lip is doing a number on my thoughts. Let me count the ways to take Madison Issac in her room.

I tear my eyes away from her and grab items from the floor. Madison takes the hangers from me one by one and places them back in the closet. We do this in silence for what feels like eternity, while Graham puts together all the drawers. He clears his throat. "Maddy, where was this picture?"

I glance back at the frame he's holding up. It's one of all of us from a few years ago. It was taken in her driveway near the basketball hoop. "Just toss it in the drawer," she says and then elbows me. "Bags, please."

"When did you start keeping it in the drawer?"

Madison looks over at Graham. "I don't know. When you started dating Karen Higgins." That's a lie.

She had that photo out a few weeks ago when we were in her room. I don't say anything, though.

"Why, though?" Graham asks.

She groans. "I don't know. Can we get back to the task at hand?"

He stops asking questions. I'm glad too because I don't want to know the reason. In fact, I'm certain if she confesses how she feels about Graham right now, I might lose it. I'm no good for her, I know this, but Graham is probably worse.

"Bryce?"

I shake my head. "Hmm?"

"Did you hear me?"

"Bags, right?"

"No, I asked if you were okay. You went pale for a minute, then you, um …" She places her hand on top of my closed fist. "I think you're bleeding."

I open my hand, and sure enough, blood smears my palm where my nails punctured my skin. I wipe my hand on my jeans. "It's nothing."

She nods and goes back to putting all the clothes in the closet. It takes us another ten minutes between the three of us to get the room all put back together. But she still hasn't found her missing keys.

"I knew I should have put them on the same ring as my car keys," she groans as she takes a seat on the floor.

I don't ask her why she didn't. Neither does Graham.

Graham and I walk to the park. I pop a cigarette in my mouth, and he puts a joint in his. He takes a long drag and then chokes out, "Are you into Madison? Seriously, bro."

I shrug. "I don't know. It doesn't matter. Her dad hates me, and she's going off to college soon. What good is hooking up with her now when in a few months we're going to be saying good-bye to each other?"

I take a hit of my cigarette, and Graham laughs. "Dude, you can't think like that. You gotta think about how much fun you can have in that short time. And why do you care what her dad thinks? That's never stopped you before."

"I can't. Madison is different. I just … Why are we talking about this anyway? I thought you told me you didn't like me hanging out with her and that she's crazy?"

He nods. "I did think she was crazy, but only because Sarah made me think it." He takes another drag from his joint and blows it out slowly. "Seriously, man, before all this shit, I thought Maddy was cool, but you know I think of her as a sister. That's why it kind of weirds me out. I mean, you're like my brother, and she's like my sister. You two couldn't be hooking up."

"Well, we're not, and we weren't, so it doesn't matter."

He smacks my arm right as I release a cloud of smoke. "I know. That's what I'm getting at. You should. I saw how she looked at you. I even saw how you looked at her and how pissed you got when I asked about that picture. Dude, if you like her, you better go get her, because rumor has it Foster is about to ask her out. You know he's only after her because she's probably the only virgin in our grade—well, besides Holly Dive, but I don't think you could pay someone a million bucks to take her to bed."

Holly is gross. She smells like she rolls in trash, has brown teeth, and is not what you would call a small girl. I finish my cigarette and he's still working on his joint when I spot Madison running up the road. "Put that shit out," I growl to Graham.

Graham gives me a look like I've lost it. "Chill. I'm almost done."

"Mads is running up the road. Put. It. Out."

He scans the park and then rolls his eyes. "Jesus, you've turned into such a killjoy."

He's right. Madison is really changing me, and we're not even together. I watch her run by step for step. She doesn't glance over at the park; she just runs. Graham elbows me. "Just ask her out."

And get buried in her backyard by her dad? Um, no, thanks. But I will say this: Jake isn't going to be dating her either. Not while I'm still living next door.

Chapter Twenty-Five

Madison

Bryce is such an asshat! This morning before first period, Jake Foster came up to me in the hall. He's kind of cute. Yes, he says goonish things, but what guy doesn't? Anyway, because of my recent shrunken-clothes situation, he's been flirting with me a lot lately.

I know it's nothing. It's simple flirting, big deal. Every girl in school flirts. But Bryce slammed Jake into the lockers. He told Jake not to look at me, talk to me, or even breathe in my direction! Then Bryce ignored me in calculus 2. *What the heck?*

In lunch, I don't know what I'm doing—or where the courage came from—but I march right up to Bryce's table. Emily yells my name as I walk right past our usual spot. I wave her off. I reach Bryce and slam my palm on the table. His troublemaking friends Marty and Seth look at me and snicker.

"Hey, shorty. I think you made a wrong turn,"

Marty says.

"Bryce, I need to speak with you. Now."

"Ohh, Bryce, looks like Minnie Mouse here might give you a lashing with a ruler if you don't obey." Seth chuckles.

I shoot them both a look. "And if you two don't shut up in about two seconds, I'm going to hit you with my backpack." Turning my attention back to Bryce, I say, "I need to talk to you."

Graham walks up to the table and plops down. "What's up, Maddy?"

"Nothing."

Bryce is looking over some drawings of some sort, possibly tattoo sketches. Clearly he is ignoring me as he turns another page. My patience has completely gone out the window. As he turns yet another page, I yank the binder from him and snap it shut.

He glares at me. "Smalls, that was just rude."

"Was it? Was it as rude as you ignoring me?"

He smirks. "Am I ignoring you? No. I was waiting for you to talk to me."

I want to smack him with the binder. "Really?" He doesn't answer, so I continue, "I would like to speak to you alone. Now."

He stands. "Next time just say that." He takes the binder from me and follows me out of the lunchroom into an empty hallway. He stops by a set of lockers. "Right here is good enough."

"Fine." I stare at my shoes and try to settle my breathing. "Did my cousin ask you to mortify me this morning?"

"No, why?"

Why? Is he serious? I fold my arms over my chest.

"You're joking, right? This morning ring any bells? And then during calculus, you acted like I wasn't even there. So did she ask you to do it? Or are you going to start finding ways to humiliate me yourself, like you did in elementary school? Because I've had enough."

He leans in close. I inhale his minty breath and almost melt. "Let me get this straight. You're pissed at me for threatening Jake Foster, is that it? The guy is a tool, and he has a rep for nailing virgins. Excuse me for making sure that asshole knew you weren't going to be another name in his scorebook. And I ignored you in class today because I don't want you getting the wrong idea, Smalls. I'm not interested in that way. You're my friend; that's it."

I feel my heart drop to my stomach. My eyes water, and I glare at my feet. I stifle a sob and whisper, "Oh. Okay."

"Smalls?" His thumb brushes against my cheek. "I'm not good for you. You've gotta know that, right?"

I nod but refuse to look up. "Stay out of my personal life from now on. If Jake wants to date me and use me, it's not any of your business."

He lifts my chin. Our eyes lock, and a tear slips down my cheek. "I'm not going to do that. I might not be good for you, but neither is he. Most of the guys in this school aren't even worthy of you."

"Yeah, and I should be the one to decide that, not you."

"Mads." He presses his forehead to mine and says in a soft tone, "You're right, but if I can stop it, I will."

I sniffle. "Why?"

"Because I like you a lot. I can't date you because

151

I'm terrible for you. I can't kiss you because I've got a past that follows me everywhere. No one wants a girl like you with someone like me. I like you enough to let you go but not to be taken advantage of by others."

I start to break free from him, but he pulls me back into a tight hug. "Madison, I swear if I could get a blank slate right now, I would. I'd do it so I could date you. But the fact is I don't. You have a future far away from here, and I'm going to be in Michigan. While you're off running hillsides and through campuses, I'll be looking out for Hailey."

I tilt my head and study his lips. They're so close. I could literally have him right this minute. So I do. I touch my lips to his. He doesn't respond at first, but then he does. He presses me against the lockers, cradling my head in his hands. His kisses are so soft and explosive I don't know if I am soaring or dying. It feels like the wings of butterflies tickling my insides while tingling sensations run down my arms. With every kiss, touch, and caress along my skin, lips, and tongue, I don't want this to end.

He eventually pulls back and stares at me. We're breathing hard, smiling, and he tucks a strand of my hair behind my left ear. "Madison, we can't do this ever again. Okay?"

I nod. "Yeah." But it's not okay. He walks away, and I wait a few minutes before I return to the lunchroom.

I notice Bryce doesn't look back at me. How can he walk away so easily? Am I really that bad of a kisser? I lean against the cool metal of the lockers and shrink down to the ground. He's right—he's not right for me. But that kiss, it's everything I've ever wanted, and I'll never have it again.

Emily finds me after school and practically holds me hostage in my own car. "All right, spill."

"Spill what?" I ask.

She looks annoyed. "You know what." I do, but I don't want to tell her. This isn't really normal because we tell each other everything. Except lately, I've been holding back. I mean, what will she think of me as soon as I let her know that I'm falling for Bryce Matthews? She'll probably ask me if I've had a head injury.

"There's nothing to tell."

She shakes her head. "Really? Nothing to tell? Last time I saw you, you were at lunch, where you bypassed our table and dragged Bryce out of the lunchroom. He came back; you never did. His cheeks were all rosy like he'd just run a marathon, soooo ... I want to know what's going on."

I roll my eyes. "Nothing is going on."

"Bullshit! I call it as I see it. I'm calling bullshit. He came by your hospital room and looked so scared. I swear he looked like he'd seen a ghost. Then at school he's been watching you. I don't think you've noticed, but I have. He watches you enter the halls, the lunchroom, hell, he even watched you get into your car a few minutes ago. So what the heck is going on?"

"Nothing," I whisper. "Well, nothing ever will. He said I was too good for him and that we aren't going to be anything more than friends."

She places her hand on my knee and squeezes. "He's not looking at you like he just wants to be friends, Maddy. He's looking at you like you're his whole world."

"It doesn't matter. He's not going to ask me out, and I'm not going to ask him. Now, I've got to get to the field for practice."

"Okay. But, Maddy"—she opens the door and gets out, looking over at me—"just be careful. I mean, if you like him, fine. But he's got a reputation for getting himself into some serious trouble. You don't want to be around when he does."

I nod, and she shuts the door. She's right. Bryce seems to know it too. That's probably why he said we won't be anything more than friends. So why does my heart still hurt?

Chapter Twenty-Six

Madison

It seems all anyone can talk about is Greg's big Halloween bash this Friday. In chemistry, a few of the girls—Hadley, Justice, and Sue—were collaborating on costumes. Apparently they're all going as Playboy Bunnies. French class, English lit, even civics has been tainted by the discussions of different costumes and plans that make me think I'm the only person who doesn't care.

Even Emily is on board for the Halloween bash and pitches me ideas in between periods.

"I'm not going!" I finally yell while walking to calculus.

She grabs my arm, causing me to stop in the hall. "This is our senior year, Madison. We're supposed to have fun."

"I've gotta find another job. My insurance is due in December, and I have to find a way to pay it."

"Well, I think it's stupid your parents make you pay for your car insurance."

"They don't make me. I want to. Besides, since I started doing it, they've given me a little more free range. I don't have to be in at ten like Kyle did. I can come in at eleven or twelve."

Emily narrows her eyes. "Yeah, but none of that matters if you're doing nothing but being a silly homebody. We need to do this, Madison. It'll be fun. And hell, maybe we'll be lucky and score dates to the winter formal."

I shrug. "I'll think about it."

We walk to class where I sigh and slump into my chair. Not a full second passes before Mrs. Vixen calls me to her desk. I approach, and she says in a low tone, "I wanted to get you a new group, but it seems your partners overruled me. Sorry. Looks like Graham and Bryce are still your partners. If you really can't work out your issues, I will pull you from the group, but you won't be put in another group."

"So I'll be by myself?"

"Not exactly. You'll have to help me grade papers, and tutor the kids struggling in class everyday in order to make up the difference in points. Remember, group work is double the grade. If you're not in a group, it's hardly fair to give you double the grade on individual efforts."

I swear this woman is trying to ruin me. I can't stay after school; I've got cross-country practice and meets. This Saturday is state where I'll be seeing the wonderful Kathy Wheeler again. I cannot be slacking.

I march back to my seat, grumbling. Graham smiles at me, and I flip him off. "What did I do?" he asks.

"You know you two have been nothing but awesome this year. I tried to get a new group, and you jackholes had to ruin it."

Bryce strolls into the room, and Graham shakes his head. "I told you we should have let her find another group. Now she's pissed at both of us. Good job."

Graham has been nicer lately, but it still doesn't mean I've forgotten his douchbaggery at the beginning of the school year. And I'm definitely not willing to hand him my notes, homework, or anything else he used to get from me before.

"So, wait, you're coming over tonight to study?" Bryce asks me. I shoot him a glare and face forward.

He swats at my ponytail, and I ignore it. But after the fifth time, I turn in my seat and snap, "What do you want?"

The whole class shifts in their seats, and all eyes seem to be trained on us. I can feel heat blossoming across my cheeks and down my neck. Bryce stares at me and smiles. "I was going to ask you what time you were coming over tonight." He doesn't even bother to whisper. I can hear people chuckling and snorting around us.

"Mr. Matthews, Miss Issac, and Mr. Nichols, out in the hall right now," Mrs. Vixen says.

Graham protests, "What did I do?"

"Out in the hall, or I'll give your group a week's worth of detention."

I hang my head and make my way into the hall. I lean against the brick wall, staring at the pebbled floor tiles.

"You know we wouldn't be out here if you hadn't messed with her," Graham whines.

"We wouldn't be in this mess in the first place if you hadn't dated her cousin," Bryce says.

I finally look up. "I'm right here. This is exactly why we're out here. I'm not invisible, yet you two treat me like I am."

Graham snorts. "Trust me. We know you are not invisible."

"No, she's right. We've been treating her differently. How would you like me to be from now on, Smalls? Want me to remain quiet whenever you're around?"

I shrug. "I don't know."

Mrs. Vixen steps into the hall. Her pale skin looks shiny under the fluorescent lights. Her hair looks darker and springier. "You three are my best students. But today I'm very disappointed in you all. You've been bickering in class, you've asked for a different partner, then you promise me everything will work out, and then you interrupt my class. What's going on?"

"Nothing. Just a miscommunication," Bryce replies as smooth as ever. "I didn't know if we could study directly after school or if we had to do it later because of Madison's schedule."

Mrs. Vixen looks at me. "Well, Madison?"

"Uh … I have practice until five," I say.

"There you have it, boys. Now, I'll give you a few minutes to get your scheduling set, and then I want you parked in your seats—and no more interruptions," Mrs. Vixen says and then walks into the class.

I push off the wall and start to follow when fingers catch and tighten around my wrist. "Where are you going?" Bryce asks.

"In there. We'll just do the usual time."

Graham isn't listening to us. He has his phone out

and is probably texting someone or playing a game the way his thumbs are moving. I focus back on Bryce and ask, "Why aren't you letting me go?"

"What are you doing Friday?"

"I'm not going to that Halloween party."

He nods. "You should."

"Why?"

He leans in. "Because there's going to be a lot of misguided youth drinking and doing things with people they'd probably never be with. Costumes are great for that sort of thing. Living out fantasies."

I shove him and walk back into the classroom. What's he getting at? He can only be with me if we're in costume? Or is he talking about someone else? Either way, it's not happening.

I'd like to say my day got better, but it only got weirder. In art class, Ms. Dyson asked me to stay after class. Normally this means you're in trouble, have to schedule time to finish a project, or need to help out with something. This could mean putting together flower arrangements or helping set up for the sports banquets. Neither of these things are fun or worth volunteering for.

"Madison," Ms. Dyson began, "I gave everyone's showcase paintings back to them today. But you won't be getting yours because it's not here. It'll be returned by Friday."

"Oh, um … okay."

"You've got such a wonderful gift. Have you ever thought about exploring it more?"

I shake my head. It's a lie. I have thought about it, but I can't. My parents will never go for it. My dad would go ballistic. "Art is doodling, and doodling doesn't pay the bills." That's what I overheard my dad tell my mom one night when she suggested I go to an art school for the summer.

"I'd hate to see a talent like yours go to waste," Ms. Dyson continues. "Please think it over. Okay?"

I nod.

As soon as I leave, I try to forget all about my weird day. But that's not easily done.

"Smalls … *Smaaaaaalls* … wake up," Bryce says as he shakes me awake.

I lift my head and peel off a piece of paper that's stuck to the side of my face. Blinking a few times to focus on my surroundings, I notice the drool stains on my homework. Gross. Fanning out the paper, I sigh, "When did you get here?"

"A while ago. Your mom let me in. I knew something was up when you didn't come over after your practice, so I decided to check on you. Rough day?" Bryce takes a seat on my bed.

I crack my neck as I tilt my head from side to side and then yawn. "I'm just beat."

He nods and lies back on my mattress. "Fair enough. How about this: you lie down here"—he pats a place next to him—"and we'll go over the homework in math. Remember, we have a test tomorrow. Double the grade and bonuses are extra points and we get to use past homework as cheat sheets."

I nod and crawl onto my bed beside him. I don't take my book, pencil, or my homework with me. Nope, just me. And I lay my head on his chest. Bryce doesn't push me off or beg me to wake up; he simply sighs. "Mads, are you really that tired?"

"Mmm-hmmm."

"You know I can't stay here, right?"

"I know," I whisper. "But I don't want you to go."

I feel his arm touch my waist, and his lips brush against my forehead. "I don't want to go either, but I'm pretty sure your dad will murder me."

I feel him stir next to me. "Don't leave." I brush my lips against his neck and clutch his shirt.

"*Maaaaaadiiiiiison*, we can't. You don't want me."

I lift my head and stare at him. "I do, though. As stupid as it is, I really do. And I know it makes no sense. Trust me, I've tried to make any kind of logic out of it, but I can't. I like you, Bryce."

He shakes his head. "No, you don't, Madison. You don't know shit about me, just the surface and the rumors, but that's it. Trust me, you don't like me." He gets off my bed, and I try pulling him back.

"Why?" I ask. "Why even come over here and check on me? And don't feed me the 'double the grade' line. We could have checked our work and answers before homeroom. So don't feed me that bullshit. You like me. Admit it."

He's halfway to my door. "Yes, I like you. I like you a lot. But that doesn't mean I'm good for you."

I nod. "Fine. Just go. I don't know why you even bothered to fight for me to stay in your stupid group if you constantly want to push me away."

He stops and turns. He marches back and growls, "Screw it." His hands cradle my face, and his lips press against mine. The kiss is rough, and it's blazing. Each time his lips brush mine, my body warms all over like I've been lying in the sun for hours. Tiny tingles run down my spine, arms, legs, and my heart pounds like a crazy drum against my ribs.

I yank him down to my bed and twine my fingers through his messy mane. He pulls back slightly, his breathing a little rough, and he coughs one time. "Mads, get your stuff, pack a bag, whatever, and come to my house."

It's like he threw a bucket of ice water all over me. Suddenly I'm awake. "What are we going to do?"

"More of this." He leans in and kisses me again. "Maybe more."

I sit up a little and shake my head. "I can't. I'm, uh … not experienced."

"I know. Well, I gathered that. I promise I won't take advantage of you. Ever. If you don't want to, we don't have to."

I nod. "Bryce, if I go, does this mean we're dating?"

He shakes his head. "No. It'll be us having fun."

He tries to kiss me again, but I push him back. "Just fun. So, what, like friends with benefits?"

"Sure." He leans in to kiss me, and I smack him.

He backs away and stares at me. "Why did you hit me?"

"Are you kidding me? I'm only good enough for friends with benefits, nothing more?"

"I didn't say that."

"But you just said we wouldn't be dating."

He nods. "Yeah, because I don't date. This is why I said you wouldn't want me. This is why I said I wasn't right for you."

I blink back some tears. "Because you won't change. Thanks. You're right; you should go."

He leaves my room without looking back. I'm so stupid to have thought Bryce could actually fall for someone like me.

Chapter Twenty-Seven

Bryce

The Halloween party is tonight. Madison hasn't spoken to me since we made out in her room and then I told her that she and I couldn't be more than friends with benefits. It was the dumbest thing I've ever said, but I can't have her falling for me. I've already fallen for her, but that's different.

She's got to realize that she and I would be a very bad deal. In the end, I'd do something to screw it up. I'd make her cry and hate me. So really, I'm saving her from all that.

I miss her lips. They were soft and warm, and tasted like cherry candy. Why did she have to smell delicious and taste so good it was like my own personal crack? Kissing her again will send me down a path neither of us will ever recover from. No, I've got to stand my ground.

For the most part, I have been. I barely look at her in class. Okay, I try not to look at her too much. But today, I break code as soon as I see her tears.

"Hey, what's wrong?" I ask, touching her left arm.

She immediately jerks away from me and mumbles, "Nothing."

"Really? Then why are you crying?"

She looks at me. There are no traces of makeup—which I love about her—just fresh tears running down her face. She sniffles a little and runs a hand under her eyes. "I just got yelled at. That's all."

"Who yelled at you?" I clench my fists, ready to pound whomever it is into the freaking ground.

She shakes her head. "None of your business."

She's shutting me out again. On a normal day, I would silently congratulate her. This is what she should be doing to me. It's what I need her to do. But I don't want her doing this to me now. I reach for her again, but she snaps, "I said it's none of your business."

"And I want to make it my business."

"Well, you shouldn't." She breaks eye contact with me and mumbles, "I can handle this on my own."

Can she, though? Probably. But for some reason I don't like that idea. Not even in the smallest amount. Graham interrupts my next round of questions, and I watch her relax a little. She seems relieved so I let her win this time. But mark my words, I will get to the bottom of this.

"Hey, man, are you heading to Greg's tonight?" Graham asks.

"I don't know," I answer.

Madison faces the board and mutters, "Sarah's going. Just so you know."

"Well, she doesn't own the guest list!" Graham grumbles. "I can be in the same places she is. Greg was my friend first."

Madison turns in her seat and glares at him. Her cheeks are puffy and red. "You sound like a two year old." I stifle a laugh because he does sound like a toddler. "In the beginning, I was going to warn you about her, but I decided everyone had to learn for themselves. You bought her whole act, hook, line, and sinker. And for the last two weeks, I've had to listen to you moan and complain about her. 'Can you believe she took that dick to our place?' 'I go to get some pizza, and there she is, like a damn nightmare that just won't leave.'" Madison's impression of Graham is spot-on. "So I was just warning you ahead of time so that maybe I won't have to hear all about it on Monday!"

She whips back around in her seat, and I chime in, "Dude, you have been super whiny about Sarah."

Graham turns in his seat. "Go screw off! Both of you. You two have never been cheated on. And one of you has never even been in a relationship with anyone. So excuse me when I say you can take your advice and shove it."

I shoot a look at Madison, who sighs and puts her head down. I know Graham is talking about her. Yeah, I figured that out already, but now it just makes me feel like more of an asshole. Just how inexperienced is Mads? She kisses like she's done it a hundred times, but now I get the feeling I might have been her first. If that's the case, I'm definitely going to hell.

In my room, I drum my pencil against my notebook while looking over my chemistry homework. It's Friday. Why the hell am I doing homework now? My door opens, and I watch Graham stroll into my room dressed like Jack Sparrow from *Pirates of the Caribbean*. He looks over at me and snatches up my notebook. "What are you doing? Get ready. We're leaving."

"I don't feel like it."

He hits me with my notebook. "Get up. This isn't like you, man. Doing homework on a Friday. Staying in instead of going to the biggest party of the year."

"Why does it matter?" I ask.

He plops down on my bed. "You'll stop being this dopey weird version of my friend if you come. That's why."

"I'm not going." I glance out my window and notice two figures in Madison's room. One is Mads; the other is Sarah. Mads is flinging her arms around like a lunatic. Sarah has her arms crossed and is smirking like she's enjoying every second of whatever is going on.

Madison launches something at Sarah and then disappears. I head over to my window and scan the yard. Graham is mumbling, but I'm not listening to him. I spot Madison storming across her lawn and into her car. She peels from the driveway, and for some reason, I have this urge to follow her. Make sure she's okay.

Yeah, I know it kind of sounds stalkerish, but there's a knot in my stomach. I grab my fitted Marlins hat and snatch up my keys. "We're going?" Graham asks. I nod. "Awesome! I knew you'd see it my way."

Not sure what way he was talking about, but at this

point it doesn't matter. What matters is catching up to Madison and making sure she's okay.

When we get into my car and start heading down the road, Graham complains, "Um, where are you going?"

"I don't know." It really isn't a lie. I don't know where Madison is going.

I roll to a stop sign. Graham looks around and huffs, "Where the hell are we?"

I shrug. I've actually never been this far west of town. We could've hopped a city line, and I actually wouldn't know. All I see is taillights up ahead, and I pray that's Madison's car. It's not until the third stoplight, when the car turns, that I finally get a better glimpse of the make and license plate. And thankfully, it is Madison.

She finally pulls over. There are a couple of rundown buildings along the street, but Madison walks to the one building that looks brand-new and out of place. There are only a few streetlights working, so the place is fairly dark. But there is just enough light to catch Maddy's expression. A scowl is on her face, and her movements seem stiff as she stomps to the entrance of the building, which looks like it was cut from marble.

Graham punches my shoulder. "What the hell? I thought we were going to Greg's, not following Madison."

"Something isn't right."

"She's at her mom's work. I'm sure whatever it is, she'll be fine. Can we freaking go to Greg's now?"

I wait a moment longer, but when Madison doesn't appear, I slowly pull away from the curb and take off.

Fifteen minutes later, we're driving to Greg's house. There are cars lined on both sides of the street. There are people in costumes making their way across lawns to Greg's parents' mansion on the lake.

Graham grumbles, "Dude, we're going to be driving a mile down the road before we find a spot."

"Want me to let you out right here? Then it'll look like you got a ride from your mom."

"Fuck off, ass." I glance over at him and notice his posture changes. His arms are folded, and he turns his head to the passenger window. He's right; it's probably going to be a mile hike back when we finally do find a spot.

I keep driving and scanning the street, and Graham yells, "Oh, that little punk ass is here tonight!"

I don't have to see who he's talking about. I already know. "Don't get in any fights." We look at each other, and I shake my head. "Let me rephrase: don't drag me into your mess. If you start some shit, you better finish it."

"You're supposed to have my back, man."

"I've had your back before. In fact, more than once. So don't pull that shit on me." I leave out the fact that he's never once had mine.

Chapter Twenty-Eight

Bryce

It takes me a while, but I finally find a spot in BFE—Bumfuck Egypt. We're not the only ones parking out here, though. About five cars pass and pull off to the side in front of mine. Graham talks to Kelly as we make the hike down the hill to the party. I've completely tuned them both out. By the time we reach Greg's, I'm in the mood for a beer. Maybe something harder in order to drown out everyone.

I make my way to the kitchen where row of liquor rest on the countertop. It's like a buffet of booze, and there is a line. I get in place. A scent of butterscotch hits me. It smells exactly like Madison. I search the room but don't see her anywhere. My mind must be messing with me. This is a costume party—and yeah, I'm not the only one who didn't really dress up—but I'm pretty sure I could pick out Madison even in costume. There's just a certain thing about her, like how she walks straight but on the balls of her feet. She rarely lets her heels touch the ground. Almost like she's a dancer or a runway model. But I don't see any of that here.

No, in front of me is a blond with thick curls. She groans loudly. "Do these people ever move? I mean, hello, the rest of us need some alcohol too."

"Sarah?" I ask.

She turns and sneers. "Oh, Lord. Look, tell Graham it was fun, but seriously, he left me. End of story."

"I'm not here because of Graham. He's a big boy and can deliver his own messages. I'm in line for a beer."

She nods. "Well, it's probably gonna take us fifty years to get our drinks."

"What did you do to Madison?"

Her eyes widen a little, and then she rolls them. "Nothing. I told her the truth. Unless you're talking about that art thing—I just thought she wasn't interested anymore because she threw out her drawings."

"You mean the ones you scribbled shit all over and then showed to Graham? That's not cool. And why would you do that anyways? Madison didn't throw a bitch fit when you painted her walls a color she hates. She didn't even go off on you for humiliating her in front of her friend. What's wrong with you?"

Sarah smiles. "For starters, it's sisterly affection. Second, it doesn't matter. She can play innocent all she wants, but she kept a secret from me. A terrible secret. So this is my way of saying thanks to her."

"What the hell kind of secret did she keep from you? Are you talking about her crush on Graham? You know Madison wouldn't have stolen him from you; she stepped aside. Not that it mattered because he was into you and not her. He sees her as a sister."

"No, that's not what she kept from me. And, honestly, it was just fun watching Graham fall for me. The way she looked physically ill every time Graham and I kissed was just icing on the cake."

This girl is sick. I need to make sure Madison stays away from her. Hell, even if she has to spend the night in my bed and I have to sleep on the floor until the end of the school year. I'll gladly do it in order to keep her safe from this little bitch. "There is something wrong with you. Stay the hell away from Madison."

"Can't really do that, Romeo." The line moves.

I grab a red Solo cup and tap it against my thigh. Sarah glares at me. "Speak of the devil. Here she comes."

I shift, and sure enough, here comes Madison, marching over to the line. I'm about to tell her to cut in front of me, but I don't want her near Sarah. Sarah's grin is creepy, but she turns when someone ahead of us shouts at her. She leaves and weasels her way to the person in front.

Someone touches me, and I turn to see Emily and Madison. "Hi. You ladies wanna cut me?"

"Thanks," Emily says. She grabs two cups. Madison shakes her head, but Emily insists. "You need this. Do you hear me? I won't let you get so stupidly drunk you won't be able to talk or do something with a dirty stranger. But you do need a few. You had a rough day, Maddy."

"I'll take you both home," I offer. I don't know why I do. I'm supposed to be keeping my damn distance. And here I am roping myself back in.

Madison gives me a look. "You don't have to."

"But I want to. Go on. I'll even watch you. I'll

make sure nothing happens to you."

Emily smiles. "Thank you, Bryce." She shifts her attention to Madison. "See? It'll be okay. Bryce will be our DD and make sure we aren't out of control."

The line moves again, and we're finally at the buffet of beverages. I was going to get a beer, but since I'm going to be driving Madison and Emily home I pour some Dr. Pepper into my cup and toss in some ice cubes. Emily fixes Madison and herself a drink. I'm not exactly sure what all is in it, but I can tell from Madison's face it's a lot of liquor.

"Go easy," I whisper in her ear as we leave the kitchen.

"I'm not easy!" she shouts back.

"No, I said *go* easy."

She glowers. "You're not my mother."

"I'd hope the hell not. I'd have a lot of explaining to do to quite a few people." I laugh.

Madison's face just sours. "I hate her."

"Who? Sarah? She seems like a real bitch."

Madison laughs. "Yeah, her too, but I was talking about my mom."

I start to ask why, but Emily whisks her off to the crowded dance floor. It's not really a dance floor, but a lot of drunks are spinning around, grinding on each other or swaying to the loud beats thumping through the surround sound in the living room. I debate whether to do the good thing, which would be to give her space. It almost happens too—until I see Jake Foster wrapping his freaking hands around her waist and pressing his abs into her back.

Nope. I will not be watching that. Sober. Drunk. It will not be happening. I march over and yank him away from her. Then I throw a right hook into his jaw. Jake stumbles a little. He drops his cup of probably beer and glares at me, raising his fists. "What the hell, Matthews?"

"Don't touch her. I told you to never fucking touch her!"

Jake shoves me and then swings his fist toward my face, but I dodge it and hit him again. My fist connects with his chin, and he falls into a group of people who have now formed a giant circle around us. The booming of a techno jam turns into a chant. "Fight! Fight! Fight."

Jake pushes off the people, and I'm about to hit him again, but my upper arm is pulled down and a small voice that quakes with fear says, "Bryce, don't. Please. Don't. Let's just go take a walk or something. Come on."

I glance back at Madison, and Jake sucker punches me right in my eye. What kind of wuss takes a cheap shot like that? Madison surprises me, though, and instead of mothering me and making sure I'm okay, she cocks her fist back and slugs Jake. He hits the ground with a loud *thud* and slumps against the floor.

I'm in shock. Madison turns to me. I snatch her hand and examine it. "Are you okay?" The skin on her knuckles looks angry. "I had that handled."

She shrugs. "Maybe you did. I just thought it was a douche move for him to hit you while you were walking away."

Chapter Twenty-Nine

Madison

Emily winks at me as Bryce and I walk by. Her contact might be coming out, though; she was having issues with it earlier. Either way, she's not the only one being all weird at the sight of Bryce and I holding hands. The crazy thing is, though, I actually like that he's holding my hand and not ashamed of who sees or what they might say.

It's not until we pass by Sarah that my insides churn and I have this dire need to flee this place. I pick up the pace to avoid that annoying smirk she has pasted on her face. Once we're outside, I sigh in relief.

"Embarrassed about something?" Bryce asks as he releases my hand, his lips drawing into a grim line.

"What? No. If anything, you should probably be embarrassed by me."

We walk down the steps. The night air is bitter and chills my nose and cheeks. I rub the sleeves of my coat, which I'm thankful I didn't take off when Emily insisted. See? Sometimes stubbornness pays off.

"Why would I be embarrassed by you?" Bryce asks.

I shrug. "Because apparently my life is a whole lot more complicated than yours could ever be." I laugh. "I think I'd prefer your parents pretending they aren't cheating on one another over the newly developed facts in my life."

We make our way over to the small beach area of the lake. A shiver runs down my spine. Do I really want to tell Bryce what lie I uncovered? I mean, for God's sake, I thought it was weird how Mom treated Sarah. I found it stranger how Aunt Catlin acted around me. But now I know, and it makes me sick. Do you know how disturbing it feels to find out the person you called your cousin is actually your sister?

"Madison." He steps in front of me so we're facing each other. "What's wrong?"

"Sarah and I are sort of … sisters. My mother is, apparently, her mom. Well, it was her egg that made it possible. And I guess my aunt felt cheated."

"Wait, what?"

"My aunt Catlin couldn't have kids because she had no eggs in her basket, so to speak. My mother decided, after she had Kyle, to donate some to her. So the test-tube experiment worked, and my mom got pregnant a couple months later with me. I guess Sarah is jealous and hates me because I apparently have the better life."

He kisses the top of my forehead. "Madison, she has to know that's not your fault."

I laugh. "You'd think, right? But she's so crazy, she convinced herself that I stole what should have been hers. So she plans on stealing everything and anything that's mine."

"Jesus, she told you this?"

I nod. "She's a monster." I take a drink from my cup and swallow down the sugary, burning concoction Emily made. A rum and Coke, I think that's what she said it was. My memory is a little hazy on that. "Do you know she took a call from Carnegie Mellon, pretended to be me, and set an interview date? She thought it was a riot watching that woman wait for me, and I never showed. That poor woman will never speak to me again. She's furious with Ms. Dyson. She told her that she'll never look at my art again. She didn't care how talented I was. In fifteen years, she's never had a student stand her up. I will not be the first and still get accepted into her program."

Tears fall. I shake out sobs and use my sleeve to wipe away snot. Once again, I'm a wreck around him. But he's holding me, and I need this. I need someone to hold me and tell me it's going to be okay. Even if it won't be. I want to hear it, believe it.

"Isn't there a way to talk to the woman? Explain to Ms. Dyson what happened?"

I sniffle and laugh. "And what? Tell her my psychotic test-tube sister is plotting revenge on my life because she thinks I stole it from her? Yeah, that will go over real well."

He shrugs. "You gotta do something. You can't let this happen otherwise she'll just walk all over you."

"I know." I kick the dirt and sigh. "Really, I do. I'm just so tired. It seems like she'll never stop."

A loud roar of *oohs* and *aahs* interrupts my next thought. Bryce and I both turn toward the noise.

Graham slams out the back door of the house holding Ryan by the collar with one hand and punching him in the face with the other. Bryce swears beside me and takes off after them. I try to keep up with Bryce's long stride but fail miserably. "Wait. Don't."

He's not listening, though, and I stay back in the shadows of the trees on the property while a crowd forms around Graham and Ryan bashing each other's faces in. Sarah, of course, isn't even trying to help stop the fight. She just stands back with the rest of the crowd, covering her nose and mouth with her hands but nothing more. Honestly, I think she's loving the fact that these two idiots are fighting for her.

Bryce marches over to Ryan and rips him from Graham's grip. All is well. It's over now. But as soon as I think this, Bryce blasts the side of Ryan's face and lets him crumple to the ground. I'm not watching any more of this. I turn and head to my car.

I hear the sirens from a distance. Someone called the cops. It could have been one of the neighbors or possibly one of the partygoers. I text two people only because I care about them getting busted for something.

> Me: Cops are coming.
> Emily: Where R U?
> Me: In my car. I'm outta here.
> Emily: Fine. I'll get a ride.

I'm not really in my car yet, but I'm not waiting for her to hike her way to me. If I did, I'd definitely be at a risk of being arrested for underage drinking and thrown in the back of a police car. No thanks.

> Me: Hi. Cops are coming.
> Bryce: Shit! Thanks.
> Bryce: Hey where r u?

```
Me: Heading home.
```

I'm still hiking to my car, but he doesn't need to know this.

```
Bryce: How much have u had 2
drink?
Me: Not much.
```

Okay, that's a lie. I've had a little more than I'm leading on.

```
Bryce: Please pull over at the
first gas station.
Me: Why? I'm fine.
Bryce: But I'm not fine with u
driving.
Me: I'm srsly fine!
Bryce: Damn it Mads! Don't do
this shit 2 me. Where r u? Ur
car is still here.
```

Son of … really? I scan my surroundings and can't see anyone. Where the heck is he? How does he know I'm still here?

"Hi."

I scream at the top of my lungs and jump at least three feet from fright.

"Calm down, Mads. You'll attract the five-O." Bryce leans in close and sniffs my breath. I cover my mouth with my hand, and he laughs. "And from the smell of you, I assume you don't want to be introduced to the back of a police cruiser." I shake my head. "Come on then."

We march to my car. "How's Emily?" I ask.

"She was bailing just like me once I got your text. I was worried you were actually driving."

I raise a brow. "Why?"

He looks taken aback. "What do you mean 'why'? I like you, Madison. More than I should. I worry about you."

A blush I'm sure the darkness is not hiding burns on my face. But reality sets in, and I know if I want to keep Bryce, we're going to have to keep this on the DL. As long as Sarah's still around, Bryce and I will have to be careful. Because Sarah is out to ruin anything that makes me happy.

Chapter Thirty

Bryce

Thank God I reached her in time. I was so freaking worried she was driving. Not that she was smashed, but still, one is enough to cause a lifetime worth of damage. So yes, I'm glad I spotted her marching up the road to her car. Actually, no, I'm very glad Greg's parents have a short loop of a drive that caused all these cars to park miles and miles down the road.

We're very close to her car, thank God, because my feet are killing me. "Smalls, I know I shouldn't but ... will you go out with me sometime?"

She looks at me with those stunning green eyes of hers. "You know you shouldn't? Why bother asking me if you're already having regrets?"

"I don't have regrets. I ... I'm worried that I'm bad for you." I might as well get the truth out there.

She shrugs. "Because we're like a horrible cliché? Bad guy falls for the good girl? But let's be real here ..."

She stumbles a bit. I catch her arm and pull her to me before she face-plants.

"Yeah, you're not fit to drive," I mutter as we continue toward her car.

"Pfttt. I just tripped over a rock. Don't get all high and mighty on me." She glares at me. "What was I talking about before I tripped?"

"Stumbled," I correct. "You were saying we're a terrible cliché."

She points her finger up to the sky. "Yes, that's right. But we would only be that if you were really a bad boy. You, you cute specimen, are not bad. No. You know what I think? I think you're really the guy who likes to play the hero. Soooo, you do something stupid and take the fall for others. Don't you?"

I'm shocked. Graham knows what I've done but never said a word. Everyone else, though, every person in this whole idiotic town, has not seen me as anything but a criminal. And here she is, picking away at the truth. "I think you've had a little more to drink than you've let on, Smalls."

"I'm right. You do that when I'm right about stuff. You purposely change the subject." She pulls out her keys, and I snatch them from her. "What are you doing?"

"Driving. Come with me."

I guide her to the passenger side and open the door for her. She narrows her eyes but slides into the seat. I shut the door and go to the driver side. Once I'm in, I start the car, and she huffs. "So … why did you help Graham?"

"Because he's my friend. He can't fight for shit. And honestly, Ryan deserved to get knocked out."

"Did he?" I can hear the annoyance in her tone.

I glance over at her. "I don't have a crush on Sarah. I did it to help Graham."

"Not the first time you helped him out, is it?"

"I don't know what you're mumbling about."

She snorts. "Yes, you do. So what did you do for him? Beat up his supplier?"

I pull into the lot near the lake and throw her car into park. I shift in my seat and stare at her. "Why are you asking me all this stuff? If I answer any of it, will it help or hurt my chances at taking you out?"

She rolls her eyes. "I need to know what I'm getting into. I can't just go out with you and run into one of your buddy's friends that you may or may not have taken a fall for. What's going to happen if they need you again? Am I going to have to find my way back home while you get hauled away?"

I am annoyed. I shouldn't be because she has a right to ask. It still ticks me off. "Look, I'll make you a deal. I promise I won't get into any trouble. Just say yes. One date. That's all. If you decide you don't want to do it again, it'll be fine. We'll act like it never happened and just be friends."

"I don't want to be friends."

I flinch a little.

"Oh. That came out wrong. I like you too much to go back to being friends, Bryce." Her eyes lock with mine. I lean in and kiss her softly.

Her lips are urgent, though. She unfastens her seatbelt and climbs over the console. Her ass hits the horn, and she mutters a curse word. I snicker, and her mouth is on mine again as she straddles me in the driver's seat. I run my hands along her back.

She pulls away slightly, and I kiss her neck. "Say yes," I murmur against her skin.

"Yes. I'll go out with you."

She grinds against me as my lips reach her collarbone. I break away and stare at her. "Babe, as much as I want to fog up these windows, we can't. And you're really doing a number on me right now. If you don't stop soon, I might have to go to the hospital for my massive case of blue balls."

She bites her lower lip. "Oh. Oh gosh. I'm sorry." She moves over to her seat again and giggles. "I wasn't thinking. I just … This is new."

"I know. That's why I wanted to warn you. We're going to take this slow, Madison. If you decide after our first date you want to keep seeing me, we're going to take this really slow. You're going to have to give me the green light on everything."

She nods and tucks some loose hair behind her ear. "Okay. Good. Because I'm a virgin at everything."

I choke on a cough. "Was I your first kiss?"

She blushes a deep red. "Not really, but I don't count the first one. That was forced and gross. So … yes."

I smile as I turn the key to the ignition. "I'm honored, Madison."

"You should be," she teases.

I wish the drive back home lasted longer than it did, but I also know that Madison's parents can't catch me driving her car home. She warned me many times in the three minutes before she passed out.

When we get to her house, I slip out of the car and open her door. She snores softly. A little bit of drool falls from the side of her mouth, and I shake my head. God, she's a mess, but she's still the most adorable thing I've ever seen. I lift her from the car and look up at her house, then over at mine.

I could try waking her, but … I don't really want to say good-bye to her just yet. So, I shut her door as quietly as I can and carry her to my room. Once I'm there, I tuck her into bed, and I take a spot on the floor beside her.

As much as I might want to sleep beside Madison, I want her consent to do it. She rumbles against the sheets and moans lightly. "Why?"

"Madison?" I shake her a little. She flails about the mattress. "Madison!" I shake her again. Her eyes fly open, and she sits up, breathing hard. "Babe, calm down. It was just a dream."

"Bryce? Why are you … why am I in your room?"

"I didn't want to ring your doorbell and explain to your mom and dad why you were passed out in my arms. So I decided to let you sleep here."

She wipes her mouth and groans. "Oh God, I was drooling. That's so embarrassingly gross."

I shrug and take a seat on the floor again. "I thought it was kind of cute on you."

Her nose wrinkles. "No, you didn't." She starts to get out of bed.

"Stay. Please."

"You want me to stay?"

I nod. "Yeah—I'll take the floor." I say it so fast

I'm not sure she hears me right.

A few seconds pass, and she sighs. "Okay, but I want a T-shirt."

"Do you promise not to drool on it?" I smirk.

She hits my shoulder. "Funny. Yes, I promise not to drool on your shirt."

I kiss her mouth. "You can if you want. I'm just messing with you."

I walk over to my dresser and grab an undershirt for her to sleep in. Tossing it to her, I say, "I'm going to get changed in the bathroom. I'll knock before I come back in, so just let me know if it's safe to enter. Okay?"

"Okay."

I reenter my room wearing flannel PJ bottoms and a tank. Madison is snuggled into my bed, and can I just say, she looks good there. I quietly shut the door and kiss her forehead. She stirs a little and whispers, "Lay with me."

"Are you sure? I can sleep on the floor. I meant it when I said we're going to take this slow."

She smiles at me and pats the empty side next to her. "Come on."

I shouldn't. It's probably the alcohol talking. But at the same time I don't want to upset her. So I grab my blanket I was going to lie on from the floor and lie on top of the covers. I use my own blanket to cover up and wrap my arm around her.

She presses against me, well, the blanket barrier. It's still nice. I kiss the back of her neck and whisper, "Good night, Mads."

"Night, Bryce." It's a simple phrase, but coming from her lips, I wanted to hear it a thousand times more.

Chapter Thirty-One

Madison

To say I stayed all night with Bryce would be a lie. Once he was down for the count, I snuck out of his room and then out the door. Did I want to stay all night? Absolutely. Why didn't I then? Because I heard a car pull up.

It wasn't quiet at all, like, roll to a slow stop, let a person get out, and gently close doors so you barely hear a thing. Nope. Whoever drove her home was as loud as possible. What woke me was the sound of trash cans crashing to the ground, along with the high squeal of someone's brakes. Bryce, amazingly enough, slept through the whole thing. Maybe if I were in my own bed I'd have slept through it too, but I didn't. I climbed out of bed as carefully as possible and went to Bryce's window. I watched a blond ragdoll crawl out of the car, and then I heard her cough hard. I looked away before I could see. After the hard coughing came the sounds of her regurgitating whatever she'd consumed. I prayed she hit our bushes and not my car.

As I gathered up my jeans from the floor and slipped into them, I wrote Bryce a note and then kissed him softly on the mouth.

Outside, I don't check the lawn or my car for throw-up. I just quickly slip into the house and hurry up to my room. At the top of the stairs, I crouch down low, because just a few feet ahead of me, zombie-walking her drunk butt to the bathroom, is Sarah. The gross sounds start all over again before I can reach my room and shut out the noise. She has the door open, so I can hear everything hitting the toilet.

I shudder while entering our room, strip out of my jeans, toss my clothes in the hamper, and settle into my bed still wearing Bryce's shirt. I inhale his scent, which must be embedded into the fabric, as I nestle deeper into my covers.

It doesn't take long before I'm sleeping again. That is, until Sarah makes her way back into the room. She's loud. Flicks on all the lights. I sit up and groan. She just keeps flinging crap all over the place. "What are you looking for?" I ask, annoyed.

"None yer biznus."

"Keep it down. You'll wake everyone up."

"I hate yo," she slurs.

I roll my eyes. "I don't care. Go to bed."

She stumbles over to me, grabs me by my collar, and starts shaking me. "I lob him. I ruin it. Evry'in."

"Jesus, are you on drugs? Did someone slip you something? Seriously, Sarah, stop shaking me like a maniac." She's scaring the shit out of me. I'm not sure what she'd do to me if she's straight up wigging out.

I free my hands, which were trapped under my comforter, and wrap them around both of her arms. She screams something about Graham. I narrow my eyes but manage to pull her off me. I cock back my fist and punch her in the jaw, knocking her out, right on top of me.

Rolling her dead weight off me, I spring from my bed and check her pulse. It's barely there. I'm in a panic. I knocked out a crazy, possibly drugged person. Do I have to watch her? Get her to a hospital? I need to wake my parents, but I'm not in the mood to answer questions like why didn't I watch her? Hell, I'm not in the mood to even look at my parents and not feel betrayed. That horrible secret … How could they? I grab my cell from the charger and call Bryce. I know he's sleeping. Hell, he probably won't even hear it ringing.

"Hello?" he grumbles.

"Hi, um, I need you to get dressed and come over."

"Babe, why aren't you here? What's going on?"

"Listen, I heard Sarah come home. I figured my parents would look for me if they saw my car and not me in my room. Sarah is too drunk to have parked correctly, and they know I'd call and tell them if I was at Emily's or something."

I see his light flick on, and he grumbles, "I'm coming. It'll be a minute, but I'm coming."

"Thank you. But fair warning, I think Sarah is on drugs. Do you still have those handcuffs from when we were kids?"

"Yeah, keep talking to me."

So I do. He asks how Sarah looks; I tell him pale, a mess of makeup, and I explain how I knocked her out.

He asks me other things, but most of them I have no answer to. Thankfully, I don't need one because he's already tiptoeing into my room. He smiles at me.

"You look good in my shirt, Smalls."

I smile back. "I'm keeping it. But enough about me. What about her?" Sarah starts to stir against my covers. My hand is throbbing from hitting her, and I thought it would feel amazing to punch her in the face, but it doesn't. I actually feel worse.

"Is she going to be okay?" I ask Bryce as he looks over Sarah. She groans and twists.

"Get a bucket. She might puke."

I run out of the room. My parents' bedroom door opens, and my mom steps into the hallway, tying up her purple robe. "Madison, what's going on? I heard a lot of racket."

"It's fine, Mom. I'm just getting a bucket. Sarah had a little too much to drink. Bryce helped me get her into the house." Well, sort of.

She makes her way to my room, and I decide to just let her see the mess. Hiding is what got us all here in the first place, right? I hurry downstairs, grab a bucket from under the kitchen sink, and then rush back to my room.

My mom is sitting on my bunk brushing the golden locks from Sarah's forehead. She turns back to me and motions for the bucket. "Set it here. Go get a cold rag. Bryce, be a dear and get me a glass of cold water with some ice chips in it. Madison, I need some aspirin too. Hurry."

I follow her instructions and leave Bryce to his task. I return before Bryce. My mom glares at me as she takes the rag and bottle of pills from me. "Were you watching her?"

"No," I say in a low tone. I drop my gaze to my feet.

"You should have been. Unless you decided not to attend the party at all, then that's a different story. But even then, you should have at least told her. She told me you were going together before I left for work."

I roll my eyes out of habit. "Really? This is how it's always going to be, isn't it? If Aunt Catlin is convicted, I'll forever be the babysitter, the coddler, and everything she does will be poor Sarah, or where was Madison? Won't it?"

"It's not like that. I just thought you cared and would protect her. You know these people better than she does. You know who is a bad influence and a good one. Why wouldn't you help her?"

"Because she ruined my future, Mom! I'm not her babysitter. I'm not her keeper. And I sure as shit will not sit here and take all this. She should have to deal with her own consequences. Isn't that what you always tell Kyle and me? We have choices, and we have to live with them one way or the other?"

She shakes her head and turns to Sarah. Bryce enters the room with the water. I turn back to my mom, but she's no longer paying any attention to me. Sarah sits up and rubs her cheek. She looks at Mom with wide, fearful eyes. Then she looks over at me. Her eyes narrow into slits. "Keep her away. She hit me."

"You were choking me!" I yell.

"Enough!" my mom says. She glares at me. "Go downstairs. Bryce, sweetie, thank you for your help, but I'm afraid it's time for you to head home."

I scowl at my mom and pull Bryce out of the room. I make my way to the living room. Bryce takes a seat next to me and pulls me into his lap. "It's going to be okay."

"I shouldn't have helped her."

"It's okay to care, Mads. Your mom is just a little scared. It's fine. Give it a few hours; it will blow over."

I shake my head. "It won't. You don't get it. She's looking at the what-could-have-been daughter. The daughter she could have had if she didn't give up her eggs to my aunt. She probably thinks she should have raised her." I rest my head against his chest and sigh. "She's always treated Sarah different. I thought it was an aunt thing, but now I know better."

"Babe, look at me." I do, and he smiles. "Your mom loves you. She probably just feels like she missed out on a lot with Sarah, so she's trying to make up for it. She probably doesn't realize it's hurting you in the process."

"Before you came over, Sarah was tearing through the room looking for something. It's probably nothing, but she mentioned Graham and love."

I study his face as he asks, "Graham? She does know she cheated on him, right?" His eyebrow raises.

"I don't know. She's completely whacked out. I mean, she was tearing through the room one minute and then choking me the next."

He nods. "That's messed up."

"I don't want to stay with her. I'm afraid she might kill me while I'm sleeping."

"Just come home with me."

I lower my voice. "I can't. My mom will probably come down here to check on me. If I'm not here, she'll freak out."

Bryce shrugs. "You could after she goes to bed.

Just slip out and come over."

It sounds wonderful. Staying with Bryce and waking up next to him in the morning. But now that Sarah's all delusional and probably going through a bad high, my mom will be checking on her like a hawk, which means she'll also be checking on me. I frown. "I can't. Mom will be watching my room all night." Then a thought dawns on me. "Ugh, Sarah's going to have my bed."

Bryce kisses my forehead. "It'll be okay, babe."

Footsteps echo off the stairs, and I motion for Bryce to go out the door. I follow him out on the porch, and we remain silent for a good bit. Then he sighs. "Tomorrow, if you aren't in trouble, I'd like to take you out. Is that okay?"

I grin like an idiot. "Yes. Text me in the morning."

He pulls out his phone and types something.

Bryce: It is morning. :)

Me: Thanks. Smart-ass!

He laughs. "Oh, man. I'm rubbing off on you."

I nudge him. "Maybe."

Chapter Thirty-Two

Bryce

I text Madison at noon. She doesn't answer, so I put on some music and chill out at my desk. As I'm completely immersed in alphabetizing my movie collection, arms come around my waist, causing me to jump and yelp like a little girl.

I turn. Her giggle fills my room. She smiles at me. "Ha. I got you."

"Jesus, Madison! You scared the living hell out of me!" I yell, but I also have to fight the smile trying to form.

She pokes my side. "You know you think it's funny."

I roll my eyes. "A little."

"A lot. But okay, you don't have to admit it." She hugs me, and a swoosh of tingles runs through my body.

I kiss her forehead. "Well, are you ready to go out on a date then?"

She nods. "I am."

I grab my wallet and keys and follow her out the door. I'm nervous. I want to hold her hand, but I'm not sure if I should. Would she pull away? Shit. This isn't like me at all. I have this kind of stuff under control. Not when I'm with Madison, though; everything makes me second-guess myself. Shirts, jeans, and now my own moves. Hold hands? Don't hold hands? This girl is turning me upside down.

I grab her hand and let relief wash all over me when she doesn't pull away. Once we're in my car, she says, "You don't have a pack of cigarettes sitting here like usual."

I nod. "I quit."

"When?"

"The day after you we cleaned up your room searching for your work keys."

She beams at me. "That's awesome! I'm really proud of you."

"Thanks. I figured it was time. Besides, this girl I really like hates when I smoke, so, eh …" I shrug like it's no big deal, but we both know it is.

"She must be so lucky."

"Oh, she is, but I'm the luckier one. She said yes to me."

She nods. "Yes, I did."

We drive into town and catch a movie first. She surprises me when she picks an action-adventure flick. It's actually the one movie I've been dying to see. Most girls I've taken to the movies either want to see some horror movie—which is fine, I'm just not a big fan— or chick flicks. No guy wants to sit through a chick flick. So yeah, when a girl picks a chick flick, we guys automatically think this is code for "makeout session."

Sorry, we do. But I was turned down a couple of times and forced to watch some really ridiculous crap.

Madison finds us a seat in the middle row. We watch the entire film in silence from start to finish. Which is another thing I love because I absolutely hate when people talk or ask questions during movies. Graham does that. He sits there and picks apart the bullshit parts in a film, like special effects or the plot. Savannah, a girl I dated a long time ago, used to talk through the entirety of the films I wanted to watch. I stopped taking her after the third time it happened, and then we broke up not long after. She claimed I never took her out. She didn't see the reason.

Once the movie is over, I take us to the Mexican restaurant in town called Agaves. "So how am I doing so far?" I ask Maddy as the waitress leads us to our booth.

"Pretty good. But you do know this is my first date ever, right?"

We slide into our seats, and I nod. Even though it's still kind of a shock to me. "I can't believe no one ever asked you out."

She blushes. "I've been asked. I just never said yes. Before, I was waiting for Graham. And now, I just … I really like the person who asked me." She lowers her lashes.

"Good. Because I really like you." But that bit about Graham bothers me. It shouldn't, but it does. If he asks her out, will I be old news or will she refuse him? I hope it's the latter. Because I really don't want to kick my friend's ass, but I will for her.

"Why do you sound bitter?" she asks as she gazes at me.

I shrug. "I'm not bitter. I just don't like the whole

Graham thing. I'm jealous, Smalls."

She snorts. "There's nothing to worry about, Bryce. I don't want him now."

I'm going to ask. I need all seeds of doubt to be squashed. "So if he asked you out right now, you'd say … ?"

"No. Because I don't want him."

I reach across the table and kiss her softly, then smile at her. "Sorry. I just had to."

"Okay." She looks down at her menu. I can see a hint of a smile and blush form. I love that I can make her do this.

I already know what I want so I just play with the hot sauce bottles, sliding one from my left hand to my right. "What are your plans after we graduate?" she asks, catching me off guard. I miss the bottle and watch it crash into the wall.

"Well, that depends. My father expects me to attend his old alma mater, University of Virginia. Of course this is only if I can keep my ass out of trouble." I wink. "But my cousin, you know, Hailey, is at Michigan State. And I've been there a few times to visit. I honestly will probably go there."

She sets down her menu. "That's nice. I mean, you at least have a plan."

"I know why you can't make a decision. Don't give me that look. I'm not making fun of you. Just hear me out. You can't make a decision because you don't know who you want to please more. Emily is going where … Florida?" She nods. "Okay, and then there is your brother, Kyle. He's at the University of Tennessee, right?" She nods again. "Then you got your parents. Your dad wants you to go to Vanderbilt; it's probably been his dream school for you ever since you got your first report card. Then you have your mom, who wants you to stay close to home. You gotta figure out what you want, Madison."

"I thought I knew what I wanted. I did. But now … I'm not so sure."

"The good thing about this decision is it's not an entirely a permanent one. Stay with me on this for a minute. I already see your brow rising, so that means you're about to argue. If—"

The waitress comes back to our table and asks for our orders. I give her both my drink and dinner order. Madison does the same, and the waitress leaves us.

"Where was I? Oh, right. Look, if you go to some school that your dad wants, you try it out for a year but are unhappy or not feeling it's where you want to be for the next four years, you can always change. Go off to Florida with Emily. See if that's where you need to be. If not there, then change again. Maybe you do need home or maybe … just maybe … you need to explore the world. You just have to choose one now if you haven't figured out what the right choice is for you. But you'll get there. You know?"

"How did you get so wise?"

The waitress sets down our Cokes, chips, and salsa and walks off. Madison pours some salsa into the two little bowls and passes one to me.

"Thank you," I say. "I wouldn't call it wise. Just knowing that as long as I'm breathing and living, I can do whatever I want. Death is the only thing that can stop that. What?"

She frowns. "I wish I hadn't act like such a snob to you before."

"I wouldn't change a thing, Mads."

Chapter Thirty-Three

Madison

The last few weeks with Bryce were amazing. He took me to the ice display in Opry Mills. I saw the whole *A Charlie Brown Christmas* cast in ice-sculpture form. It was truly fantastic. He took me to the art museum, which I thought might have bored him to tears, but he seemed really into it.

Today is Monday, though, and the upcoming week is Thanksgiving break. Bryce says he'll be in Michigan visiting Hailey. It's only going to be four days, but still, I'm already missing him, which is stupid because he's sitting right beside me as we drive to school. This is the first time we're driving to school in one vehicle since we started dating.

When Bryce said we were going to take it slow, he wasn't kidding. He hasn't even held my hand in school. We say hi in class, but we've been kind of acting like, well, like we aren't a couple. So last night, while we were talking, I mentioned it. And so he offered to drive me to school today.

"Emily was okay about getting a ride? I can still go pick her up," Bryce says.

"She said it was fine. Her words were this: 'Maddy, you know how I feel about third wheels. Just remember locker time is for us, not him.' So you can't hang out at my locker before class."

He laughs. "Girls and their secret locker time. Got it. Any other rules I need to know about?"

I smack his shoulder. "Shut up. And no."

"Good. Because I get to take up every other spare minute of your life forever and ever … or until you dump me," he teases.

I roll my eyes. "Somewhere in there I have to shower and shave my legs, mister, so no."

"For real though, just be honest with me, and we'll be fine," he says as we pull into the school parking lot.

"I will. You have to do the same."

"Always." He kisses me lightly, and my heart melts at how even his gentle kisses make me all swoony.

He slides his hand into mine, and we walk like a sappy, happy couple all the way to my locker. He flashes a smile at me right before he lets go of my hand as we reach Emily. Bryce pecks my forehead. "See you later." Once he walks off, I open my locker and glance over at Emily.

I must be grinning from ear to ear because my jaw is starting to hurt. Emily squeals. "Oh my God! That was so cute!"

"He is so sweet. I told him last night how I wanted to hold his hand or at least sit with him at lunch, and he said okay. Em, why did I hate him so much before?"

"Uh … he threw gum in your hair, and you had to get your locks all chopped off. People thought you were a boy. Then there's that bad-boy rep of his. He has an attraction to trouble. Oh, and the water balloon thing. That was awful. Oh God, and the whole rumor about you wanting to hook up with Danny What's-his-face. Barftastic!"

I nod. "Yeah, but … he's not, though. Trouble, that is. Em, I think … oh God, I think I'm falling for him."

"Are you?" Her eyes widen.

I shrug. "I don't know. I mean, I thought I was in love with Graham. But that was over a long period of time; it wasn't instant. He was really nice, and we had fun. As soon as he turned into an asshat, I felt miserable, yes, but I don't think it was heartbreak from him not loving me. It felt just like when Kyle does something to disappoint me. You know?"

"Brotherly. I get that. And with Bryce, if he disappointed you?"

"I think I might be devastated because it's more than trust, it's love too. You know?"

She nods. "I get it."

Everything in my life is fairly great so far. Maybe Bryce is right after all. I don't need to stress about college or my future, I just need to take a chance. Don't try pleasing everyone else, just choose what I love. So before second period, I hurry to the guidance counselor's office and grab the "college, universities, and more" binder. I flip through each page and write down all the art schools I can.

At lunch, I sit at the table and start researching some of the schools using my phone. Bryce sits down beside me, and Emily soon joins. She looks a little annoyed at me. "What?" I ask, lowering my phone to the table.

"Locker time?"

"Oh. I'm sorry. I didn't need anything from mine. And I, uh … I wanted to, um … get my list together." I show her my college list.

She raises a brow. "Didn't you apply to the ones you wanted already? Are these like fallback schools or something?"

"No, um … I, uh … didn't apply any." I bite my lower lip.

"Shut up! Seriously? We had a plan, Maddy. I can't believe you're telling me this crap now." She stands up. "Best friends for life, my ass!" She marches off.

"Em! Em, come on!" She keeps walking but not without flipping me off.

"Hey, Mads, look at me," Bryce says. He grabs my right hand. I turn to him and sigh. "It's going to be okay. She'll get over it."

"Will she? She seems pretty ticked off. Maybe this was a bad idea."

He shakes his head. "Babe, it's not a bad idea. Can I see the list?"

I show him, and he smiles. "Mostly art schools?"

"Yes." I say it like I'm unsure because I kind of am.

He squeezes my hand again. "They'll be lucky to have you. Any one you choose."

Will they? I can think of at least one school I can see myself at that will probably think differently. I frown. "I want this one." I turn my phone to Bryce. "But I think I messed up. I mean, I didn't mess up, but someone made sure that I'd screw my chances." I cast a look over to Sarah.

He follows my stare. "If someone were to talk to

Ms. Dyson—"

"No, Bryce. Don't. I'll apply, and if they accept me, great. If not, it's fine, it wasn't meant to be."

He nods. I have a feeling, though, that he's not going to listen to my request. We get through lunch without much more drama. Bryce walks me to class holding my hand, and when we get there, Graham glares in our direction. "Did I call this, or did I call this?"

"Knock it off," Bryce growls.

"No. I'm not going to knock it off."

Bryce drops my hand and takes a step toward Graham. "Knock. It. Off."

"No! Does she know what you plan on doing this weekend?"

I blink at Graham and then glance at Bryce. He's breathing hard and flexing his fists. "Aren't you going to Michigan to visit Hailey?" I ask, confused.

Graham shakes his head. "Bryce here is planning on saying fuck this to his probation and getting thrown in jail. Tell her now, so someone can talk sense into you."

"Bryce?"

Bryce looks back at me. "It's not what you think. We'll talk about this later. I promise." He glares at Graham. "You should have stayed home, buddy."

"She needs to know. You're doing something stupid!"

Bryce slams into a seat, and I slowly lower myself into mine. Graham doesn't say another word, and Bryce just looks angry the entire time. When the bell rings, he plows his way out of class. At the end of the day, he's not even in the parking lot. I look around for him, but he's gone. Em is still mad at me and left already, so that just leaves me with three options: the bus, which is currently making its way down the road, walking, or finding a ride with one of my classmates.

I'm about to walk. I'll curse Bryce with each step too. How could he just leave me? I'm mad at Graham too. If he hadn't ticked Bryce off, then I wouldn't be walking. However, what if what Graham said is true? Would Bryce have ever told me? And what the heck am I supposed to do with that information?

I start down the sidewalk, gripping the straps of my backpack. My thoughts are so jumbled, I don't notice the gray Chrysler following me until someone shouts, "Madison! Hop in."

I glance over at Graham and flip him off. "This is all your fault!"

"Madison, be reasonable. I'm trying to be nice and give you a ride home."

I stop walking and grumble, "Fine." He opens the passenger door, and I slip into the seat. "I'm still mad at you."

"That's fair. Buckle up."

I do. "Why did you tell me about Bryce?" I'm kind of glad he did, but I wasn't too crazy about the *way* he told me.

He sighs. "Because he wouldn't. Look, Bryce has done things. Not necessarily himself. But he has a tendency to stick up for or take the fall for others. And he can't afford any more strikes on his record. You're probably the only person who can talk some kind of sense into him. He's not a superhero."

"What exactly is he going to do?"

"You met Hailey, right?" He glances at me and then back at the road.

"Yeah."

Graham's jaw tightens. "Her ex-boyfriend beat her.

A lot. One time so bad she was in the hospital. What's really fucked up is she wasn't dating him anymore. He just jumped her as she was walking to her apartment. The cops put him away, and she has a restraining order against him. Anyways, the dude got out and has found strategic ways of stalking Hailey."

I cover my mouth. "Oh my God! That's awful. Are the cops not doing anything about it?"

"They do what they can." He shrugs. "Bryce knows, and he plans on beating that asshole into a coma, or worse. He'll do anything to protect the people he cares about."

"But … if he's on probation, and he beats that guy up or worse …" I shudder thinking about it.

"Exactly. I like Hailey. She's a cool person. But even she can't talk Bryce out of hunting that guy down. I think you can, though. You're the something he's afraid to lose." Graham pulls up to my house, and I thank him as I get out. I glance over at Bryce's house and notice his car in the driveway, but I refuse to go over there. Yeah, Graham says I should talk to Bryce, and I should. But I can't.

I stroll into the house and up to my room. I pull out my books and work on my homework. After homework, I start on more college applications. After the eighth application, I look up from my laptop and over to Bryce's window.

He's pacing, staring at something in his hand. The pain in my chest deepens. Why isn't he calling me to make sure I got home okay? Why isn't he telling me he's not going to do anything crazy?

I slam my computer shut and close my curtains as he looks over at my window.

Chapter Thirty-Four

Bryce

What's wrong with me? Everything! I left the girl I'm falling for at school without a freaking ride. That's a dick move on my part, and I know it. I'm surprised she hasn't posted a sign on her window that says, "Burn in hell, fucker," or, "I hate you, prick!"

When I look up from my phone and over at her room, I notice her staring out at me. I'm about to call her right then, but she slams her curtains shut. Damn it. I ruined it. My chance with her just went straight down the toilet. And for what?

Freaking Graham couldn't keep his damn mouth shut. I notice he gave her a ride home. My blood boils at the thought of her sitting in his car. It shouldn't because it's my own fault she had to fetch a ride with him in the first place. Still, that doesn't make it any better.

I pace my room some more. If only there were a way

to keep Hailey safe and that asshole behind bars, I'd do it. But because of overcrowding, they let Darren Hicks out. For assault, stalking, and harassing, he should have been in there for five years. That little shit got six months. He's also supposed to follow the restraining order my cousin put out on him, but it seems that punk found a way around it.

So of course I want to go up there and teach him a lesson. One that will require him to be locked up—in a hospital, in a coma, or six feet under. There is no reason a piece of garbage like him should be allowed to walk the streets. Hailey is scared to death to leave her dorm room.

I just wish Madison would understand. Yes, I should have told her, but I was worried she'd react just like she did. I don't want to lose her.

Skimming the numbers in my phone, I push down on one and listen to it ring.

"Hello," Hailey says in a low tone.

"Hi. How are you holding up?"

"Okay." I can tell she's lying. I clench my jaw.

"Screw break. I'm coming early."

She pauses. "Bryce, promise me you won't do anything stupid."

I pace my room, snatching up my bag from the floor and setting it on the bed. "I'm not going to do anything that little shit doesn't deserve."

"Damn it, Bryce! I know you want to protect me, but you can't do it if you're hauled off to jail. Threaten him if you want or punch him a few times but don't do anything too rash. I'm serious. I can't lose you. And think about Madison."

I stop grabbing clothes from my closet. "Don't

bring her into this. She's already pissed off at me, and I've probably lost her for good." I turn from my closet, my arms full of clothes, and just about jump straight out of my skin. Madison is standing in the middle of my room with her arms folded, glaring at me.

"Jesus, Mads, what are you doing?"

"Oh, is she there? Go talk to her, Bryce. I'll talk to you later. Tell her I said hi!" Then the line goes dead.

I lower the phone and slowly make my way toward the bed. "I'm an asshole. I know. I shouldn't have left you at school like I did. I just ... Madison, please stop looking at me like that. I'm trying to apologize."

"I don't want an apology. I want to know why you're doing this. Any of this. We were supposed to be honest with each other, and everything would be fine. You said that! Yet hiding things like this is the exact opposite of honest. You need to tell me this stuff."

I drop the clothes and hug her. I kiss her forehead, then say, "I'm sorry. I really am. You're right. I should have told you the moment I knew. But I was scared. I can't lose you, Madison. I'm in love with you."

She backs up and stares at me. Her arms drop to her sides, and she's trembling. "What?"

"I love you, Madison. It scares me because I know eventually this will all end. It scares me even more that you might not feel the same way. But you have to know."

"Bryce, I'm not sure what I'm feeling anymore. I'm mad you left me, but I'm more upset and hurt that you kept this from me. You told Graham but not me. Why?"

I look down at our feet and glower. "Graham was in the car when I got the call Friday. He overheard me say, 'Don't worry about it, Hailey. I'll take care of it.' He knew I was going to Michigan and knew you and I were spending a lot of time together. Especially when he asked if I wanted to come hang out over the weekend. I told him I couldn't because I was taking you out." I glance up at her. "He told me to tell you, and I said I would. But I didn't."

"So he told me instead. And now you claim to love me. Is that supposed to make me forget?"

I take a step closer. "No. Madison, I really do love you. I've loved you since kindergarten. I loved you when you pricked your finger on that stupid rose bush your mom has on the side of the house and you practically fainted at the sight of your own blood. Do you remember? We were five. I rushed inside and grabbed a Band-Aid, and you said I was your prince."

"But then you stuck gum in my hair."

"Because when I told you I liked you, you screamed that I had cooties and ran away."

One side of her lip quirks up. "I'm sorry."

"Madison, I swear I was going to tell you. I mean it. There are three things very dear in my life: you, my family, and Graham. If anyone harms or threatens those things, I will not stand around and watch. You asked me not to, but I did it anyway. I told Ms. Dyson to call her friend and get you another interview. You were still sick from that snakebite, and that's why you missed. Yes, I lied, but it was better than the truth and more logical."

Her eyes widen. "Bryce. I ..." Tears form, and I gently wipe one away. "Don't go. Please don't go without me."

"Madison, I'm leaving tomorrow. I don't think

your parents would be very pleased about you leaving with me. I know your dad would hunt me down and kill me."

She rest her head on my chest and whimpers against the fabric. "I don't care what they think. I'm not leaving you. I love you."

This time I pull her back slightly and stare at her. Tears still stream down her cheeks, and I ache for it to stop. I kiss her mouth, and at first, it's gentle and light, but she deepens the kiss. I moan against her mouth and guide her to the bed. In one fluid motion, I shove my bag and clothes to the ground to make more room for Madison and me.

My fingers roam her body without removing any of her clothes. I swore I would take things slow with Madison, and I'm keeping that promise. She presses her lips to my neck and exhales against my skin. God, I've never been so turned on in my entire life.

I break away from her. "Sorry. We … have … to … pause."

"Why?" she asks all breathy.

"Because I don't want to break any more promises." I get up and stride across the room. I stand near my dresser, giving us ample space.

She straightens her shirt as she sits up and then says, "I'm still going with you."

"Babe, you can't. I need you to stay here."

"Because you're going to get into trouble?"

I shake my head. "I don't exactly plan on it, but if I must to protect Hailey, I will."

She frowns. "Okay." She stands up and heads to the door. She pauses and looks over at me. "Can you promise me something?"

"Anything."

"Turn him in to the police. Let them do their job."

I tear my gaze from hers. "You don't understand, Mads."

"You're right, I don't. I guess you've made up your mind then. Good-bye, Bryce."

"Good-bye?" I stare at her. "Are you ending us?"

"I don't know. Just … call me when you get there."

She doesn't wait for my answer; she just leaves.

Chapter Thirty-Five

Madison

I haven't talked to Bryce since he left. I don't know what I was thinking, telling him I loved him. Yeah, I do love him, but … he still left. I understand he wants to protect his cousin. Believe me, I get that, but why hasn't he called me?

Sarah wanders into our room and snaps, "What?"

"Nothing." I slump into my chair and stare out at his window. I don't know why. Duh, he's not there. But I can't stop staring.

"Boyfriend finally figure out just how nunnish you are and leave you?"

I swivel in my chair. "Don't you have a flight to catch?"

She sneers at me. "No! I'm staying here for Thanksgiving. Got a problem with that?"

"I don't know. Do you plan on getting tanked on wine before or after dinner? I'd like to know so I can choose a good time to leave and not stay to clean you up this time!"

She stalks over to me. "You know what, Madison? I'd watch it if I were you. Pissing me off will not end well for you."

I roll my eyes. "Please. What more can you do to me, Sarah?"

Her grin turns evil, and she strolls over to the door.

Once she's gone, worry sets in. Crap. I should watch what I say around that little she-devil.

Kyle plows through the front door like an oversize caveman Thursday morning. He almost runs Mom over with a heap of laundry that, no offense, smells like it's been sitting in sewage for months. I plug my nose and make a sour face as soon as he drops the bag beside me and wraps me up in a hug. Oh, sweet Jesus, I think I'm going to die from the disgusting boy odors coming from him.

"Shower much?" I groan as he puts me down.

"Yes," he says and shoves me away.

"I can't tell."

He mocks me and then says, "I was driving for a while. Cut me some slack."

"Whatevs. Go take a shower. You smell worse than a pig barn."

"Bite me." He finds Dad and hugs him. He hugs Sarah too and then marches upstairs.

The phone rings. I pick it up since I'm closest and Mom is now busying herself in the kitchen. And Dad, well, he's flipping to football. "Hello?"

"You have a collect call from Arizona Correctional. Do you accept the charges?"

"Yes?" I say, completely unsure if my parents are taking my aunt and uncle's calls or not.

A woman with a deep and scratchy voice answers. "Hello?"

"Aunt Catlin?" It should be her, but it doesn't sound like her at all.

"Madison. How are you, honey?"

"I'm fine. Happy Thanksgiving."

She grunts like a truck driver and asks, "Is your mom or Sarah around, honey?"

"Yeah, hold on." I clasp my hand over the receiver and yell for Sarah first. I'm sure she wants to talk to her mom. She comes down the stairs and glares at me as I hand her the phone. "It's your mom."

"That's not my mom!" She knocks the phone away from me, and I pick it up.

"Sorry, Aunt Catlin. Sarah seems to be in a mood. Hold on, here's Mom." I hand the phone over to Mom while taking the spoon from her and stirring the stuffing.

While I stir, Mom talks in hushed tones. It's making eavesdropping a lot more difficult. I'm almost about to give up when Mom shouts, "That's beyond ridiculous, Catlin! I can't afford to do any more than I already have."

My father enters the kitchen with an alarmed look. He studies my mom, and then glances at me. I turn my attention to the stuffing. Whatever is going on is not good.

A shadow clouds over me. "So, squirt, why are you making the stuffing? And why is Mom crying?" Kyle asks.

"Aunt Catlin is on the phone."

"Oh."

He takes the spoon from me and scoops a spoonful of stuffing. He's about to put it in his mouth when Mom comes over and snatches it from him. "Kyle! No taste testing! Get out of my kitchen." She glares at me. "And you, I thought I taught you better."

I shrug. "He stole it out of my hand."

"Just go entertain yourself somewhere else."

I scowl at her and walk out of the room. I head up the stairs to my own room. Once I'm there, I sigh and call Em. "Happy Turkey Day," I say when she answers.

"Uh-huh. You too."

"Em, are you still mad at me?"

She huffs. "I don't know. Lately you've been a totally different person, Maddy. You aren't applying to Florida like we planned. You're falling for Bryce, the guy you couldn't stand most of your life. What other stuff have you been holding out on me on?"

"Nothing. Well ... I don't think you'll have to worry about Bryce and me anymore."

"Why?" she gasps. "Listen, I'm sorry for being a total bitch lately. I don't want you two to break up. Mads, you're really happy."

I sniffle. "He hasn't called me since he left. He told me he loved me, and he left, Em. He promised to call me, and he hasn't."

"I'm coming over. This is like—wow—huge! He said he loved you? Maddy, I'm so excited for you."

"Um ... Em, aren't your parents going to go, like,

crazy if you leave the house?"

She grumbles, "I don't care. I told you before, this is wow-huge shit!"

We hang up, and I wait.

She arrives at my house in ten minutes. My mom looks at me from the kitchen as I answer the door. "Madison?" she calls as I lead Emily inside.

"She's only staying for a little bit, Mom. Don't start. Please." I want to tell her I'm having boy issues, but I don't want her butting in. The last time she gave me boy advice, the kid laughed at me. Never again.

Em and I run up to my room, and I shut the door behind me. Sarah is sitting on the top bunk brushing her damp hair. Apparently she got a shower. Wish she was still there. I don't want her listening to my conversation.

"Um … Let's go to Kyle's room."

Em blushes but follows me out into the hall and into my brother's room. It's empty, well, aside from his suitcase, which is popped open on the bed. Em looks about his room like it's a treasure chest. She has no idea that I know she has a major crush on my brother. Every girl does, except me, because that's gross. Girls used to try to become friends with me just to get to my brother. And that's just plain disturbing.

Em hasn't ever admitted to having a crush on Kyle, but I can tell. She gives off little hints, like asking, "When's Kyle coming home?" Or whenever he had his latest girl toy over, Em would try to sabotage their alone time. And sometimes I would help because it was funny.

I think she doesn't tell me because she's scared. I'm not weirded out by the idea of Em and Kyle; however,

I would be really protective of Em. If he hurt her in anyway—not that he'd physically hurt her—but if he broke her heart, I'd hate him for it. And I don't want that.

Em takes a seat on the corner of his bed. "Does it feel weird when he's gone?"

"No. It's quieter. I don't hear the sound of this all day long." I pick up the small plastic basketball and toss it at the tiny hoop hanging on the door. The ball hits the cardboard backboard with a *thud* while the plastic rim makes a *blunggg* sound. "Remember how he'd do this for hours before game nights? It used to drive me nuts. Especially on a Saturday morning. I mean, those are for sleeping in."

"Yeah." She says it all dreamy, though.

"Anyways … I want to talk to you about something."

She smiles. "About what you're going to do when Bryce gets back?"

"He told me—no, he promised—he'd call me."

"And he didn't?"

"No. Em, he was going to do something crazy. I tried to talk him out of it, but he was just so set on it. There was no talking him out of it. So I let him go. But he hasn't contacted me once, and I'm worried. What if he's hurt or something?"

Emily shakes her head. "Did you call him?"

"No because I didn't want to sound needy," I admit. "You know I've never had a boyfriend before. I'm scared I'm going to do all the wrong things and lose him."

"I don't think that will happen. The boy worships you. Give him a call, Maddy; he's probably just waiting to hear from you first. In case you're pissed off at him. Guys are weird like that. And when you ask them, 'Hey, why didn't you call?' You know what they say? 'I thought you were mad at me so I waited for you to call.'"

"That's just ridiculous."

She shrugs. "I know. But that's how they are." She shoves me. "Call him."

I pull my phone from my back pocket and find Bryce's name. Mentally counting down to three, and risking talking myself out of it, I double tap his name. Emily smiles and watches me the entire time the phone rings.

Two long rings and then voice mail. Voice mail? Ugh!

Chapter Thirty-Six

Bryce

Hailey glares at me as she hands over my phone. "Bryce, honestly, I should hit you. I told you not to get into trouble."

"Was he or was he not stalking you?" I say it as calmly as possible. I pulled up to Hailey's place Tuesday night, and that freaking asshole Darren was sitting in his car staring her place down. He was just waiting for her to come out. He tried telling the cops he had a date that lived in that building and he was waiting on her. He told them that he had no idea Hailey lived there.

I got out of my car and stormed right up to his. I told him to get outta there before I busted him up so bad he couldn't walk. Some nosy neighbor heard me shouting at that asshat, and the cops showed up. Of course, right before the boys in blue rolled in, that freaking jackass got out of his car and took a swing at me. I ducked, and he missed me by so much he actually punched out his own back window.

Because it was a domestic disturbance in a residential area and the moron was bleeding from his own injury, I got hauled off to the police station too. I called Hailey as soon as I got a chance. And she's pissed at me. She was pissed at me as soon as she got the call.

"Ten minutes. You couldn't even be in town ten minutes without getting arrested. Your mom is going to have my hide."

"Calm down. I didn't lay a hand on him. He did it to himself. I ducked, and he took out his own window. End of story."

"Mrs. Gable says you threatened to pull off his limbs and beat him with them if he didn't leave. She didn't know who you were. And she also didn't know why you were threatening him." Hailey looks annoyed. "Madison called."

I glance down at my phone. "I can't talk to her right now."

"Well, if you're finished playing hero, I need your help on some stuff and then you're calling her."

"I've been in jail for two days. I just want a shower and a change of clothes."

She shrugs. "Whatever."

She drives us back to her apartment. I head to my duffel bag and then to her shower.

She shouts at the door while I step into the hot running water. "So are you and Madison a thing now? Last time we talked you were taking her to the ice show!"

I squirt shampoo in my hand and rub it in my hair,

yelling back, "Can't you wait until I'm out of the shower?"

"Nope! So are you dating?"

"Yes!"

"Yes what? You are dating?"

I rinse the soap, lather the rest of my body with body wash for men, and then condition my hair before answering her again. Once everything is rinsed away and I've stopped feeling like a dirtball, I get out and dry myself off. I slip into my sweats and a T-shirt and hang the towel on the towel rack. I crack open the door to let out the steam. Hailey opens the door wider and glares at me. "Well, are you going to answer?"

"Yes, we're dating. Well … we were. We probably won't be when I tell her why I haven't called her."

Hailey shakes her head. "Stop with the drama stuff. She'll talk to you. Just be honest. Don't fib or skate around the reason. Because then she'll be mad at you and probably will leave you."

I glower at her. "Thanks." I squeeze toothpaste onto my toothbrush and wash the foulness from my mouth. How anyone can stand not brushing their teeth on the daily is beyond me. While I'm brushing, my cousin decides to plant herself right beside me, giving me very little space to move or rinse out my mouth. "Could you back up into the hall or something?"

"You have to promise to call her."

"Why does it matter so much?" I ask, spraying a bit of toothpaste foam.

She wrinkles her nose and wipes her cheek with the back of her hand. "Because I like her. She's good for you. Maybe this one can keep you on a straight path. I want to see you go far, Bryce. You're a good person.

You just do dumb shit."

"Thanks for the vote of confidence." I shake my head and rinse out my mouth. After I spit and turn off the water, I ask, "You really think we're good for each other?"

"I don't know about you for her," she teases.

I shove her. "Shut up."

"I'm joking. I don't know her very well, but I think you could be good for a lot of people. Just have to pick the right people."

I tip my head back and then walk out of the bathroom. I take a seat on her couch and sigh. My phone sits on the coffee table, silent, screen black, and it is so haunting. I pick it up and call Madison.

It rings four times, and then her voice comes through the phone. "Hey, you've reached Madison. I'm not able to take your call at the moment. Leave me a message at the beep. Or text me."

Her damn phone beeps at me, and I hang up. I text her.

> Me: Hi. Call me.
> Madison: No.
> Me: Why?
> Madison: Ignoring my calls is an asshole move. I know ignored calls. It rings twice and then you get a voice mail.
> Me: Madison I'm not saying this shit through txt.
> Madison: Happy Thanksgiving. I've gotta go.
> Me: Madison I was in jail.

My phone rings, and I answer it because it's her.

"Hi."

"What the hell do you mean you were in jail? What did you do?"

"Nothing. Okay … Not technically nothing. I threatened him. He was stalking her house."

Silence.

"Madison?"

"I can't. Bryce, I swear, I thought I could, but I can't. I worried so much. Really worried. I haven't slept but a couple of hours. My stomach is in knots. I've been waiting to hear your voice. You were in jail. Not that this is really surprising, I just thought … God, Bryce, I thought if you were with me you'd make more of an effort to not get yourself into trouble. Clearly I was mistaken."

I grip my hair and sigh. "I love you. I am making an effort."

"Really? Then why are you there and not here? Why didn't you do something like, I don't know, take Hailey to your house? Graham was right; no matter what, you just always want to play the superhero. And that's fine, but I'm not the right person for this. I can't support you and try to figure out my future."

Tears start to form. I'm not a crier by any means, but this girl is busting my heart into a thousand pieces. I swipe away at a few tears and swallow hard. "Fine."

"I've gotta go," she says. "Bye."

"Bye," I choke out.

I slam my phone against the coffee table and weave my fingers through my hair. Tears fall, and I don't care to wipe them away. Hailey clears her throat, but I refuse to look at her. I know one thing: I'm never doing this again. Love is for idiots. Lust is fine. It's not dangerous. It doesn't make your heart feel like a train hit it at full speed.

"Bry?"

"I don't … want … to talk."

"Okay." I hear the floorboards creak. Her feet stamp the hardwood floor, and the creaking drifts farther and farther away.

I sniffle and look around the room. Pale yellow walls surround me. I hate the sun and anything bright. Why? Because brightness reminds me of Madison's smile, her freaking laugh, and the way the sun would bring out the secret things about her. Like her hair. It turns from a dark brown to a reddish brown in certain parts in the sunlight. I knew I'd lose her eventually.

She's not the first to tell me she loved me. But she is the first I said the words to. It doesn't matter much now, though. I lean back on the couch and stare up at the ceiling. I curl my upper lip and then look back at my phone.

After a couple of minutes, I get off the couch, swipe under my eyes, and then search my cousin's stash of liquor. The cabinets are empty, and the freezer is tapped out too, but the fridge has a twelve-pack of Corona. Score. A few of these and I'll be saying, "Madison who?"

Chapter Thirty-Seven

Madison

I want to call him back immediately. But my brain is yelling at me not to. Everything else is begging me to. I can't, though. I won't.

There is enough drama and bullshit that I still need to deal with in my already crazy life. I can't have a boyfriend who's in jail. I can't be one of those girls. Having a boyfriend this late in high school is just stupid anyway. Isn't it? I mean, yeah, there are a few school dances coming up, like the winter formal, sweetheart dance, and prom. But none of that really matters.

Emily is into all that stuff, not me. And besides, we were eventually going to call it quits, right? He's dead set on Michigan State. He made his choice, and now it's my turn to make mine.

I sluggishly make my way into the dining room and do one of my Thanksgiving chores, which is to set the table. Might I add I do this rather slowly too. It's like my body just doesn't want to get anything done. Mom slaps her spoon against a pot. "Maddy? Are you feeling okay?"

I shrug. "I'm fine."

"You don't look fine. You look like you've been crying."

"I broke up with Bryce." I set the last of the silverware down and look up at my mom. She stares at me like I'm a lunatic.

"What do you mean, honey?"

What do I mean? What does she mean what do I mean? Hello, I was dating the bad boy next door. Dur. I fell in love with him, but he broke my heart when he decided to go against my wishes and get himself into trouble. Well, worse than that, he got thrown into jail. I can't tell her any of this, though, because she'll start in with the "I told you so" crap. And who is ever in the mood to hear that? No one is ever in the mood to hear that.

I give her an eye roll. "Never mind. I'm going to my room."

"Dinner's almost ready."

"I'm not hungry. Can I eat later?"

Her eyes widen, and she closes the space between us. She places a hand on my forehead. "Oh, you feel kind of warm, and you are looking flushed. Are you feeling okay?"

"I don't know."

She kisses my forehead and tells me to go up to my room and lie down. So I do. I'm thankful the room is empty and everyone is downstairs. This way, I can cry without feeling like someone might see or walk in on me. I locked the door just in case. If Sarah needs to get in here, too bad. Mom won't yell at me too much for it. Of course, I honestly don't care if she does. It'll just be the icing on this horrible day.

It's midnight when I wake up. Yeah, apparently I cried myself to sleep. I didn't think that was a real thing—apart from babies, that is. I check my phone and see I've got three missed calls. Two from Bryce, one from Graham. The last two were ten minutes ago. There are a few voice mails, too, but I ignore them.

I have twenty unread text messages. I don't even read them; I just call Graham first. He answers after the first ring. "Hey."

"Hi," I say. "You called?"

"Yeah, um … Were you sleeping?"

"Eh. I kind of went to bed at six. Don't ask. What's up?"

I hear him huff. "So you haven't talked to Bryce?"

"Earlier. He said he got out of jail."

"Yeah, well, you might want to call him. He's completely lit. And that's when he does really stupid crap."

I groan. "Did you talk to him?"

"For about twenty minutes. He kept saying how I was right. That you were a train wreck and he never should have gotten involved."

What kind of response could I possibly have for that? Nothing. I sigh, and eventually we hang up, and then I rummage through some of the text messages. Some are Happy Thanksgiving texts from teammates and friends. But then I have a few from Bryce.

> Bryce: I hate this.
> Bryce: I was Fine without u.
> Bryce: I Love U!
> Bryce: Fine Don't Answer!
> Bryce: Madison, I'm better with u. Please Madison, talk 2 me. I love u. I just … fuck. I don't know. I'm stupid babe.

God, he probably thinks I hate him. I don't. I love him. Too much, apparently. Enough to make me cry and miss Thanksgiving dinner and dessert. I exhale sharply and tap his name twice. It rings a few times and then, "Hiiiii!"

"Hey. I was sleeping when you called and texted."

"Suuure you were."

"What? Are you drunk?" I know he is, but I want him to confirm it.

"Why you car?"

"Um, because I do. Bryce, listen to me. Please don't do anything stupid."

Something breaks. He curses and then says, "I dow need you to tal me wha to do."

"I know. But I love you, and I'll be really sad if you hurt yourself."

"Na you dow."

"Yes, I do. I cried myself to sleep. I really don't want us to be over. You just … Bryce, you doing this kind of stuff and getting into trouble is what worries me. It makes me think this is nothing more than a passing good time for you."

"You not. I luab you. Fuck, I cried. Like a boy. Over you. I neva said I luab you to anybady."

I bite my lip. If he had said this when he was sober, I would melt into a big puddle. Right now, I'm not feeling this conversation. In fact, I'm not sure if anything he's saying is really the truth or just a bunch of lies. "Okay. I just wanted you to know that I wasn't ignoring you. I'll talk to you tomorrow when you're sober. If you answer the phone."

"Fine."

I don't know if he thought he hung up, because I hear something hit a surface of some sort. Then I hear deep snoring. I mean loud and throaty, so I whisper, "Bryce?"

He doesn't answer, so I click the big, red end button and lie back against my pillow. I'm worried about him. Is his cousin watching over him and making sure if he pukes he won't choke on it? I stare at my phone, and then I get out of my bed.

I pace the room. Sarah's blond hair peeks from the covers as she shifts in bed and groans, turning onto her side. "Graham, please," she whimpers.

Before, that would have bothered me. Now, though, I don't care. Weird. I glance out the window and stare out at the darkness. There is a soft glow coming from Bryce's room. I miss him. I lower my stare to the driveway and see it's vacant of the one car I long to see.

Chapter Thirty-Eight

Madison

One more week of school, and then it's winter break. Emily and I have been hitting up stores on the weekends, so all my Christmas shopping is basically finished. Yay!

I make a quick trip to my locker between third and fourth to grab something. I stop at my locker and almost die at the sight before me. Sarah and Bryce are in deep conversation at a locker across the way from mine. She touches his biceps, and I see red. He hasn't talked to me since our last phone conversation almost two weeks ago.

I shouldn't care. He's trouble. She's a bitch. I should be happy if they get together. She'll think she's doing it to make me miserable, but honestly, she'd be doing me a favor. I tear my gaze away from them long enough to get the papers I need.

Slamming the door shut, I glance back at them.

Sarah is pressing her mouth against his. My folder slips from my grip, and all the papers in it spill onto the floor. I kneel down and start scooping up the pages as fast as possible. Anger swells in my gut while my head spins.

I lied. She wouldn't be doing me a favor. This is killing me. My eyes water, and I can't really see through the blurred tears whether I got all the papers or not. I don't care, though. I just take what I do have and run down the hall to class.

Mrs. Vixen calls me over to her desk and asks, "Are you okay?"

"No. Can I … May I go to the office and call my mom?"

"Sure, honey. Let me write you a pass."

As soon as she writes the pass, I hand in my papers, gather my things, and flee from the room. I'm not even two steps into the hall before I ram right into someone and fall backwards. My ass slams into the hard floor, and a hand drops down to me.

"Hey. Where are you going?" Bryce asks in the most causal tone ever. Like he's so innocent and perfect. Like he wasn't just making out with my test-tube sister a few seconds ago.

I slap his hand away, stand up, and then slap him as hard as I possibly can. "Don't talk to me ever again!" I scream as my palm makes contact with the side of his face.

"Madison?" He rubs his cheek while he tries to stop me from moving around him.

"Let me leave!"

He walks after me. "You need to tell me what the hell is going on!"

"I don't have to tell you anything. I'm not playing this stupid game with you!" I storm ahead of him. At least I think I am ahead of him. He's actually matching me stride for stride.

"Will you stop for one second? Please."

"No."

He catches my wrist and whips me toward him. I almost lose my balance, but he grips my waist and rights me. "Listen to me."

"Let me go," I growl.

"No. I know you're mad at me. I know I'm an idiot." He's right so far. "And I know I shouldn't have gotten out of my car and threatened to kick Darren's ass when I saw him outside my cousin's place. But the fact is I did do it. I can't take that back, but I'm begging you to at least give me another chance."

If he had just did that, and not made out with Sarah a few minutes ago, I would have said yes. But since this isn't the case, I sound out the syllable slowly, "No."

"Why?"

"I saw you with Sarah. You're a jerk! I can't be with you ever again."

He shakes his head while his eyes widen. "No! You have this all wrong. She attacked me in the hall. She caught me off guard, kissed me, and then I pushed her away. You apparently weren't watching closely enough."

"Really? She attacked you? Because I saw you two talking. Then kissing."

"She kissed me. I shoved her away and asked her what the hell she was doing. She told me she was trying to make you mad. I told her to leave you alone. She laughed and tried to kiss me again."

I narrow my eyes and shove him away. God, I want to believe him. I do. But I can't. I know what I saw. But it is Sarah, and she's been doing everything in her power to make me miserable. What if what he's saying is true? I obviously can't ask her, because she'll just lie either way.

He looks defeated and doesn't block my path anymore. Screw them both. This is too much drama for me, and you know what? I'm out. Deuces, bro. Never again. I make my way to the office and call my mom.

"Honey, are you okay?"

"I think I'm coming down with something," I say weakly.

"Okay. Put Mrs. Butterfield back on the phone."

I hand the phone over to the main office lady, Mrs. Butterfield. Her name kind of fits her. Not that she's fat or anything, but she looks like a grandma and smells like a peanut-butter cookies. Seriously, how can anyone not love that scent?

Her red-painted lips curl upward, and she says, "Madison, I hope you feel better soon. Are you able to make it home safely?"

"Yeah, I can drive. Thanks."

"Okay, dear. I'll let the staff know you've left for the day. Get some rest and eat some soup."

I nod. Although I'm pretty sure soup can't cure a broken heart.

Chapter Thirty-Nine

Bryce

She doesn't answer the phone when I call. She doesn't answer my texts. I'm not losing her. She might be done, but I'm not.

I sit in front of my laptop, trying to think of ways to get Madison back while I Google it. Yes, I said that. I'm freaking Googling how to get a girl to forgive you. And seriously, I'm not the only idiot who ever Googled this before, so ha. I scan the information, and some of it looks like crap. Seriously, this advice is really crap.

Annoyed, I decide to do something else. I'm about to place an order for roses to be delivered to her house when my dad comes into my room. I spin in my chair and ask, "Yeah?"

"Son, I think we need to talk. It's about your mother and me."

"You're leaving her for your secretary?"

I haven't really seen him for months. Glimpses of

him here and there, but not long enough to study him, and damn, he looks old and tired. Bags under his eyes. More grays in his hair than I can count. He doesn't look surprised or upset that I blurt out my response. Normally, I'd watch my manners. I'd address him as "sir." But why should we kid each other now? He hasn't stuck around, and whenever he did, he'd tell me I was worthless and going to end up being nothing because of all the trouble I got into.

"Well, yes. I want you to know this isn't your fault."

I snort. "I know it's not my fault. I'm not married and screwing a girl fourteen years younger than me."

"That's enough!" My dad rubs his hand down his face. "Your mother tells me you've been hanging out with Madison Issac. Hopefully she's been a good influence on you."

I lean back in my chair. "Been the best. Especially right here." I pat my lap and grin.

My dad shakes his head. "I don't know why I bother."

"I don't either." I whip my chair back around and hit send on my order. Using his reflection in the screen, I watch him leave. I slide over to the far side of my room and grab a notebook from my stack. My mom—I love her to death, but she goes overboard on school supplies. If the list says three, she buys ten. Why? She says you can never be too prepared.

I slide back to my desk and start writing. Well, I write, and then I tear out the page and crumple it up. Then I start over again. I continue this process until I get the right words and phrases. I haven't done this since first grade when she shot me down cold. But I'm older. Wiser. I'm even hotter. Yeah, I said it. So maybe this one will be my saving grace.

I don't come out of my room until I have completed the best and sappiest love letter ever written by a man. Dear God, if this doesn't work, I hope you drop a crater on my head. Immediately would be awesome.

Emerging from my room, I go downstairs to the kitchen. My mom sits at the island, drinking a glass of wine. Excuse me—it actually looks like she's finishing off a bottle by herself. "Mom?"

"Hmm."

"Did you eat anything?"

She shakes her head. "I'm not hungry, honey. There are leftovers in the fridge. Did your father talk to you?"

Um, about those leftovers … I ate those last night. But I'm not going to tell her this. I'll get a pizza in a little bit. "Yeah, he did."

"What an asshole! I mean, I've known for months. But that prick just kept saying it was my imagination. The nerve of him." She dumps more wine into her glass and then stares at the bottle. "Bryce, please get another bottle down for me. This one seems to be empty."

I don't point out it's because she drank it. I do, however, grab her another bottle. If she wants to get drunk, hey, go for it.

She takes a sip from her glass and swallows. "Don't become a liar, Bryce. That's one thing I can honestly say you aren't. You make bad choices, but you aren't a liar."

"Thanks."

"I like Madison. I haven't seen her around much. Are you two okay?"

"We're fine, Mom," I lie. "I'm just about to head out to go see her." I'm hoping to get a glimpse of her as I get into my car. Maybe I'll get lucky and she'll speak to me.

"Have fun. Be back at eleven." Now I know my mom is hammered because it's a school night and she usually wants me in at nine thirty every night.

Madison isn't outside. She doesn't appear to be in her room as I lurk in the driveway and stare at her window. I'm officially creepy. I need to quit.

I get into my car and head down the road. My stomach growls and seems to get louder as I pass by a food place. Long John Silver's. I love the place, but today I'm not feeling my usual. So I keep driving, and my stomach keeps grumbling.

"I know. Jeez, man." What the hell? I just talked to my own stomach like it was a little kid.

I pull into Zaxby's. I walk in and place my order and then go have a seat. As I'm waiting, Emily walks in, Madison following. Madison's eyes are bloodshot and puffy. Emily keeps talking to her, and Madison simply nods.

Emily would know what to do. She's Mads's best friend; she'd definitely know how to win Madison back. This is, of course, if my flowers and love letter fail miserably. The flowers are due to arrive at school on the last day before break. And the love letter is currently burning a hole in the back pocket of my jeans.

Emily looks about the joint, and I duck down

before she sees me.

"Order 82."

Son of a bitch. That's me.

The guy calls out again, raising his squeaky voice another notch. "Order 82!"

I look up. Emily and Madison are ordering at the front, so I hurry up, grab my food, and head outside. I've gotta get Madison back because there is no way I'm going to keep dodging places just to avoid her glare.

Thankfully, she doesn't seem to notice me in my car. I'm not stalking the joint like a perv. I just didn't want to drive and eat at the same time. Also, I don't want to go home in case my mom is still eyeing the front door like a vulture.

"I hate him, Em. And then … I love him. I'm pathetic," I hear Madison say. "Why can't I just forget about him?"

"Because he was your first boyfriend, Maddy. Of course you aren't going to forget him"—she snaps her fingers—"like that. And he lives next door. You know, next time, you should probably pick someone that resides outside of your neighborhood. Did you know …" I can't hear the rest because she's inside Madison's car.

It doesn't stop me from watching them from my rearview mirror. Madison tips back her head and then wipes her hand under her eyes. Damn it. Again and again, I make this girl cry. She dumped me, though. She told me we were through, not the other way around. I want her so freaking much, if she'd just take my call or talk to me she'd see that.

I drive home. My food looks unappealing, I force down a few fries and give up. Driving through my neighborhood, I stop at the park.

I toss my food in the trash and head toward the merry-go-round. I sit down on the cold metal surface. With one foot hanging off the side, I push, sending myself into a slow spiral. The night sky is filled with stars, and while the angles of the sky change with each spin, I wish I had a cigarette. Not really for the taste or something to do but for the release. That's why I started smoking; it helped me not snap at my worst moments. Right now, I'm almost there. I need control over my life again, and at this point, it seems I've got none. My cousin has a stalker I can't do anything about. The girl I want isn't speaking to me because her … I don't know what to call her … but whatever, she kissed me. She kissed me, and I've never ever hit a girl, but she was damn close to being the first. Then there's my mom and dad and all their dumb shit. I can't. Everything is turning into a shitstorm, and I can't seem to find the exit. And, being on probation, I'm damn lucky I'm not going to be in a fuckload of trouble for my Michigan trip. My assigned case officer said I was lucky the guy did it to himself, otherwise I would be in jail right now.

The merry-go-round moves slower, as if it's about to come to a stop. I push off again. My butt is feeling a little numb from the frigid surface, but I don't care. The cold helps me think in a way. Maybe I should hold off on the letter. It's too late to cancel the flowers. That's okay.

I launch myself off the merry-go-round and head back to the house.

Chapter Forty

Madison

Today is the final day of school before we have almost three weeks off for winter break. People here are acting nuts, even the teachers are not in a teaching mood. Each class so far has been, "Today is a free day. You can watch ..." I've seen some of *Christmas Vacation*, *Jingle All The Way*, *A Christmas Story*, *How the Grinch Stole Christmas* (the Jim Carrey version), and *Christmas with the Kranks*. Like I said, it's been a really lazy day. It's going on sixth period, and I just want to cut out early.

I slump into my assigned seat and avoid looking at Bryce, which I've been doing for every class we share. Good thing is he hasn't tried to talk to me. It makes ignoring him that much easier.

Graham is speaking to me again. Weird, right? It's like the deranged cycle of my life: lose a friend— gain a frenemy, gain a friend—lose them, lose—gain,

gain—lose. I lay my head down on my desk, indicating I'm not in the mood to talk, but Graham shakes me.

"Hey. Someone's calling your name."

I look up and see a cute guy in a brown button-down with "Flander's Florist" stamped on the pocket carrying a huge bouquet of roses. Most of the class is making kissing noises or *ooh* and *aw* sounds. My face feels like it's on fire as the cute delivery boy says, "Are you Madison Issac?"

I swallow. "Yes."

"These are for you. Happy holidays." He places the enormous vase of roses on my desk, and I just stare at them. They're not one color. In fact, there's one of each: yellow, red, green, pink, pink and yellow, white, purple, blue, the list goes on.

I glare at Bryce. "Did you send this?"

He doesn't answer.

This only makes me madder. Why won't he just answer me?

"There's a card," Graham says as he points to the top near his side.

I turn the bouquet, and right as I reach for the card, Bryce snatches it from the clip.

"Give it back!"

"No," he snaps. "I want to see who you've been giving your attention to since it sure as hell isn't me."

What? He didn't send this? Who did then? I chew on my thumbnail and stare at the multicolored roses. I should toss them in the trash, but they're pretty and I've never gotten roses before. It's ridiculous, I know, but I'm touched that someone got them for me. But I'm also creeped out. They seem to be from someone I don't know. At least I don't think I know them, because

Bryce still has my card. I motion for it back. "Give it."

"Dude, just give her the damn card," Graham snaps.

Bryce smirks. "Here." He hands it over but doesn't say a word.

I read it and frown. The card is sweet, but the sender signed it, "You own my heart."

I turn back to Bryce. "You seriously didn't send this?"

"I told you I didn't."

Why would someone sign the card like this? Apparently the one person's heart I'd like to own didn't send this to me.

The rest of the day, I carry around my vase of roses. Thank goodness I only have two more classes. Because if one more person asks me who sent the flowers, I might scream. Especially when I hand over the card, and they ask, "Well, who do you think sent them?" Yeah, as if I have a clue.

"Wow, who's the lucky man?" Emily asks as she reaches me in the parking lot.

I shrug. "I don't know. Can you help me with the door, though?"

She laughs. She takes my keys from me and unlocks the door, then helps me with the trunk. I wiggle out of my backpack straps while holding the vase. Emily tosses her bag in my trunk and eyes up my roses. "Ooh, a card. May I?"

"Knock yourself out. It's super sweet, depressing, frustrating, and creepy at the same time."

She raises a brow while taking the card and flowers from me. "Why?"

"Just read." I climb into my car.

She gets into the car, too, then unveils the card,

and reads, "I could have sent a rose, but that won't do. Not when I feel all of this for you." Emily giggles. "Red: I love you. White: I wish to be worthy of you. Pink: Thank you. Yellow: Remember me. Yellow with red tip: Friendship. Orange: Desire. Red and yellow: Happy. Peach: Gratitude. Lavender: Enchantment. Black: Farewell. Blue: The unattainable. These are just some of the things I feel. You own my heart."

Emily flips the card over and then looks at me. "That's it? Well, it's certainly not an early birthday gift. Speaking of your birthday, what are we doing?"

"No, not a b-day gift. And I'm not sure I want to do anything."

"Well, we're doing something." She waves the note. "This is straight-up the sweetest, craziest thing ever. Why did they sign it like this?"

I grip the steering wheel. "I don't know. But you see why I'm a little frustrated?"

"Uh, yeah. Who do you think it is?"

"I thought it was Bryce, but he acted like a total asshole in class. Plus, he said it wasn't him."

Emily opens her mouth but snaps it shut as soon as the back door to my POS opens. "God," Sarah whines, "I swear you pick the only spot in no man's land, Madison, and say, 'OMG, there is the best spot in the world, let's park here.'"

"Shut. Up," Emily snarls. "Boohoo, you got some exercise in. You know there are children in some third-world country who have to walk thirty miles with no shoes."

"Good for them" is Sarah's retort. I just drive and try to tune them out. But they continue to bicker back and forth.

I know Emily is just trying to stick up for me, but I wish she wouldn't. It's annoying to go to school and then get into a tiny space and hear nothing but arguing. When I reach Em's house, I'm actually thankful she's getting out.

Sarah leans forward as I'm backing out of Emily's drive. "She forgot her flowers."

"They're mine."

"You bought yourself flowers?" Sarah asks in that "oh, man, you're pathetic" tone.

I roll my eyes. "I didn't buy them. Someone else bought them."

Sarah grumbles, "Graham was going to get me flowers." I should inquire about this, but I don't. That's what she wants, and I'm not in the mood.

I park in our driveway, grab my flowers, and head inside. My mom is coming down the stairs as I'm going up. She makes a noise that sounds like a swoony sigh. "Is there something you'd like to tell me?"

I move past her and groan, "No."

"Fine. Be like your brother, all secretive."

That statement really ticks me off. I'm nothing like Kyle. He's a male whore. Most of the girls he did date only lasted three weeks. One managed two months, but that's it. And all the breakups were disasters, because when my brother dumps someone, it's like a tornado just ran through town. The girl would not only call the house constantly for a month straight, she'd drive by—slowly. A sobbing mess, the girl would sometimes bring her friends along—who, in some cases, were hooking up with Kyle. Some girls would even be stupid enough to sleep with him at a party just to try to win him back. I know all this because I was the last resort. They'd cry and confess everything to me, as if I had the magic power to fix it. I don't.

I sneer at my mom and slam the door to my room behind me. I set the flowers on my desk and reread the card. Why would someone send this and leave it anonymous? A part of me wants—no, is dying—to know who sent this. The other part is grateful for not knowing. I mean, they could be from Danny Livingston. I shudder at the thought.

I toss the card down and pick up my drawing pad just as my phone begins to ring. "Hello?"

"Madison Issac?"

"Yes," I say to the person on the other end of the line.

"This is Hilary Vanworth. I'm the director of the art program at Carnegie Mellon University."

I straighten and twirl a lock of my hair. "Oh, hello."

"Good afternoon. I was wondering if you'd like to reschedule your interview with me?"

"Really? Um, yes, that'd be great. I can meet you wherever."

"Would you be willing to travel to our school? It's a distance, I know, but you could take a tour of the grounds. Personally, I always find seeing things in person so much better than on a screen or in a photo, you know?"

I nod. Then stop, because—doh! She can't see me. "Yes. I agree."

"Miss Issac, I must warn you now, I do not normally give second chances. You'll be the first. Do not make me regret it. Talk with your parents and call me back with a date, and we'll schedule a time. Does that sound fair?"

"Yes, Ms. Vanworth. Thank you." We hang up, and I squeal!

I run out of my room, almost colliding with Sarah, but somehow sidestep her and hurry down the steps into the kitchen. My mom is at the stove stirring a pot of something delicious. I can't pinpoint what it is, but my mouth is watering.

"I don't know, Caitlyn," my mom says into the phone. "She doesn't want to visit. I can't force her." She smacks the spoon against the pot with such force I think it's going to snap. "You know what? I'm about fed up with what you think I'm doing to her, Caitlyn. You're damn straight she's a part of me, and all you do is make me out to be a monster. I'm done. You can rot in prison for all I care. Don't you dare call here again!"

I try to back out of the kitchen, but my mom spots me. She smoothes her hair back and smiles at me. "Hi, honey."

"You okay, Mom?"

"I'm fine." She sets the phone back on the charger and walks over to the stove. She picks up her spoon and starts stirring again. "So how was school? Besides the enormous bouquet you don't want to talk about, that is."

I pick up an apple from the fruit bowl in the middle of the kitchen table and take a bite. "It was okay. I've, uh …" I chew some more and then swallow. "I got a call from a professor at this school. It's in Pennsylvania."

"Uh-huh, that sounds nice," she says.

"Mom, are you listening to me?"

She stops stirring. "Madison, I'm having a really rough day. The last thing I want to talk about is college."

"That's fine." It's really not. Lately, she hasn't

seemed happy for me about anything. I shake my head, grab my coat, and leave the house.

Normally, I'd sit on the porch or run, but I don't want to. Instead, I lean over the railing and stare back at his tree house. Ugh. I shouldn't, but it's not like anyone will know I'm there. He's not even home.

I rush across the lawn and head deep into his backyard. I climb the ladder and shut myself inside. Taking a seat on the floor and staying away from the windows, I look at the walls surrounding me. In the corner is a pile of envelopes. I crawl over to them and pick one up.

It's addressed to me. In huge letters that start on one end, and the N in my name is close to the corner of the envelope. It's sealed shut. I shouldn't open it. But then again, it does have my name on it so it's technically mine. Right?

Chapter Forty-One

Madison

I debate whether to open the envelope for a while, and then I close my eyes and tear into it. Removing a handmade card from the envelope, I read, "Will you?" on the outside. I open it up, and the inside says, "Be mine forever? Check box: Yes. No. Maybe." The inner child in me giggles. My seventeen-year-old self raises a brow and asks, "Why would he ever put a maybe box? That's hardly helpful."

I reach for another envelope. As I snatch one up, I hear, "Yeah, I'll be there tonight."

Shit! That's Bryce. I scan the area, and there's literally nowhere to hide. So as the door starts to lift, I scurry over to it and slam my body on top.

"What the fuck? Let me call you back."

If he uses both hands, he'll knock me off. I know this. So I start pulling things to me. Like his box of CDs and his box of random crap, like yo-yos and baseballs and footballs. This still won't be heavy enough. And I can't stay up here forever. I just want to be up here until my dad gets home or Kyle—he's supposed to get home for winter break today.

"Madison! Get the hell off the door!"

"No. Go away."

I hear him growl. "It's my fucking tree house."

"Well, I'm using it."

"I'm counting to ten, and then I'm busting in. If you get hurt, it's your own fault." I think he's joking, but then he starts counting, "One, two, three …"

I push the boxes off the door and scurry into a corner. The door flies up and smacks the wall. Bryce shakes his head at me. "What's wrong?"

"Nothing is wrong."

"Really? You only hide in here when there's something wrong. So what is it? Spit it out because I don't have all day."

"Where are you going? Hot date?"

His lips press into a grim line. "Something like that."

My heart stops beating. My eyes begin to water, and I drop my gaze to my knees. "Oh. Well … um … okay." I swallow back my shame. "I was just waiting for my dad to get home. My mom is in one of her moods. It's nothing. I'll, uh … leave."

I start for the door, but Bryce grabs my hand and pulls me to him. He wraps his strong arms around me and breathes, "Why are you constantly running away from me?"

"You have a hot date."

"Yes. I'm going to work on a 1969 Camaro." I look up at him, and he smirks. "It's a car, Smalls."

"I know what it is! Why would … why would you have me thinking it was a girl?" I wipe my hands under my eyes, and he just smiles bigger.

"Because it is a girl. She's cherry red. With a black interior."

I punch him in the shoulder. "You know what I mean!"

"Are you jealous, firecracker?"

"Don't call me names."

He touches my jaw and then runs his hand through my hair. "I can't call you 'firecracker'? Or Smalls? What about beautiful? Or mine?"

"I'm not yours," I mumble.

He kisses my mouth, and oh man, it feels amazing. His mouth on mine. I've missed this. I melt into his arms and press myself against him. I feel him through his jeans. I want him so bad.

I numbly work at the zipper on his coat. He pulls back slightly and asks me in a breathy tone, "What are you doing?"

"You. I need you."

"Madison. We … should … talk."

I nod and continue ripping off his coat. His lips are on my neck and work their way down. His hands bunch up the hem of my shirt and begin to lift in one fluid motion. I yank off his shirt and run my fingers along his muscles.

Bryce moans and pulls my hands away from his rockin' abs. I begin to pout, but he nips my lower lip with his teeth. He draws back and pushes our clothes into a pile. As I'm beginning to wonder if maybe I'm taking this too far, he pulls the pins to the windows. Wooden slates of wood slam down, shielding the light and covering the tree house in darkness. Bryce lifts me and then lowers me down to the floor. He shuts the entrance door and flips the latch, locking us inside.

My eyes adjust to the darkness. His hands find me and continue to touch and grab my ass. He lifts my lower half and sheds the rest of my clothing. His hands move up my thighs, and he whispers, "I'm going to kiss every inch of you, and then I'm going to make love to you, Madison. But if anything gets too intense, you need to tell me to stop."

"Okay."

And, wow, does he deliver on his promise.

He lies beside me, stroking my hair as I rest my head on his chest. The reality comes crashing in all at once. "I had sex."

"You were amazing," he whispers as his lips brush against my temple.

What did I do? Oh my God. I sit up, a little self-conscious, and use my shirt to shield my nakedness.

"Mads, look at me." I do. "Babe, what's wrong? Are you okay?"

"I'm fine," I say in a shaky voice.

"You wish we hadn't done it, don't you?"

I shake my head. But really, I'm not sure. I mean, I loved it. It was with someone I loved. My only regret is that we're not together. We're not in a relationship. I feel like a horrible slut.

He sits up and pulls me to him. "It's okay. You can tell me."

"I'm fine," I lie. I gather up my clothes and put them on quickly. He's doing the same. But I'm pretty certain we're hurrying to get clothes on for different reasons. I stand by the door and then throw it open.

Bryce stares at me. "You wanna talk about this before you go rushing off?"

"No. I have to get home. This was fun. Thanks." Okay, I could officially high-five myself right in the face for that one. *This was fun? Thanks?* Jeez, it wasn't a casual date. We had sex. He took my virginity, and I said *thanks*. Oh my God. I need to leave before I say anything else just as lame.

I'm halfway across the lawn when Bryce yells, "Madison! Wait up."

I don't. I start running and then fly into my house. Kyle hurls off the couch as I'm booking it up the stairs and into my room. "Where's the fire, Maddy?"

"Fuck off!" I slam the door and curl up in a ball on my bed.

I hear knocking, and then my brother's voice booming from downstairs. "Aren't you out of school for three weeks? Why do you need to see my sister?"

I throw a pillow over my head in order to drown out the sounds of shouting. And then my door bursts open, and I sit straight up, hitting my head on the top bunk. "Ow! Son of a bitch!"

"Are you okay?" Bryce rushes over to me and cradles my face with his hands. My brother pulls him away from me.

"Don't touch my sister, man! She's fine."

"Damn it, Kyle! She just smacked her head off a

metal bar," Bryce snaps. "Why don't you go beat off in your room or something?"

Kyle pushes Bryce right into my desk. "Don't fucking talk to my sister! She doesn't need you hanging around her. You'll just ruin her life."

Bryce shoves him back and raises his fist. I knead my fingers into my scalp and scream, "Stop it! Just stop! Kyle, get out. Bryce, go to the shop and work on the car. We'll talk later."

"The hell you will!" Kyle yells at me.

"Kyle! Out!"

He glares at me and takes a seat at Sarah's desk. Whatever. As long as he's not shoving Bryce or yelling about idiotic crap.

Bryce takes a seat on my bed. He pulls me to him and starts examining the top of my head. "You got a small cut, Smalls. Take a shower, put some ice on it, and I'll call you a little later." He glances over at Kyle. "Make sure she doesn't get dizzy."

"Bite me, Doctor Fuck-up."

Bryce looks back at me. "Are you feeling lightheaded or dizzy?"

"No."

"Good." He kisses my mouth, and my brother launches himself out of the chair and straight at Bryce. But Bryce stands, shoves Kyle out of the way, and leaves. Kyle follows. I lie back on my bed and think about what has transpired in the last two hours of my life. I got an interview to talk with the art director of a college I really believe I want to attend. I lost my virginity. And Bryce kissed me in front of Kyle, causing him to go bananas.

My door slams shut, and Kyle stomps over to me.

He takes a seat at my desk and just glares at me. "I thought I told you he's bad news and to stay the hell away from him!"

"Kyle, I can see who I want."

He points at me. "Not him! Jesus, have you lost your mind? He's going to be in jail by the time you graduate. For what, who knows? But you don't need to find out."

"Who cares? Our family tree has jailbirds in it too. Or did you forget why my room has a bunk bed in it?"

"That's not even funny, Maddy. I'm saying this to protect you. Look, guys like him, they prey on girls like you. Innocent, sweet girls, just like you. I'm telling you this for a reason. He's only going to hurt you."

I shake my head. "You don't know him, Kyle." But then again, neither do I.

Chapter Forty-Two

Bryce

I made love to Madison in my freaking tree house. Jesus. I'd give anything to take it back and choose a different, more romantic spot. But it's too late. I don't regret being with her at all; I just hope she's not regretting anything. She just ran out of there like nothing ever happened. I know I'm going to sound like a chick for a second, but she better not pretend nothing went down between us.

As I'm driving to Hector's, the body shop in town, the image of Madison lying underneath me takes over my thoughts. She was amazing. Tight as hell, so freaking wet, and just ready for me. Thinking about it is making me hard all over again. Damn it, I might have to take a quick break and rub one out in the bathroom when I get there. At least I've got some stellar images to jerk off to, like Madison's face as she had an orgasm. Her eyes locked with mine wide and trusting, then she arched back and screamed my name. It was the sexiest thing I've ever seen or heard. After our adventure in the tree house, I wanted to tell her I sent the roses. That was the plan. But she ran, and then Kyle was hovering like a vulture. Freaking asshole.

I pull up to the garage and hurry into the bathroom to relieve myself. Once I'm finished, I wash my hands, step out, and nod to Hector.

"Hey, amigo!" he says. "You came. Thought you'd be over earlier."

"I got tied up in something," I answer with a shrug. Hector waves me over to the cherry beauty taking up space in the garage. "She's a sexy beast," I say.

"Yeah, she is. Come on. Get underneath her and check her out."

I work at the shop until nine—that's closing time—and then swing by my house and call Madison. She doesn't answer my calls, so I text her.

> Me: Hey u. How r u feeling?
> Mads: Tired. My parents are being jerks.
> Me: Because of me?
> Mads: No. Me. I have an interview in PA and they're telling me I can't go. It's too far. And art school is a waste of money.
> Me: Mads screw them. I'll take you. When do u have 2 go?
> Mads: This Friday. I was going to leave Thursday. Stay in a hotel and look around.
> Me: Ok. Wait, when do u turn 18? Dec 24th or 25th?

Mads: 24th. Why?

Me: Because I'm still on probation. And I don't need 2 add kidnapping 2 my record. We'll leave Thursday. Okay. Meet me in the park at 9am.

Mads: Bryce, I can't ask you to take me. I can drive myself.

Me: I know. I want 2.

Mads: You know earlier was just sex. It doesn't mean we're back together.

I read her text and wince. We're not getting back together. "Just sex." But that was not "just sex." I made love to her. We'd never have "just sex."

Me: Ok. I'm still taking u.

Mads: Fine.

Me: Good night. Sweet dreams.

Mads: Night. Same to you.

She's going to be stubborn. I expected that. It's okay, I've got a plan. As long as she doesn't keep surprising me and I can keep surprising her, I'll win her back. And this time, there won't be any letting go. I won't mess up. I won't give her a reason to run. Madison has me. All of me. Problem is, the girl has no idea.

It's Christmas Eve. It's the last day for shopping, and of course I'm in the mall hunting down gifts. Most of them are for Madison. Hailey is with me, which is really becoming more of a pain in the ass than a help. "What about this?" Hailey giggles as she holds up a piece of see-through lingerie.

"Yeah, that will go over real nice." I tug her out of Victoria's Secret and down the crowded hall. "Will you try to be helpful? I need something special for her birthday. I also need something for Christmas, and a couple gifts for our road trip."

"Why not get her flowers?"

"I did. Look, she's more special than flowers. I need something that's perfect for her. Are you going to help or not?"

Hailey groans. "I said I would. Jeez. I swear, if she doesn't take you back, I'm changing my number and you're not getting it."

"Why?"

She pulls me into a bookstore. "Because you being in love is kind of scary."

I glower. "Why are we in here?"

"For these!" She grabs some books off the shelf and hands them over. "They're art books. You said she's into art."

I flip through some and start putting some back. I keep two and check out. The next store we go to is Kay's. Hailey points at a bracelet. "You add charms to it. So make her a charm bracelet that's unique to her."

I find a paintbrush, a tiny runner, a heart, and then I pick out an Eiffel Tower charm. After I pay for this, we head over to Michael's, the craft store. Hailey finds a whole art kit. I'm not sure if it's any good. The salesperson I asked said she thought it was good, but her bored facial expression was sending off a different vibe. Here's to hoping, though.

On the way home we stop at Target, and I pick up a couple of things for my mom and Hailey when she isn't looking. Screw my dad. As soon as I'm home, I lock myself in my room and start wrapping. Yes, I can wrap. It might not be what you'd call Hallmark-worthy, but it's decent. I slap on name tags and bows after I finish each gift; this way, I won't forget and assign the wrong gift to the wrong person. I've done that before.

Snatching up my phone, I text Madison.

> Me: Happy Birthday! Can u come outside for a minute?
> Mads: I'll meet you in your tree house.
> Me: Ok. C u.

Inside the tree house, I wait. My ass is freezing. We got a cold front last night, and it's just hanging around. The temps are in the low thirties. The door to my tree house opens, and I say, "Hi."

I want to press Madison against me. But I've got to give her some space. That's the only way this will work. She smiles at me and takes a seat near the window. She runs her hands across her legs, and I toss a thick blanket over to her.

She raises a brow. "What's this?"

"To keep you warm." I adjust it so it's draping over her legs.

"Thank you."

I nod. "You're welcome. I don't have a cake for you, but here is this." I hand over one of the gifts I brought with me.

She looks at it and smiles. "You didn't have to do this."

"I know. But I wanted to."

"Thank you." She unwraps it slowly and gasps once the paper falls away. "Bryce, this is amazing. Thank you." She hugs me with the books still clutched in one hand and then kisses me.

"You're welcome."

"It's the best gift I've gotten all day. Well, besides Em's. She got me art and nail supplies. My dad bought me new track shoes. And my mom … She got me a snowflake necklace. No need to point out how much I hate Christmas-type gifts on my birthday, but who cares?"

I laugh. "Well, I'm glad I made a good call."

"That you did." She looks around for a second and then shivers. "Do you mind if we go inside? I'm so cold."

"Yeah. Here." I grab the blanket and wrap it around her shoulders while I take the books and move down the ladder after her. When we reach the bottom, we go to my house. I lead her to the living room. Not really our usual place, but again, I need to keep this light.

"Want some hot chocolate?"

She nods with a huge grin. "Please."

"Marshmallows?"

"Of course I want marshmallows. Who doesn't like them in cocoa?"

We both shout out, "Graham!" and then I start laughing. "He's such a weirdo."

"That's not even human," Madison says.

"Right. It should be a law. Must have marshmallows with hot chocolate, or you'll be exiled."

Madison giggles. It's the cutest noise ever made. I get off the couch and enter the kitchen. It takes me a little longer to make the hot chocolate because I'm making it from scratch, the only way I actually know.

Madison enters the kitchen and sets the books down on the island. "Do you need help?"

"No. I got this. Sit down and just bask in the deliciousness."

She laughs. I continue to melt the chocolate slowly in a pan. I carefully add warm milk to the pan and stir.

"Did you literally melt down candy bars?"

I turn the heat to low and look back Madison. "Yeah. Why?"

"I don't know. I've only seen the powder way and the syrup way. I've never seen anyone make hot chocolate using actual bars."

"Well, the trick is to add warm milk. Not cold. If you add cold milk, your chocolate can become hard, and then it's not as easy to make into chocolate milk."

She smiles. "Aren't you full of surprises?"

I laugh and stir until the milk is a deep chocolate color. I pour it into two mugs, toss in a bunch of tiny marshmallows, and then top it off with whipped cream. I hand her mug to her and watch her eyes widen.

"This looks delicious."

"Try it."

She takes a sip. Whipped cream blots the tip of her nose and across her lip. I crack up as she sets the mug down. "What?"

"You have …" I lean in and decide to kiss it off instead of tell her. As soon as I'm done, I say, "You had whipped cream all over your face."

"Oh." She covers her mouth with her hand. A deep blush spreads across her cheeks, and I plant a kiss on her forehead.

Chapter Forty-Three

Bryce

Christmas morning, all I want to do is sleep in. My mom, on the other hand, wants us to have a family breakfast, open gifts, and drive to her sister's house. All this is fine, except for the fact that she wants to start our day at seven thirty in the morning. And do you know what she says to me when I grumble and put a pillow over my head? "Bryce, you have to keep yourself in an early-mode routine. This way, when you have to go back to school, it'll be easier to get up."

I see the logic in this, I do, but fuck it. We're on break for a reason. Sleeping in is always the top-choice thing to do. Getting up any earlier than ten is for the birds.

She won't leave me alone, though. She opens the blinds. Makes a crap-ton of noise. I actually wish she'd drunk herself to sleep last night. But yesterday was Dave's night, so she spent the evening with him. When she's with Dave, she doesn't drink. Ironic, I know.

"I'm up! Jesus Christ." I throw the blankets off and grab some clothes. I move out of my room and into the bathroom down the hall. Once I shower and change into my clothes, I head downstairs.

At the bottom of the stairs, I glance out the big picture window facing Madison's house. Usually my mom has the curtains closed so no one can see in or out, but today, for some reason, it's open. I can see directly into their dining room.

I catch a glimpse of someone entering the dining room in a skimpy outfit. So, of course, I'm curious and staring like a pervert. I take a seat on our huge leather couch. As I adjust my position to get a better view, I notice it's Madison in the skimpy outfit. She takes a seat at the dining-room table and flips open a laptop.

Why doesn't that girl ever sleep in? Wonder what she's looking at? And fuck, what I would give to bend her over that table right this second. I'm getting excited just thinking about the positions and ways I could have her.

Then my mom has to bust my train of thought with, "Breakfast first, then presents."

"What?" I blink at her.

"Breakfast. Kitchen. Come on."

I move away from the window and follow my mom into the kitchen. There is a big, buffet-style layout of breakfast foods. Yeah, I eat a lot, but this is like we're feeding twenty of me. "Mom, who else is coming for breakfast?"

She gives me a puzzled look, sinks down into a chair, and starts crying. Damn it! The last thing I want to do is deal with this crazy-ass episode of hers. "Mom, it's cool. Never mind. Maybe, um … maybe we can invite Aunt Gretchen to our house, and they can have breakfast with us."

"We can't," she wails. "They went to your uncle Barry's brother's house." She lifts her head, and then she moves away from the table toward the liquor cabinet.

"That's okay. I have a better idea. Madison is up; I'll invite her over. Will that be okay?"

My mom pauses. "Her mother is probably cooking."

"Yeah, she's probably making dinner. Think of how much we'd be helping out if we brought them breakfast. Less cleaning. Gives them more time to spend doing whatever." Come on. Take the bait, woman.

She nods. "It would be like my gift to them, huh? Okay. Go over and ask Madison and her family to join us for breakfast."

"I will, but you should probably stay out of the liquor."

She looks at the cabinet and then over at me. "You're right. I'll just set out some plates and move this into the dining room."

I grab my coat off the hook by the door, slide into my boots, and shuffle next door. Madison is still on her laptop when I ring the doorbell. She opens the door slowly. "Bryce, what are you doing here?"

"Look, I've got a … uh … situation."

She raises a brow. "I can't help you with that. I told you it was a one-time thing."

"Not that! God, what's wrong with you? Look, my mom is kind of going through a spell. You'd be helping me out by making sure she doesn't have a meltdown." I rock on my heels. "Will you have breakfast with us?

Or at least take some home and you and your family can eat it this morning? She made too much, and she's really upset. And today, of all the days in the world, I don't want her getting depressed over it."

Madison turns from the door but leaves it cracked. She's gone for, well, it feels like forever, and my ass is freezing. She returns, wearing yoga pants and a hoodie, with not only herself, but Kyle, too. Great.

"She said you had food?" Kyle asks, but there is still an unmistakable glint of hate in his eyes.

Madison smacks his chest. "Don't be an ass or you can stay home."

"Nah, it's cool," I say. "My mom made enough to feed two football teams."

"My kind of mom," Kyle chimes in. "Lead the way, Brycey!"

I swear if he calls me Brycey one more time, I'll knock him on his ass.

We stalk into my house and make our way to the dining room. My mom has it all decked out with the fine china, silverware, and way more plates than we need. She enters carrying a huge casserole dish. "Mom, you remember Madison's brother, Kyle, right?"

"Yes, hi. Come sit down, help yourselves. I'm sure Bryce told you about our little mishap this morning. I thought my sister was coming here. Apparently, they're at her husband's brother's house in Elizabethtown. No one tells me anything until the last minute."

Kyle nods, but I don't think he's really listening. He piles his plate with food as he makes his way around the table. Madison is doing the same, not exactly piling on heaps of food, but she is putting a little bit of everything on her plate. I wait until they both get what they want, and then I fill a plate. My mom smiles and pulls me aside when I come near her. "Thank you."

"No worries, Mom."

"Hey, Mrs. Matthews, these potatoes are the bomb!" Kyle says with a mouthful of food.

Madison kicks him. "Swallow first. Jeez, you act like you grew up in a barn!"

"Screw off, Mom!" he snaps back.

"Thank you," my mom says. "There's plenty left, so really, help yourselves. And if you wanna take some back with you, please do."

"Awesome!" Kyle says.

I take a seat next to Madison. Kyle looks over at me but doesn't say anything. He doesn't even give me a dirty look, which kind of surprises me. Madison sets her plate down and asks, "Where are your cups?"

"Shit!" I say. My mom glowers at me. I cringe. "Sorry. Um, what do you want? Juice, water, milk?"

"Juice would be great," Kyle says.

I wasn't asking him but okay. Madison follows me into the kitchen. "Sorry about Kyle. He asked me where I was going. I told him you invited me to breakfast. He asked why, so I told him how your mom made too much and it was only you two here to eat it. He said he was starving, so I told him to come. He'll eat three helpings if you let him."

"I won't stop him." I grab three cups and fill one with juice. "What did you want?"

"Milk."

I smile. I pour milk for me and her and then hand her a glass. "Thank you," she says in a quiet voice.

"You're welcome."

"I'm sorry for my bitchiness this morning."

I shrug. "It's fine."

"I don't want this to be weird."

"Then don't make it weird."

She chews her lower lip. "But it is. I mean … I feel like everyone knows."

I can't help but smirk. "Seriously, Smalls, you're worrying about nothing. I'm not going to go telling everyone. First, because it's no one's fucking business. Second, I'm not like that. Third, I don't want you to feel awkward around me. I love you." I peck her forehead and leave her in the kitchen with those thoughts.

She comes storming into the dining room, grabs my arm, and yanks me into the living room. She pulls me all the way to the far corner where the tree is. Her hand slaps my chest, then my arm. It doesn't hurt. She scrunches up her nose; her skin is turning pink, her eyebrows drawn together. She hits me a few more times. I try holding in my laughter, but it slips out.

"Ohhh! You make me so mad!" This time she slaps my face.

I back up and stare at her. "Why are you hitting me?"

"Because you're laughing at me. You hurt me. I don't know if I can trust you. I'm trying. I want to. But then you just go and say those words to me. Then you laugh at me."

"Sit down." I guide her to a chair near the tree. I snatch a present out and hand it to her. "I'm not going to stop saying I love you. Because I do. And I'm laughing at you because you look adorable as hell when you're pissed off."

She unwraps the gift. "You shouldn't have gotten me anything else."

"But I did." Once she opens the art kit, I say, "Merry Christmas."

She throws her arms around me and kisses me. "Thank you."

"Madison, any school will be lucky to have you."

She smiles. The art set is clutched to her chest as she whispers, "Thanks for believing in me."

"Anytime."

Chapter Forty-Four

Madison

Today is my long drive to Pennsylvania. My parents still have no clue I'm going. I don't care. Call me selfish or crazy, but it's my future. They're trying to squash my dreams before they even get started.

I sit on the park bench waiting for Bryce. I must be insane. Spending almost eight hours in a car with Bryce, then possibly sharing a hotel room? Yeah, what was I thinking? And let's not forget the fact that I keep thinking about our act in the tree house. That deliciously dirty deed.

Again, what is wrong with me? I don't know. But I hope it's out of my system soon. I can't keep thinking about Bryce and his sexy body. I can't keep wishing we were together because I know it's impossible. Come graduation, he's going in one direction, and I'll be going in another. This will never work.

His car slowly pulls up to the curb, and he smiles at

me. "Morning, sunshine. Ready for Pittsburgh?"

I nod and roll my small suitcase to his trunk. He gets out, places my bag in the back, and shuts the trunk, and then we're off. He glances over at me once in a while, and I hate the silence between us. "Do you wanna listen to some music?" he asks.

"Sure."

He plugs in his iPod and pushes play. A song I'm not familiar with fills the space. "What is this?"

"Like it?" he asks.

"Yeah."

"It's called 'Shots' by Imagine Dragons."

I nod. "It's got a good beat. I could run to this."

He chuckles. "Only you would take a song meant for mellowing and turn it into exercise music."

I glare at him. "Oh, don't make jabs at me. I know perfectly well you weren't just blessed with your sexy abs." I cover my mouth and look out the window. I can feel his eyes on me, but I refuse to look over at him. Of all the things to let slip, I let that come out. Jeez, I'm such a dork.

The music becomes softer, barely a hum in the car, and he says, "So you think I'm sexy?"

"Don't."

"Well, you brought it up, Smalls. Not me."

I glance over at him. "Yes. You know you are. Happy?"

"Maybe." He smiles like he's satisfied, though. "And to in answer your assumption, yes, I work on cars. Sometimes those parts are a bitch to lift. Plus, Graham makes me go to the gym with him so he can stay in shape for baseball."

"Ha! I knew it."

He laughs and shakes his head. "Oh, this is going to be a fun ride."

Eight hours and thirty minutes later, we pull into the Quality Inn. Bryce surprises me by grabbing our luggage and opening all the doors for me. It makes me gushy inside that he's being such a gentleman.

I step up to the desk and check in, and then we go up to our room. Bryce stares at the king-size bed, and I say, "We can share. I won't have you sleeping on the floor."

"Look, I'll get my own room if you're uncomfortable."

"No. I'm not uncomfortable." I throw my arms around him and squeeze. "I don't know how to do this. It's still so new." I look up at him. "I don't want you to leave me, though."

"I'm not going anywhere, babe." He runs his hand through my hair and sighs. "We should probably get some dinner. What do you think?"

"I think that sounds great."

We leave and head to this cute little bistro called The Porch. We sit at a high table, and I look over the menu. Everything looks delicious. My stomach grumbles. It smells amazing in here. "What are you getting?"

He peers over his menu. "I don't know. It's hard to choose. What are you getting?"

"I don't know. Everything looks so good."

"Yeah, it does. Well, you know what that means, right?"

"No, what?"

He sets his menu down. "It's up to our waiter."

"What? No."

"Or you can play the choosing game. Cover your eyes and run your hand up and down the menu. When I say stop, that's what you'll get."

I laugh. "That's ridiculous too!"

He grins. "I think I like it. I'm covering my eyes. Tell me when to go and stop."

He places a hand over his eyes, and I laugh harder. He looks so silly. He makes a sideways V with the fingers over his eyes and peeks out at me before saying, "Come on, Smalls. I'm waiting for my countdown."

I straighten in my chair. "Okay. Since you want to be goofy. Go."

He snaps his fingers closed, shielding his eyes completely, and begins running his finger along the menu. After I count to three silently in my head, I say, "Stop."

He uncovers his eyes and nods. "Bacon cheeseburger with blue cheese crumbles. Awesome. You do it."

"No."

"Come on. Live a little."

I scowl at him. "I live just fine."

"Do you?"

I cover my eyes. "Okay, count me down."

He tells me to go, and I run my finger along the pages. I probably look utterly silly, but it's kind of fun. "Okay, stop."

I do. Opening my eyes, I see my choice: a Greek chicken wrap. I can deal with that.

"Admit it, that was pretty fun and easy, huh?"

I roll my eyes. "Yes, it was fun. Happy?"

"Very."

The odd thing is, I believe he's talking about more than just our choices in food. And even odder, I hope he is, because I'm happy to be here with him.

My phone buzzes in my purse, and I glance down at the caller ID. I swallow. "It's my parents."

"Answer it."

"But …"

"Look at me, Mads." I gaze at him. "Answer it. It'll be fine. I'm right here. We're close to eight hours away from them. Just be honest, and everything will be fine."

"But what if—"

He grabs my phone and slides the answer button. He hands the phone back to me. I hear, "Madison! Where in God's name are you?" as I draw the phone to my ear.

"Hi, Dad. I'm in Pittsburgh."

"Pittsburgh? Pittsburgh! What the hell are you doing in Pittsburgh? I thought we said no to this trip. You deliberately defied us!"

"Dad, this is my future."

"No! Your future is at one of the schools I picked out for you. This is not part of the plan, Madison! That boy has been corrupting your head. I knew this would happen."

I shrink in my seat. Bryce moves around the table and holds me to him. I want to sob, but we're in public. I'm not going to cry in this place. My dad won't make me feel bad. "I'll be home on Sunday. You can punish me then, but I did use my own money, and I left my car there. So you can't be too mad at me."

"You better not hang up on me, Madison. I'm not done talking to you."

"Well, I'm done talking to you if you're just going to scream at me." I hang up and shut my phone off.

Bryce kisses my forehead and then returns to his seat. Even if this trip turns out to be a waste, I'm glad he's with me.

Chapter Forty-Five

Bryce

Back at the hotel, I slip into the bathroom and change into a pair of boxers and a clean nightshirt. I brush my teeth and step into the room. Madison is bundled under the covers with one of the art books I bought her.

I've never been nervous about going to bed, but this is different. I'm not sure what to do: a. sleep as far away from her as possible; b. hold her close; c. fool around a little; or d. just go with the flow. As I approach the right side of the bed with caution, I decide on a., because in the end, she's going to have the final say. Always. So if I just keep to my side like we agreed, everything would be fine.

My phone rings, and I answer it while sliding under the comforter but on top of the sheets. "Hey, Graham."

"Dude, where are you?"

I'm not sure how to answer this. Should I say I'm

with Madison in Pennsylvania? "I'm, uh … out of town."

"Really, man? You're supposed to be at Greg's. Remember? The Ho-Ho-Ho party."

Okay, Greg has some weird dress-up parties. Halloween is one thing. But at this one, Greg dresses up as Santa and asks all the girls to sit on his lap. He even asks if they got what they really wanted this year. I swear the dude is a freaking clown. The girls come dressed up too, sometimes as sexy elves or Mrs. Claus. A naughty version of Mrs. Claus.

"Yeah, sorry I'm missing it." I'm really not.

"Fuck, I've gotta go. Someone said the cops are coming."

I hang up and put my phone back on its the charger. Madison sets her book down and shuts off her light. I look up at the ceiling and sigh.

There's a rustling next to me, and then she whispers, "Bryce?"

"Yeah?" I'm still looking up at the ceiling. I need to be good. Stay on my side. She hasn't really said it, but I think she regrets us sleeping together. And I can't have her regretting it every time.

"Thanks for coming. And for earlier today, with my dad … I just … I need you to know that I really am grateful."

I look at her. She leans in, and I follow. My hand brushes a strand of hair from her cheek, and then the curve of her mouth finds mine. I need more, though, so I deepen the kiss, with my tongue sliding against hers. She moans and rolls on top of me. As she straddles me, she grinds against me, and I'm about to lose it.

I press my head into the pillow and place my hands

on her shoulders. Pushing her back slightly, I pant, "What are we doing?"

"I don't want to fight my feelings any more, Bryce. Can't we just have fun until graduation?"

"Be fuck buddies?"

She pauses for a second. Possibly mulling the words over in her head. She won't agree. This is Madison. She's top in our class. She's safe. A tease, maybe, but never a slut.

"Yes. Only it's with no one else. We aren't dating. But we won't go screwing other people."

My eyes widen. I can't believe she said that. She's got to be joking. I'm waiting for the laugh, but it never comes. "Madison, you really want to be friends with benefits?"

"Why not? Logically speaking, we'd both be saving ourselves from heartache. After May thirteenth, we'll be done with high school. Then what? We'll have the summer, where we'll try to stretch out our good-byes, but that will lead to fights. Which in turn will make us be impossibly stupid. We'll break up, get back together, and then end up breaking up long-distance. So this saves us all those stupid steps."

I'm shocked. Impressed. But mostly I'm shocked. Who the hell is this girl? "If that's what you want, I'm in." Even though I've got a really bad feeling about this. I've seen the movies—this shit doesn't end well.

She leans in and places kisses on my lips and down my jaw. "Yes."

I yank off her flimsy tank top and suck on her boobs. She grinds against me, and fuck, I need her. Right now. But I can't take her too quick. She'll think this is all I wanted from her. I don't want to go too slow either because then she'll know I want more than this and she'll run away again. So I keep chanting *medium speed, medium speed* in my head. I know it's dumb as hell. But it's the only way to keep her until I can convince her that the two of us could work.

She moans, "Please. Now. I need you now."

"Shh," I tell her as I guide my hand past the waistband of her shorts and undies. She's so wet, it's turning me on even more. Especially when she rocks back and forth against my fingers and palm.

"Oh, Bryce, please," she begs.

I roll her underneath me, rip off the rest of my clothes, and slide on a condom. Then I yank her shorts and underwear off and give her exactly what she wants. After we've both been satisfied, I continue kissing her until she falls asleep beside me. Then I get up, dispose of the condom, and put my boxers back on. I crawl back in beside her, wrap my arm around her waist, and press her against me. I could sleep like this forever.

Slivers of light making their way through the crack in the curtains wakes me. My hand brushes against her bare ass. She rolls toward me, grabs my hand, and guides it to her sex. I shouldn't, but I oblige her and give her what she wants all over again.

When we finally leave the bed, I ask, "Wanna shower together?"

She shakes her head. "Don't get greedy." She gets

her shower first. Once she's finished, I take mine.

Madison is rushing about the room when I step out in a towel. She's already dressed in a businesslike suit, brushing her hand along the hemline. She examines herself in the mirror on the wall and then heads to the door. "Um, are you forgetting something?" I ask.

She looks back at me. Her eyes widen, and she shakes her head. "I just thought you'd want to stay here."

"Stay here?"

Madison chews on her lower lip. "Yeah, I mean, it's my interview. It'll be boring." But the way she says it makes me think there's something more she's not telling me. Like maybe she's embarrassed by me. It pisses me off too. I'm tired of people looking at me and feeling ashamed.

"You know what, go to your interview," I snap.

"What's your problem?"

I narrow my eyes. "Right now, you are. Always looking at me like that. I knew you wouldn't see me as anything other than a piece of shit. You got what you wanted, didn't you? Slumming it with the bad boy next door. Let me ask you something. Did you fuck me because you wanted to? Or was it just another way to piss off your family because they're not paying attention to their fucking golden child anymore?"

She storms over to me and smacks me in the face. It stings, but I don't give a fuck. It's the good kind of sting, the righteous kind. I grin at her. She lifts her hand to smack me again, and I grind out, "You better watch it. Or you might be walking your pretty ass back to Tennessee."

She backs up. "Go screw yourself!" She leaves the

hotel. I ponder whether to leave too, but I stay and wait. I'm pissed the entire time. I knew better. Knew not to try and win her back. Knew not to even try dating her in the first place. She'll never see me as anything other than an asshole delinquent, and you know what? She and everyone else can kiss my ass!

Chapter Forty-Six

Madison

I hate him! Who the hell does he think he is? Did I enjoy having sex with him? Yes. Did I do it to piss of my parents? Possibly. At first, maybe. But now, I don't know. But screw him for saying any of this to me.

I stomp my way across campus to the Frick Fine Arts Building, thinking about none other than Bryce Matthews. Ugh! I clench my hands into tight balls. I want to punch him in his face so bad. What was I smoking? Hooking up with Bryce Matthews was a terrible idea. Yes, when he's not in his asshole, grumpy mode, he's incredibly sweet. And he's hot as hell. His body is just, God, droolworthy. But then that asshat has to turn around and ruin everything!

I force my way into the building, and then it happens. Everything that enraged me becomes a distant memory. Beautiful pieces of art surround me, and it feels amazing to be around so much beauty. I step up to a replica of *The Starry Night* and want so desperately to trace the brushstrokes with my fingers. Obviously I don't, but I still want to.

"It's wonderful, is it not?" a voice breaks in from behind me.

I startle and turn toward the sound, clutching my chest. A tall woman with a long, thin face and faded blond hair pulled back in a tight bun stares at me. "You must be Miss Issac, yes?"

I simply nod because this woman is so intimidating. Her stern features remind me of a strict grandma with a large paddle in hand. Ready to crack butts if one person is out of line. "I'm Hilary Vanworth. Come with me," she says.

She leads me to an office deep in the back of the building. She directs me to a chair, and I take a seat. I watch her move around her desk and sit down in the oversized chair. She rests her folded hands on top of what looks to be a desk calendar. Her dark eyes bore into me, like I'm nothing but paper. Transparent paper, to be exact. And honestly, maybe I am transparent—everyday, ordinary—and it hurts more than I'd like.

Who am I really? I'm just Madison Issac. There's nothing special about me. I'm a decent runner. I'm smart, but there are people brighter than me out there in the world. I wish Bryce was here. He paints me as this extraordinary person, and it makes me feel great. Amazing even. Like I need to be that person always, so that he never sees me as I really am, which is how Sarah and my family see me. Plain. The good girl. The pretty one. Not beautiful or wonderful. Just pretty.

"Miss Issac, I must admit, when Ms. Dyson sent me your work last year to consider, I thought it was dry. It needed more. I wasn't sure if you had it in you. Then something changed. She sent me your latest pieces, and I must say, whatever has gotten into you has really inspired the passion and drive I'm looking for. So tell me something, Madison, what did you feel when you walked into the gallery today?"

"This is the part where I'm supposed to suck up to you, right?" Oh my God, I just said that out loud. I shake my head and quickly recover. "Sorry, that came out wrong."

She grins at me. It's worse than her stern gaze. How that's possible, I'm not sure, but I might pee my pants soon. "Go on," she says.

I swallow. "When I walked in here today, I was livid with a boy. A boy who brings out the best and worst parts about me—it depends on the day. But as soon as I entered this building, my anger disappeared. I was calmed by the beauty of the work hanging on the walls. I was also a little intimidated by it."

"Why is that?"

"Because it's amazing. I only hope to be, aspire to be that wonderfully talented."

She smiles again, showing off her coffee-stained teeth. "Why should we accept you into our program?"

"You shouldn't."

She stares at me. I don't blame her; she probably thinks I'm an idiot. I sound like one even to myself. But I am being completely truthful. I don't deserve to go here. Yes, my grades are acceptable. But so what? That doesn't make me the next van Gogh, Sophie Anderson, Rachel Whiteread, or Picasso.

"There will always be better, talented, more passionate people than me that come through these doors," I go on. "But I will never get enough of seeing the world differently. Seeing the shapes, colors, and the contrast in lights. I'll always be that odd kid who's on the edge of normal, but still odd enough to never fit in. I believe this is where I'll finally fit in. Grow, learn, and never once feel like I have to hide my quirks, flaws, and weirdness."

She stands. Shit. I said something wrong. Why did I have to get all nerdy and weird for a minute? She moves around her desk, and I have the urge to crawl under this chair and just die. "Miss Issac, I'd love to have you in our summer program. It starts the last week of June and ends a week before the fall semester starts."

I blink. "R-really?"

"Yes. I find your honesty refreshing. I actually admire that you didn't try to impress me with your list of accomplishments. I love that you showed me humility and strength. I believe you'd be a great fit for our program."

Wait, what? She likes me? She doesn't think my outburst was moronic? I want to pinch myself and faint all at the same time. It feels overwhelming and dreamlike. How is this even possible?

I stand up and resist the urge to hug her. I do shake her hand, and she walks me to the door. "I'll be sending some paperwork to your home address."

"Um ... can you send it to Ms. Dyson? It's just, my family is, um ... really against this."

"Say no more. I can send it to Ms. Dyson. Have a safe drive. I look forward to seeing you in June."

"Same here. Thanks!"

I run out of there so excited to tell Bryce the good

news. Back in the hotel, I slide my key card into the slot and push open the door. He's sitting on the bed, a pack of cigarettes next to him, an almost empty six-pack of beer on the table by the TV.

"What the hell is this?" I ask, picking up the bottles.

"Beer. That's what the box says if you'd read it, smarty-pants," he slurs.

"Why are you doing this? Please tell me you didn't smoke in here."

"I didn't." He glares at me. "You sound like my fucking mother."

I slam the six-pack down. "You know what? I was going to tell you about my amazing day and apologize to you, but forget it. Give me your keys."

He leans back and gives me a sly grin. "Come over here and get them, sweetheart."

If he thinks he can scare me, he's got another think coming. I straddle his lap and push him back against the bed.

"That's it," he purrs. "You want me, don't you?"

I do want him but not like this. Not when he's trashed and acting like a total douche. He slides his hands up my thighs, and I smack them away. "Knock it off." I shove my hands into his pockets, grazing his erection. Jesus, this boy is like a damn machine. I pull out the keys and a lighter.

Bryce gives me a sly smile. "I wish you'd stop fucking with my head, Smalls. My life was awesome without all this shit."

"Don't worry. We'll go back home, and you can hook up with some girl and forget all about me." Even as I say the words, they leave the worst taste in my mouth, like dirt. Do I want him hooking up with other girls? No. But I also have to let him go. This … this has been toxic for both of us.

"Damn straight!"

My heart twinges. I move around the bed, grab all my things, and throw them into my bag. I don't care about being neat; I just want to leave this place. Bryce is no help. He's closing his eyes and muttering incoherent crap while I shove all this shit into his bag.

I lug the bags out one at a time. I place one in the trunk, shut it, and go back to the room to grab another. And then the only thing left to put in the car is Stupid, who's now passed out on the bed.

Great! How am I going to carry him to the car? I glance around the room and spot the ice bucket. I pick it up, fill it with cold water from the sink, and then stand over Bryce. The bucket hovers over his head; all I need to do is tip it, and boom. I squeeze my eyes and turn my hands.

The water splashes all over. Bryce sits up, sputtering and cursing, and he turns his rage to me. "What the fuck, Smalls!

"We're leaving."

"Then wake me up! Don't fucking try to drown me! What the hell is wrong with you?"

I place the bucket on the table and head for the door. Bryce is still fuming. Beads of water drip off the tips of his dark tendrils. He's so unbelievably hot it's disgusting. I stare at his mouth for a second as his lips part. "We need to leave."

He scrubs his hand down his face, snatches his coat, and moves for the door. We don't talk. He starts to open the driver's side door, and I snap, "No! I'm driving. Get your ass over there." I point to the passenger side.

"I don't let chicks drive my car!"

"Too freaking bad! You should have thought of that before you got all trashed."

He folds his arms and presses his lips into a firm line. "Fine," he growls.

He slams into the passenger seat. His eyes are watching my every move. How do I know this? I glance over at him once in a while. His attention is either on my hand, which is on the shifter, or the steering wheel. It's uncomfortable. I feel like I'm in driver's ed all over again or lessons with my dad and Kyle. Kyle would purposely sit in the middle seat in the back and gaze over my shoulder to tell Dad every time I went over the speed limit.

"Could you put some music on?" I ask.

"I could, but I don't want to."

I glance over at him, and he snaps, "Watch the road, Madison!"

"I know how to drive a car, Bryce. I do have one."

"I know you do. You've got everything. You've got your whole future mapped out. You've got a car. You've got what you wanted from me. Guess we're officially even, huh?"

I grit my teeth. He's really ticking me off. "I guess we are."

"Great!" He flips on the radio. A loud booming and a person screaming pours from the speakers.

I almost ask him to turn it down, or off, because it's giving me a throbbing headache. But I decide to suffer through it. Eight hours and I'll be home. Bryce can go screw himself, and I can focus on school.

Chapter Forty-Seven

Bryce

It's been a month since our trip to Pennsylvania. I've been spending my weekends at Greg's, drinking, smoking, and chilling with whoever. One night, a little redhead named Kenya sits down on my lap. She leans in, smelling like roses or some flower scent, and shouts in my ear, "I really like you!"

"Yeah?" I say. My gaze drops to her tits, and I say, "I really like you." It's bullshit. I don't know her enough to like her, but I do enjoy her cleavage in my face.

She giggles. It's so typical and, well, predictable. Yawn fest. Whatever. I grind her against me, and she leans back. I'm about to place my mouth on her breasts when I see Madison stalk by. Emily is with her, and a couple of dudes trailing behind. I move Kenya from my lap. "I gotta get a drink."

"I want a rum and Coke."

I almost tell her I wasn't offering; instead, I nod and head off toward the kitchen. Madison stands to the side while Emily makes a few drinks. The dudes keep elbowing each other and chuckling about who's getting which girl tonight. The douche with the hipster shirt and skinny jeans says, "I'm down for the dark-haired girl. But she seems like the relationship type."

I clear my throat. "She is. Madison just got out of a five-year relationship. She's looking for marriage, boys."

Hipster dude's eyes widen. "Marriage? I'm not looking for that kind of shit." He looks over at his friend. "Fuck that. Didn't you get details on this girl?"

"Man, Em never said anything about her friend having a boyfriend. Just try to play it cool."

"You guys don't go to Portland, do you?"

"Nah, man, we're over at East Roberston."

I nod. "Well, Madison's ex is a big-ass dude, and he plays on the lacrosse team. You don't want to let him see you talking to her. He'll just plow you right into a wall and beat you unconscious."

I shouldn't have done it. Scaring the shit out of this little fuck is damn fun, though. He looks around the room and glares at his friend. "I'm not getting beat up over that. She's barely a six."

Okay, this guy is clearly an asshole and needs glasses. Madison is a fucking twelve. Her gaze finds mine right as her date leaves the room. I try not to smirk, especially when she marches over to me. "What did you do? Where is Charlie going?"

"Charlie Brown realized he forgot to feed Snoopy."

She gives me a puzzled look. "What?"

"That's what you wanna date? A douche in skinny

jeans who probably tells people he's in a band and wears eyeliner?"

She scowls. "It's none of your business."

"It is my business. I need to let you know my tree house is off limits."

"I don't want your stupid tree house."

I lean in and brush my lips on her earlobe. "I bet your panties say otherwise. I bet they're aching to be on the floor of my tree house."

She gasps as I nip her ear. Something shoves me into the counter, and Madison backs up. I glance over at Emily, who takes Madison's arm and tugs her away. "Leave her alone, asshole!"

I return to the living room and notice Kenya is chatting up someone else. Fuck it. No love lost there. I run into Graham and say, "I'm out, man."

"What? You're leaving?"

"Yeah, man. Just not feeling it tonight."

He nods, and I head home.

Chapter Forty-Eight

Madison

He's a freaking jerk. I avoid him at all costs. It's been months since the last time I spoke to him, which was at Greg's party. Once school started back up, I deliberately changed groups. Mrs. Vixen found someone willing to switch. My heart and head couldn't take being around him.

At that party, I thought I'd explode. Literally. When his mouth was on my ear, I wanted to melt into him and beg him to come back to me. I was weak and stupid. Thank God Emily was there to keep me from doing something so foolish.

Since then, I dove into schoolwork and have been running my routine every morning, and I've been good. A little better every day. Okay, yes, I spy on his room for a few minutes before I go to sleep every night. Is that wrong?

Yes, it is.

Do I think about climbing in his tree house just to see if he'd come join me? Yes, I do. Do I do it? No. He made it clear he doesn't want me. In fact, at that stupid party, he had some girl sit in his lap and probably took her to bed, so there you have it. I was nothing to him.

I'm trying to move on. I'm trying not to think about his smile, his lame jokes, or the way his hair felt running through my fingers. It's hard, okay?

I stop by the mailbox and grab the mail. I sort through it. A cringe-inducing squeal of metal makes me wince and glance over at the mailbox next to me. Bryce's towering body is there, yanking out pieces of mail, and then he slams the rusted mailbox door.

I watch him cross the street back to where our houses are and enter his house as if I weren't even there. The tears pool around my lower lashes, and I march into the house before they can spill. I hate how much he affects me. I hate that he tortures me and then treats me as if I'm nothing but empty space.

I set the mail down and grab the letters for me and Sarah from the pile. Entering my room, I barely notice the person on the floor, working through what looks like math problems.

"Jesus, Sarah, you scared me. Why are you on the floor?" I hand her her mail.

She takes it and drops it beside her. She flips her pencil over and starts rubbing the eraser against her notebook fast, as she swears under her breath.

"You okay?"

"No, nerdball! I couldn't get this shit even if I tried. I mean, who gives a shit about fractions? When am I ever going to use them?"

"I don't know," I say. I see the frustration on her

face, and it sucks me in. Slumping down next to her, I say, "Probably never, but I can help if you want."

She snorts. "You help me? Please. If my own teacher can't help me, how could you?"

I shrug. "I don't know. Tell me what you get and what's confusing you. We'll go from there."

"Fine."

I point at the problem. *5/8=A/24. What is A?* "Okay, look. On these, it's simple—if the bottom number is different, then we have to solve for this first. So, what we do downstairs, we must do upstairs. Eight times what gives us twenty-four?"

"I don't know, three?"

I nod. "Yeah. So remember the rule 'what we do downstairs, we must do upstairs.' So if we multiply by three here"—I point to the eight—"then we have to do what up here?" I point to the five.

"Multiply by three?"

"Yes. See? You got it."

She writes down the answer, and we work through some more problems. When we finally finish, she smiles. "Aunt Heather was a good teacher, huh?"

I make a stink face at her. "Mom is horrible at math. I had to learn tricks from Google."

"What? Seriously?"

I nod. "Yeah. Dad's not so bad, but he couldn't help me after geometry."

She laughs. "Wow. So you really are just a little nerd like Kyle says."

I pull myself up from the floor. "I guess."

"Hey, Madison, I heard about you and Bryce. I know it's probably a little late to say this, but I am sorry."

"I saw you kiss him," I say bitterly.

She bobs her blond head. "Yeah. But he pushed me away. He told me he was in love with you and that Graham was his best friend. He said a lot of other things after, but I mostly remember that he loved you. So what happened?"

"I don't know." I plop down on my bed. "The future happened."

"Madison, you can't be serious. You of all people should know how quickly life changes in the blink of an eye. You're supposed to live in the now moments. Not worry about the stupid future, a thing that hasn't even happened yet."

I laugh. "Well, okay, Miss Expert. Then why did you cheat on Graham?"

"This isn't about me."

I narrow my eyes at her. "I know. But humor me. Why?"

Her blue eyes find mine, and she shakes her head. "If things get close to me, they turn to shit. My parents are in jail. My life is a mess. I'm not going to college because I pissed my chances away. Who needed school when I had tons of cash put in my bank account weekly? That was my frame of thinking. That's why I just didn't care enough to try. Graham is smart. Like, really smart, and he's going places. I can't follow him. But I also didn't want to dump him either. And when he said he loved me, I freaked. Like, really freaked out. So I decided to show him I'm not worth his love."

"That's beyond stupid! Sarah, you know you can still go to community college if you get semi-decent grades. Sure, you might have to play catch-up for a while, but it's better than some shitty job you'll hate for life. As for Graham, you two could have made it work. He's only going to be at the UT in the fall."

"Enough about me. What are you going to do about Bryce?"

"Nothing. Have you seen him lately? I just went out to get the mail. He was getting his at the same time. He acted like I wasn't even there. He does that all the time now. Can I blame him? No. I did request a group change in calculus 2. And I haven't spoken to him since that party. We're just … better this way."

She and I sigh at the same time. Sarah moves up to her bunk, and I shut off the lights. I tiptoe across the room and stare out the window. Bryce stalks past his window, and then he pauses and looks directly over at me. I hit the floor and crawl to my bed. Sarah grumbles. "What are you doing?"

"Nothing. It was nothing. Night."

"Night, weirdo."

Chapter Forty-Nine

Bryce

The hardest thing in the world is to forget she's there. I smell her sweet butterscotch scent, and my blood begins pumping. I want to hold her. Press her body to me. Kiss that spot on her neck that makes her arch into me and whimper.

I want it so fucking much it hurts. I've tried moving on. But it's impossible when every girl reminds me of Madison in some freaky way. None of them are her, though. I need *her*.

I flip through my mail and open up the packets addressed to me. I read each letter. *Congratulations … We are very pleased … We are excited to …* From schools I've applied to. I pick up my phone and call Hailey.

Graham throws an elbow in my side. "We're graduating in two weeks."

"Yup. But we've gotta get through exams first."

He growls. "I know. You know who has amazing study guides for this shit?"

I glare at him. Of course we both know who has amazing study guides. I glance out my window. "Try calling her. She probably doesn't hate you so much."

"Yeah, but I'll look like a fucking asshole if I ask her to help us study. Forget it."

I snatch my phone from my charger and call her.

"Hello?"

"Hey. Didn't think you'd pick up."

"Kind of busy right now. What do you want?"

I sigh. "Are you free to study this weekend?"

"Nope. I've got, um … shit—sorry. I have something to do with my family. Sorry."

I pinch the brim of my nose. "Madison?"

"What?"

"I'm sorry."

She laughs. "Are you drunk?"

"No."

"Took you long enough. And you could have said it to my face." Then the line goes dead.

"Mads?" I look up at Graham. "She hung up on me."

He smirks. "Yeah, that's what girls do when they're pissed off."

"I guess I shouldn't have waited five months to apologize, huh?" The sad part of this is I'm not sure what I'm saying sorry for. She told me we were done. She looked at me like I was some dark, shameful thing to hide in a closet—her secret lover or whatever.

"Bro, I don't know, but don't tell them that. They

never let you live it down if you do. Remember Lisa from White House?"

"Yeah." Lisa was a hot-ass cheerleader with blond curls and a big ass.

"I fucking used the line 'I don't remember why we're fighting' on her, and she went absolutely ape-shit crazy. She threw food at me in the food court at the ghetto mall." He shakes his head. "I thought she'd get over it. But a few months later, I see her at McDonald's. She's working the drive-thru, and she leans out the window and tosses my large Coke in my lap. The she says, 'Ooops, sorry. I can't remember why I did that.' Yeah, whatever you do, don't ever use the words 'don't remember' when apologizing."

I stifle a laugh. "Dude that's messed up."

"I know."

A car honks then, and I look out my window. Graham smacks my chest. "Holy shit! Is that Maddy?"

Sure enough, it is. She's wearing high heels and a tight, short skirt. Her purple top is cut low—fuck, I can spy the cleavage from my room. She hobbles a little to a red convertible with the top down. I can't tell who's in the back, but it looks like Emily is the driver.

"Who the fuck is with Em and Mads?" I ask as I clench my jaw.

Graham mumbles, "Dude, I don't know. I can't see from up here. Why do you care so much? In two weeks we're done with school. We've got our whole summer planned out: lake, possibly take a drive to the beach, stay in a condo, hit up some fine, bikini-wearing honeys, and then off to school we go, bro."

He throws out his fist, and I tap it with my own. I don't tell him why it pisses me off that some guy might be out with Madison right now. I don't tell him that I want to smash and break every bone in that tool's body.

I take a seat back on my bed and run my hands through my hair. The frustration is killing me. I grab my last gift to Madison and say, "I'll be back."

"Where the hell are you going?"

"I've gotta drop something off. I'll be five minutes."

He waves me off. "Whatever, man. I'm gonna start playing some Zorge."

"Go for it." I run down the stairs and out the door. I hurry up the steps to Madison's house and ring the doorbell.

Kyle answers the door with an apple in his mouth. "What's up, scab?"

"Is, uh … Madison home?" I know she isn't. I just saw her leave. But he doesn't know I was watching her.

"Matthews, what do you want with my sister?"

I step back as he comes out onto the porch. "Kyle, I know you hate me. Why? I don't know. I honestly don't care. But I need to drop something off."

He sizes me up. We're about the same height, probably same muscle mass too, so I know if he throws a punch at me, I won't be going down easy. "All right. But I'm going to be keeping an eye on you. If you go anywhere near her underwear, I'll murder you."

I give him a look. "Dude, I'm not going to be looking through her drawers."

Sarah opens the front door right as Kyle and I are about to head inside. She looks at me with a raised brow. "Bryce, what are you doing here?"

"I came to drop something off for Madison."

"Oh, you just missed her. She went to the movies with Emily."

Kyle grunts. "Fucking assholes," he mutters.

The guys with them are assholes? Why didn't he go pound the shit outta them then? Fucking Kyle, what a dick. Sarah takes the box from me. "Come on. You'll have to set it with her boxes."

"Boxes?" I ask as I follow her up to their room.

Kyle snorts. "Didn't she tell you? I thought you and Graham were like her best buds or something. Maddy's leaving after graduation. She's living in an apartment in Pittsburgh for the summer."

The whole summer? I'm not going to see her? How the fuck can I win her back if she's gone for the whole summer? No. I know I've waited too long and probably lost her to some douche in skinny jeans, but I'm not giving up.

"What movie are they seeing?"

Sarah shrugs. "Some horror flick, I think. I don't know. Started with an S."

"Which theater?"

Kyle answers, "Gallatin."

I rush out of the house clutching Madison's gift, and hop into my car. Graham is probably going to kick my ass when he realizes I left. Then again maybe Zorge will keep him busy enough not to notice. I just hope he doesn't forget he's in my house and light a joint. My mom will go ballistic on him, and then on me when I get home.

I speed like crazy and get there in twelve minutes. There's a crowd of people lining up outside to get in. I spot Emily near the doors. Madison is beside her. It's now or never, man.

I rush up to the crowd and hear a whole lot of people bitch and moan. "Hey, you can't cut the line, asshole!" someone yells.

Madison turns to me, and I say, "I need to talk to you."

"Bryce, I'm kind of busy," she mumbles.

Some fucking bleach-blond, muscled assface puts his hand on my shoulder. "Hey, man. Can't you see she's already taken?"

"Get your fucking hands off me, fuckwad." I shove him off me and then stare at Madison. "Is it true? Is he your new boyfriend?"

"Jesus, Bryce, lay off," Emily snaps. "She's on a date. Go hump a skanky cheerleader."

"I'm not talking to you, Emily! I'm asking her."

Madison looks up at me. Tears are glistening in her eyes. "It's just a date."

I pull her out of line and over to a bench. She stares at me. I swear she's about to cry. I rub my thumb under her eyes and whisper, "Baby, I'm so sorry. I was an asshole. And I know you deserve better than me. But I can't waste another minute not telling you how I feel about you, Madison. I love you, and it scares the hell out of me. I worry about you all the fucking time. I think about you every second of every day. I just … I needed you to know that." I hand her the jewelry box, and she takes it but starts to sob. "Baby, please don't cry. Please. Just take it. I got it for you before our trip. I meant to give it to you then, but I wanted it to be special."

She opens it and frees the bracelet.

"Madison!" Emily calls out. "Come on!" Maddy looks back at her and then nods. She wipes her hand under her eyes and sniffles.

"I've gotta go. Thank you, though. I love it." She pecks my cheek and runs off.

Chapter Fifty

Madison

"Today is the big day!" Mom sings as she enters my room and observes me and then Sarah.

My mom sticks her thumb in her mouth and approaches me. I dodge her. "Ew. No. What are you doing?"

"You've got a little smudge. I was going to fix it."

I shake my head. "I'll do it myself."

Sarah laughs, but Mom turns and tries to do the same crap to her. Sarah squeals and leaves the room. Mom sighs. "Are you nervous?"

"About what? The speech?"

Mom nods. "Are you?"

"Very."

"You'll be fine, sweetie. I'm very proud of you. You've gotta leave here in ten minutes." She exits my room. I'm not alone for long.

Kyle knocks on my door. He gives me the stink

face and then hugs me. "Don't trip. Remember, Dad's recording."

I frown. "Don't remind me."

"You'll be fine. I think you should moon the crowd after your speech. That would be hilarious. Right?"

I punch him in the arm. "That would be so you. I'm not doing that."

"Such a party pooper." He rubs his arm. "Love you, sis."

"Love you too."

Once he's gone, I stare at myself in the mirror and take a deep breath. I can do this. I grab my speech and head out the door. Sarah and I are heading over in my car. My parents are buying her a car next week when I leave for Pittsburgh. I can't believe I won't be here for the summer.

I still haven't spoken to Bryce since he gave me the bracelet. I've worn it every day, though. I think my problem is I'm not sure what to say or how to begin anymore. Next week, I'll be in a different state. In the fall, he'll be in Michigan. That's close to six hours apart. My car is barely going to survive the few trips back home for the holidays, let alone a six-hour drive to see him. So, yes, I took the chickenshit road and haven't spoken to him.

Sarah and I drive to the school's football field. In the middle of the fifty-yard line is a stage. On the left of the stage is seating for the band. In front, there are two sections of chairs. Ten in each row to the left and right, and nine rows deep. The first ten chairs on the right are designated for speakers. I sit down in the last chair.

As students pour in and take their seats, and parents

fill the seats behind the graduating class, my hands begin to shake. "I'm going to puke," Trevor Davis says as he rushes out of his seat and hunches behind the stage.

Something smacks my shoulder, and I turn around. Emily plops down in someone else's seat and pops a bubble of gum against her lips. "What's happening to poor Trevor?"

"I think he's throwing up."

"Nice." She chomps on her gum. "Ya nervous?"

"A little. I wish everyone would quit asking me that."

She kisses the top of my head. "You'll be all right, sugar pie!" She stands, sliding a pair of sunglasses on, and asks, "Hey, have you talked to Mr. I-Love-You-So-Much yet?"

I shake my head.

"Well, even though I think he's an asshole for how he dealt with the situation, it took some nuts to tell you that stuff. You should at least talk to him. Or not." I frown at her. She smiles and skips off to her seat.

I scan the students. Graham puts his hand up. I wave just to be nice. If I think about it, I have no idea why I ever had a crush on him. Coming down the aisle, with his cap in one hand, sunglasses shielding his eyes, and his dark hair in the sexiest bedhead I've ever seen, is Bryce. My heart pitter-patters at the sight of him. It's difficult to breathe as I look at him.

Graham elbows him, but I quickly dart my eyes to the stage. Our principal, Mr. Saxon takes the stage. He taps the microphone. "Testing, testing."

When it works, he smiles. "Good. Welcome, friends, faculty, family members, students, and this year's graduating class. We've got a lot of lovely people today who will be giving words of wisdom and advice that I hope you will take with you into the future."

I sit there and listen to all the people talking, and then our names are announced. One by one, we walk across the stage. It's when my name is called that I stand up with wobbly knees. *Walk up there and get your damn diploma,* I chastise myself.

I make it to the third step before I stumble. A hand grabs my arm, sending tingles throughout my body, and rights me before I do something embarrassing like crash and burn on stage. I glance back and smile at the face that easily haunts my dreams. "Go on, Smalls." He winks. "You're holding up the line."

I take my diploma and return to my seat. I watch the rest of my classmates do the same one by one, and then I'm called up on stage again. The crinkled-up paper rests in my hand. I take a deep breath and put on the biggest smile I can muster.

Mr. Saxon helps adjust the microphone for me, and then he motions for me to begin.

I clear my throat. "Hi. I'm Madison Issac. I've had classes with some of you. With others, I've only ever shared the halls. But today, we're all here together for a reason. We did it. No matter what we might have been in high school. The cheerleader. The football player. The track star. The teacher's pet. The bad boy. The bookworm. Point is, no matter what, we all walked the halls. We took the classes. We might have had some laughs with Mr. Hamilton. We might have had a lot of fun with Mrs. Montgomery. Her drama lessons in English were truly inspiring." I take a deep breath and prepare to finish my speech. "Beyond this, we're going out into the world. What awaits us is adventure, discovery, and who the hell knows. Whatever it is, we'll face it head-on. Dive right in. Because this is our adventure, and we need to make it amazing, people!"

Everyone claps and cheers. They toss their hats high in the air. It's over. The end. As I walk off the stage, Emily grabs me and hugs me. "Ready to party?"

I giggle at her enthusiasm and say, "Yeah."

Everyone seems to flock to Greg's. At first I thought I was ready for the party, but now, I'm not. People are brushing up against me. Sweat seems to hang in the air. And I just want out. I find Emily and yell, "I'm leaving."

"But this is our last day together!" she whines. "From here on out, you'll be packing and all busy."

"Em, I love you, but I'm seriously tired."

She pouts but hugs me. As I'm walking out the door, I bump into a block of muscles. I look up and see Bryce smiling down at me. "Mads, where are you off to?"

"Home."

"Oh. Okay." He follows me out.

"Are you not going in?"

"Nope."

He walks me all the way to my car. He helps me with my door. He leans in, and his breath skates across my lips. I shut my eyes and wait for his lips to touch mine. It doesn't come. His mouth brushes my cheek.

I blink, and he is no longer in front of me but walking away. My heart sinks. Was this our good-bye?

Chapter Fifty-One

Bryce

*T*hree months later …
     Dudes are carrying in flat screens and computers, and girls are directing guys lifting couches into the large brick building where I'll spend the next nine months of my life. I pick up my two duffle bags and head on in through the crowded doorway.

A short woman in a bright yellow t-shirt shouts into a bullhorn, "Freshmen, please follow the right side of the taped area! Second-year students, you're on the left! Stop at the tables and pick up your packets and key cards!"

Some lanky dude holding a desktop computer monitor bumps into my side. "Sorry. People are pushing from behind."

"It's fine. Need a hand with that?"

He starts to shake his head, but someone pushes him again and he stumbles forward. He loses grip on his computer monitor, and it almost comes crashing to the floor. I reach out and grip it. "Thanks, man. Assholes. I swear they're everywhere," he says.

"Yeah, they are. Hey, jackasses!" I say loudly. "We're all moving at the same time, so stop shoving."

Lanky Guy pales. A deep voice behind us shouts, "I'll come up there and bash your fucking face in if you don't move!"

"Let it go. I don't need to make enemies my first day here," Lanky Guy says. "The line is moving."

We start to move forward, and a guy about six feet tall with big-ass arms comes into view. I take one of my hands off Lanky Guy's computer and flip off the asshole. "You're dead, you fucker!" he yells.

"Let it go. I don't need to make enemies my first day here," Lanky Guy says. "The line is moving."

We start to move forward, and a guy about six feet tall with big-ass arms comes into view. I take one of my hands off Lanky Guy's computer and flip off the asshole. "You're dead, you fucker!" he yells.

Lanky Guy swallows. "What did you do that for?"

"He's not going to do shit. He's trying to impress the girls in front of him." We start moving again, and I say, "I'm Bryce, by the way."

"Max. I'd shake your hand but ... you know."

We walk up to the table and get our packets, and it turns out me and Max are actually in the same room. Once we drop our stuff off in our tiny room, we head back down to my car and grab the rest of my things. Max is on the floor by the time I'm finished setting up his computer.

"Hey, man. Is it cool if I unpack later?" I ask. "I gotta go see someone."

Max moves his wire frames up his nose. "Yeah, that's cool, man. See you later."

I leave the building and walk about ten minutes across a few streets and a long stretch of lawn. I glance down at my phone and stare at the text from Graham. I'm heading to my destination when I see her. She's walking down the sidewalk to a large building. She's carrying a big, black briefcase.

I sneak up behind her, grip her waist, and turn her toward me.

"AHHH! FUCK! My eyes!" A burning liquid eats away at my eyeballs. My tears feel like fire spilling out. I try rubbing them, but it's not helping.

"Oh my God! You scared the living hell out of me, Bryce! Bryce? Wait, why are ... "

I can't really see what she's doing; she's blurry as hell through the stinging tears. "What the fuck was that? Mace?"

"Yes. My brother gave it to me. You're real? Like really real?"

"Madison, I can't see a thing! Yes, I'm real. Jesus, does this shit stop?"

She latches on to me, at least I hope it's her, and guides me up some stairs. "Sorry. The elevator is broke. I'm so sorry. Why would you attack me from behind, though?"

"I wasn't thinking. I was just ... so excited to see you. Fuck, this shit hurts. I'm not sure whether I like your brother or hate him right now."

"You're lucky I didn't use my rape horn on you."

I don't know if that would have been worse. I just know, right now, I never want to be sprayed with that shit ever again. She pulls me into a room and says,

"Take off your shirt."

"Babe, right now is not the time to get me naked and take advantage of me," I tease.

She smacks my arm. "I'm going to bend you over the bathtub and wash out the pepper spray. I don't want to get your shirt wet on accident."

I let her take off my shirt and hear her gasp. "Babe, I want to kiss you."

"What if I'm in a relationship?" she says. "It's been three months since I've seen you." I hear the water pouring out of the faucet.

My heart pounds in my chest. Jealously courses through my veins. She better not be in a relationship. I won't be able to stomach it. Sit back and watch some other guy make her happy? The thought makes me clench my fists.

"Bend over the tub." I do as she asks.

"Are you in a relationship?"

She guides my head under warm water, and I spray water from my lips while holding my breath. She pulls my head back. "How are you feeling?"

"Better. Are you going to answer my question?" I ask, keeping my eyes closed.

Something fluffy touches my eyes and rubs against my cheeks. I yank it down, opening my eyes, and capture her mouth with mine. I run my fingers through her hair, and she pulls me out of the bathroom. We hit the couch, and she gasps. "Why are you here?"

"I go to the University of Pennsylvania."

Her eyes widen. "Really? What about Hailey and Michigan State?"

"It's fine. Hailey's taking a semester off school. Her grades slipped after the whole Darren shitstorm, so she's back home in Nashville. She might transfer here once I get settled."

"But why here?"

I roll my eyes. "Do I have to spell it out for you?"

"Yes. I don't know if you've met me, but I'm a little dense when it comes to love."

I smile. "I love you, Madison Lynn Issac. You're the only girl for me, and you have something of mine. You're carrying it with you right now." I lift up her wrist and point at the heart on the charm bracelet I gave her. "I promise, no matter what happens, I'm here for you. Always."

She kisses me hard and pushes me back against the couch. Her lips leave mine and trail sweet kisses up my jaw to my ear. "Bryce, I don't want anyone but you." And those words are exactly what I wanted to hear.

ACKNOWLEDGEMENTS

Each day I am grateful and blessed to have such support from all of you wonderful readers. Thank you for being a part of this amazing journey with me. Every one of you holds a special place in my heart for I know without any of you none of this would ever be possible. Thank you!

To my awesome family, and my two incredibly awesome children, you inspire me to be the very best version of myself I can be. You push me to do better, make me laugh, and are always there encouraging me each and every day. I love you so much.

My friends, fellow writers, and CP's without you I don't think I could have gotten through some days. You're always in my corner listening to my frustrations or helping me make my work shine even more. Thank you for being my eyes and ears you all are truly the best!

Of course, I can't forget my wonderful and super amazing publisher, Georgia McBride, and the entire staff at Swoon Romance. Without you this book wouldn't be possible so thank you for believing in me.

Special thanks to: Jason, Ethan, and Leeah. Josie Glauser, Tracey Chapman, Clarissa Grimes, Nikalete Fellows, Mandisa Fullwood, Courtney Bivens, Angie Ball, Georgia McBride, Mandy Schoen, Sheri Larsen, Kelly Mooney, Annie Cosby, Jana Armstrong, and Michelle Aker.

NATALIE DECKER

Natalie Decker is the author of the bestselling YA series RIVAL LOVE. She loves oceans, sunsets, sand between her toes, and carefree days. Her imagination is always going, which some find odd. But she believes in seeing the world in a different light at all times. Her first passion for writing started at age twelve when she had to write a poem for English class. However, seventh grade wasn't her favorite time and books were her source of comfort. She took all college prep classes in High school, and attended the University of Akron. Although she studied Mathematics she never lost her passion for writing or her comfort in books. She's a mean cook in the kitchen, loves her family and friends and her awesome dog infinity times infinity. If she's not writing, reading, traveling, hanging out with her family and friends, then she's off having an adventure. Because Natalie believes in a saying: Your life is your own journey, so make it amazing!

OTHER SWOON ROMANCE TITLES YOU
MIGHT LIKE

EDGE OF SOMETHING MORE
THERE WE'LL BE
REDEMPTION
BARREN

Find more awesome teen romance books at http://
www.myswoonromance.com/

Connect with Swoon Romance online:

Facebook: www.Facebook.com/swoonromance
Twitter: https://twitter.com/SwoonRomance
You Tube: https://www.youtube.com/swoonromance
Instagram: https://instagram.com/swoonromance/
Request review copies via swoonromancepr@gmail.com

EDGE OF
SOMETHING
MORE

Andi Loveall

a novel

BOOK THREE IN THE TOGETHER SERIES

THERE WE'LL
Be

BESTSELLING NEW ADULT AUTHOR
ALLA KAR

In his life, there can be no compromise.
In hers, there is only one rule. Love hard.
Redemption
Bestselling New Adult Author
ALLA KAR

Forget. Cope. Survive.

BARREN

Elizabeth Miceli